Seminal Murder

Mary Vermillion

Quest Books

Nederland, Texas

ISBN 978-1-61929-049-5

First Printing 2012

9 8 7 6 5 4 3 2 1

Cover design by Donna Pawlowski

Published by:

Regal Crest Enterprises, LLC
3520 Avenue H
Nederland, TX 77627

Find us on the World Wide Web at
http://www.regalcrest.biz

Printed in the United States of America

Acknowledgments

Lots of folks have had a hand in Mara's third adventure. I want to thank Regal Crest Books and its head editor, Cathy LeNoir, for publishing *Seminal Murder*. I want to thank Pat Cronin and Erica Spiller for editing my novel, Donna Pawlowski for designing its cover, and all the writers and staff at Regal Crest for their warm welcome. I'd especially like to thank Lori L. Lake for helping me find a publishing home with Regal Crest.

I'd also like to thank the many people who offered me their expertise and support as I researched and wrote *Seminal Murder*. Dr. William A. Davis and Dr. Amy Sparks — of the University of Iowa Hospitals and Clinics Obstetrics and Gynecology Department — taught me about IVF and other reproductive technologies. Dr. Sparks gave me a tour of both the old and the new Centers for Reproductive Care at the University of Iowa Hospital. Janet Kaufman shared her story and, as she's often done since we were graduate students together, her enthusiasm for my projects. My friend Gina Glass, a Physician Assistant at the University of Iowa Hospital, answered many medical questions. She and her spouse, Martha Wilson, critiqued and proofread my manuscript, and more important, generously shared their own story, a story that resulted in their four beautiful children. Ellen Hart, Joan Opyr, and Lori L. Lake offered me much-needed moral support and advice about the world of publishing. Creative Girls Eileen Bartos, Marjorie Carlson Davis, Mo Jones, Tonja Robins, Mary Helen Stefaniak, Kris Vervaecke, and Ann Zerkel workshopped my novel. Marjorie, Tonja, and Kris, twice! Mount Mercy University supported my writing with a sabbatical and several Summer Scholarship Awards. My colleagues and students at Mount Mercy continually sustain my writing in all kinds of ways.

Last, but far from least, my partner, Benjamin Thiel, enriches my writing and my life with his wisdom, love, and buoyant sense of humor.

Dedication

For LGBT parents and for my family, Benjamin Thiel and our three delightful cats

Every sperm is sacred! Every sperm is great!
If a sperm is wasted, God gets quite irate!
~Monty Python

We want to assist you in maintaining control.
~www.cryolab.com

Chapter One

WHEN THE ELEVATOR doors opened, I saw that the maternity ward lobby swarmed with baby-worshippers. Flanked by their own offspring, they bore Mylar balloons, bouquets, and every species of stuffed animal. One little hellion parted the crowd, twirling a diaper bag as if it were his partner on *Dancing with the Stars*. This mayhem was the last thing Anne needed. If only she would stay on the elevator with me and let it take us away.

The elevator doors were closing. The diaper bag vanished, then the toddler, then everything but one pink balloon. Had Anne decided I was right — that now was not a good time for her to visit a newborn? No. She thrust her arm between the doors, and they slid back open. Some friends spied us and waved. When Anne stepped toward them, I had no choice but to follow.

"Anne!" Inez proclaimed. "Mara!" She smothered us with hugs. "The entire community is here."

Even though there were enough people for a gay pride rally, my girlfriend wasn't among them. Nor was Anne's.

Inez's partner, Becky, nodded her greeting as she kept watch on their son, Diego, a three-year-old poster-child for ADHD. He was plucking the petals off a bouquet that someone had unwisely allowed him to carry.

"Diego," Becky said, "those are for the new baby."

Diego kept plucking.

Anne squatted next to him and smiled. "Such pretty flowers. May I hold them?"

He shook his head vehemently.

"Did you get a haircut?" she asked.

If he did, it was at Cowlicks-R-Us.

Anne stroked his head, and he dashed behind his moms.

"It's so great," Inez said, "Sophie and Esther getting pregnant on their first try."

Anne's smile faded. She eased herself back up.

"Talk about lucky," Inez continued. She gave Becky a teasing smile. "They even chose their baby's donor super fast."

Anne folded her arms over her chest. The sleeves of her sweater left her delicate wrists exposed.

"We took forever choosing," Inez said.

I should have been interested — I was developing a radio series about artificial insemination — but all I could think about was how hard this conversation must be for Anne. She watched a wobbly toddler clutch her mother's knee. Diego offered the girl a flower. When she rejected it, he used the stem to probe the inside of his nose. Anne shook her head at him, and he pulled it out.

"Inez," Becky said, gently chiding, "it didn't even take us a month to choose Diego's donor."

The boy resumed his nasal explorations. Perhaps his mothers should have deliberated a tad longer.

"Diego Sanchez-Smith," Becky said firmly. "Give me that."

He handed her the ruined flower.

"And the rest."

He scowled and thrust the ragged bouquet at her. "I wanna go."

"Not until we've seen the baby," Inez said.

"Esther is allowing only four visitors at a time," Becky explained.

Sophie's partner, Esther, was a notorious control-freak. She probably had the baby's nap times planned out on a spreadsheet.

"How long have you been waiting?" Anne asked.

"Forever," Inez said.

"Half an hour," Becky corrected.

Anne and I didn't have half an hour. In twenty minutes, we were due on the other side of the sprawling University of Iowa Hospital. My friend, Dr. Grace Everest, had agreed to meet us in her lab, the Center for Advanced Reproductive Care. She was reluctantly abandoning her Sunday "swim club" with a retired paramedic who shared her penchant for vigorous exercise and brunching so I could interview Grace and Anne about an endowment to fund fertility treatment for low-income women. Grace had dreamed the endowment into being. Anne and the Women's Center she directed were helping to fund-raise. I was helping with publicity by including the endowment in my series about artificial insemination.

Anne smiled sadly at Diego again, and we excused ourselves.

"We can't be late," I said. "Let's come back after the interview."

Two little girls ran past, squabbling about who the new baby liked best.

"Or better yet," I said, "let's wait until Sophie and Esther are back home. We can bring them a casserole."

The lines between Anne's eyebrows made the number eleven.

"You could wait until Orchid gets back," I said, "and visit the baby with her." The suggestion wasn't easy for me to make. I hated the fact that Anne and Orchid were partners. Nearly four years ago, they'd hooked up exactly twenty-three days after Anne had dumped me. Anne and I had been together five years. Numbers like that are not good for a girl's self-esteem. Nor does it help that Orchid is my boss.

"She may not be back for days," Anne said.

Orchid was helping her parents move to a retirement community in suburban Chicago. "She'll want to see the baby," I countered.

"Mar-Bar!" My housemate Vince emerged from the crowd near

the front of the baby-viewing line. He waved a pink and blue feather boa through the air. "Anne!" he called, sashaying toward us.

"I want Sophie and Esther to know I'm happy for them," Anne said. "I want to *be* happy for them."

"Diego!" his mothers shouted in unison as the boy reached for Vince's boa. Diego attempted to flee with it and smacked into a woman with a camera.

"An accessory is not a toy." Vince's stage voice silenced the crowd, and Diego let the boa fall to the floor. Vince retrieved it and, literally smoothing his feathers, once again approached us. "Ladies," he said, "it's my turn to meet the new baby. Care to join me?"

Anne nodded eagerly. I wasn't sure whether to thank him or curse him.

THERE WASN'T MUCH to see. The baby—not yet named—slept in Sophie's arms, blanket up to her chin, and hat nestled over her eyebrows. But that was enough to keep Anne entranced. She took her eyes off the baby only long enough to congratulate the mothers.

"She has eyelashes to die for," Vince said.

"And Sophie's hair," Esther added. She reached over the bed where Sophie rested and gently moved the baby's hat. The kid did have lots of hair for a newborn.

"Won't be long before you're buying barrettes," Vince said.

"Not me." The only thing Esther ever did with her own hair was get a monthly buzz cut.

I asked Sophie how she was feeling.

"Unspeakably happy," she said, beaming at Esther. Then they both glanced at Anne, and the beaming stopped.

"Of course Sophie is tired," Esther said.

I took that as an excuse to bow out, but Anne kept gazing at the baby, her eyes sad behind her heavy-framed glasses. I wanted to touch her, run my finger along her chin and tuck her hair behind her ear. But since she'd left me, there was a vast list of things I could no longer do. And since she'd begun her monthly visits to Grace's lab, the list had morphed into a complex set of conversational rules.

Thou shalt not ask Anne how she is feeling.

Thou shalt not complain about PMS or anything menstrual.

Thou shalt not mention pregnancy, not even that of your housemate's guinea pig.

Thou shalt not discuss children or anything related to children—your nieces, your friends' offspring, your stash of Girl Scout cookies, or your incisive analysis of gay sub-texts in Disney movies.

Thou shalt not appear to avoid any of the aforementioned topics.

I joke, but, really, it's not funny. Most of time when we're hanging out, I have no idea what to say, and Anne fills the silence with sagas about her dog's latest hi-jinks. If she weren't keeping an audio diary for my series on Grace's lab, I'd know precious little about her quest to become a mother. And, truth be told, the more I hear, the less I understand. Sometimes, when we're huddled over a tiny table at the Java House, I see the never-ending disappointment in Anne's beautiful maple-syrup eyes, and I wonder why she's torturing herself.

The baby whimpered and squirmed in Sophie's arms. Anne looked away from her, and I looked away from Anne, only to find Vince watching me. He says I'm the one torturing myself. It's one of our standing arguments. "Why do you need to understand her?" he asks. "Why do you keep trying to be friends when you know you'll always want more?" I remind him that I have a girlfriend, but he shakes his head as if he knows my own heart better than I do.

Esther cleared her throat and checked her watch. I checked my own. Anne and I had three minutes to get to Grace's lab.

Chapter Two

AS THE ELEVATOR descended, Anne pressed her lips together and fingered the crystal she always wore around her neck. *If we were going to meet anyone but Grace, I'd reschedule.* The elevator dinged, and in came a woman with a toddler on each hip. She also had a little boy who was trying to remove the toddlers' shoes and socks. When we reached the first floor—after two more stops, three more passengers, and a footwear incident—Anne took off before I could say anything. Her legs are much longer than mine, so I struggled to keep up as she zipped past the info desk toward the walkway that connected the Pappajohn Pavilion to the Colloton Pavilion.

Despite the walkway's floor-to-ceiling windows and the jungle gyms outside the Iowa Children's Hospital, I felt trapped in the belly of the beast. The UI Hospital is a behemoth—five vast buildings sutured together. Anne and I would have to negotiate three more lobbies before reaching the General Hospital, where Grace's lab was housed.

As we barreled past the mirrored walls of the Colloton Atrium, Anne strode gracefully, her caramel-colored hair upswept from her long, elegant neck. I skittered after, glasses sliding down my nose, my hair a garish red mutiny. A patient-transportation vehicle swerved around us. I called after it, hoping for a ride, but it continued down the hall, blue light flashing. Anne sped up. We raced by a snack kiosk and a fully appointed coffee shop. I tried to inhale the scent of mocha and cinnamon, but I was winded. We were in the main lobby, nearly to Elevator C, when Anne stopped and announced that she needed to center herself.

"Now?" I asked.

Her face crumpled like she was going to cry.

I didn't want to desert her when she was hurting, but I didn't want to be later than we already were.

"You go ahead," she urged. "There's no need for both of us to be in the dog house."

True. Grace treasured relentless punctuality. She'd told me so when I'd been a couple minutes early to a book club I'd just joined, Grace's book club. She wasn't praising me; she was making a preemptive strike against tardiness.

GRACE WASN'T IN her office, so I walked down the lab's narrow hallway and checked the few rooms that were open on a Sunday. My shoes creaked on the over-waxed floor. Fluorescent lights glared on beige cinder-block walls. In the main office, the room next to Grace's, the lights were on, but the office manager's desk was unmanned. In front of it was a metal cart, the type hospital employees use to discreetly transport everything from meals to cleaning supplies to God-knows-what. But there was no employee. And there was no Grace.

I tried the door across the hall. It was locked. I called Grace's name, softly at first, then louder. Although she didn't admit it, she was hard of hearing. She never asked you to repeat yourself. Oh, no, she issued commands. "Again! Once more!"

Next to the locked door, two prep rooms were open and lit, but Grace was not among the microscopes in either room. I moved past them, past several closed doors, toward the window at the end of the hall. The steel wool sky was even more depressing than the lab itself. A bomb shelter, that's how Grace described it. She'd long been begging the bureaucrats for a new lab.

Where was she?

I checked her office again. The clock behind her desk said 1:10. I'd been five minutes late, max. Even Grace would have waited that long.

Between her office and the double doors that separated the lab from the rest of the hospital was the cryo room, where frozen sperm was stored. I knocked on it and called her name.

No answer.

I stared at the yellow sign that said "Cryo room. Please keep door closed."

When Grace had given me a tour of the lab, she'd taken me in that room briefly, tapping pointedly at the sign as she ushered me through the door. What would she say if she caught me opening it unnecessarily? "This door is never opened casually," she'd said. Was my search for her still casual? I closed my eyes against my own question and headed back to the other end of the hall.

Outside the lab's lone window stood Boyd Tower, the oldest part of the hospital, surrounded by newer buildings. In the distance, across the Iowa River, was another piece of the nineteenth century, the county courthouse. Scattered between these gothic structures were the Pappajohn Business Building, the Old Capital's golden dome, and a couple of five- or six-story hotels.

Something squeaked, but the hallway was empty. I held my breath, listening. My heart thumped, but I heard nothing else.

The closed door nearest me featured cartoons. "Call me crazy," one sperm said to the other, "but before this is over we'll all be in a rubber room." That's where I'd be too if I didn't get a grip. I pulled out my cell to check for a message from Grace, but the phone wasn't working.

Grace probably hadn't hung the cartoons. She wasn't the sort to decorate a door. In the largest cartoon, a woman said, "Thanks to medical technology, artificial insemination makes it unnecessary for women to have to deal with men. Personally, though, I think it takes away the best part of the reproduction ritual. Dinner and a movie." Grace definitely hadn't posted that. She met her late husband in Ghana when they were both in the Peace Corps. Their first date was a long walk under the African moon. Their second involved an accidental encounter with a bush pig. No dinner and a movie for those two.

Another cartoon was titled "Ovary Action." A woman said, "What do you mean, that time of the month?" She'd buried a hatchet in her husband's head.

Orchid would have deemed the cartoon misogynist and heterosexist. Anne might have found it funny once. But no more. Not after a year of trying.

Now she was somewhere in the hospital, trying to dry her tears, worried about delaying the interview, while I read cartoons.

I scribbled a note to Grace, tossed it on her desk, and went to find Anne.

SHE STOOD IN the main lobby, her back mostly to me, with a young guy in a lab coat. He seemed transfixed by her soft rush of words, and neither noticed my approach. As I got closer, I overheard her announce that she was on day sixteen, the longest she'd ever gone.

Anne was the closest she'd ever come to getting pregnant, to making her dream come true, and she was confiding in some stranger instead of me.

As Anne's confidante crossed his fingers and grinned, I recognized him from Grace's lab, and that eased the sting. But just a bit. When Anne turned and noticed me, I was glad she seemed flustered. I hoped she was embarrassed that I'd caught her dawdling.

"Kyle Bremmer," the guy announced. He gave me the once-over with his intense dark eyes and offered me a too-firm handshake.

Anne fiddled with her crystal necklace. "Kyle processes my sperm," she explained.

I'll never get used to Anne talking about "her" sperm, but I introduced myself and reminded Kyle that we'd met when Grace gave me a tour of the lab.

"Oh yeah," he said. "Public radio, right?"

It was easy to see why Orchid called him the frat boy. His hair was meticulously spiked, and even in his lab coat, you could tell he pumped enough iron to give his body some interesting edges. He had the charm of James Bond, and the swagger of an entire Super Bowl team.

"I'm supposed to be interviewing your boss right now," I said, "but she wasn't in the lab."

Kyle frowned. "She was there when I left."

Since my cell wasn't working, I borrowed Anne's and punched in my own number so I could check for a message from Grace. As I heard my own voice telling me to leave a message, I struggled to remember my voicemail code, and I gazed outside at the cement plaza wedged between the Carver Pavilion and the General Hospital. It was empty save for a few leafless trees in concrete pots and two women arguing. I recognized the tall one right away. Celia Spires. The eldest daughter of Reverend Leo Spires and also his second-in-command.

The minister and his band of merry moralists had long protested Grace's work, but they stepped it up after Iowa legalized gay marriage. "If these people didn't have children," Leo Spires said, "no one would dream of calling them families." Then, after Grace went public with her endowment for low-income women, Spires went really crazy. He bemoaned the degradation of marriage and fatherhood, the hoards of men who would commodify vital parts of themselves. Daughter Celia chimed in whenever she had an audience, spouting fear of radical feminism and the homosexual agenda. She decried the unnatural manipulation of women's bodies. This, from a woman who lived in alligator stilettos and skirts that were narrower than her mind.

The woman arguing with Celia Spires was old enough to be her mother. Stocky with frizzy gray hair, she wore a tie-dyed sweatshirt that sported a huge peace sign. She waved a finger in Celia's face, maybe protesting Spires' protest. Someone needed to. Grace simply scorned the reverend and the hateful signs his minions waved near the hospital's main entrance. "Fools," she'd say. "Who has time for them?"

Grace hadn't left me a message. Nor did she answer when I called her cell, her office, or her home.

Anne and Kyle leaned against the back of a sofa, surrounded by ferns too green to be real. I returned Anne's phone and spoke to Kyle. "Did Grace say anything about her plans for today?"

He shook his head.

Behind him and Anne, Celia Spires hurried toward the hospital's main entrance, her face flushed, her fists clenched.

"It's a long shot," I said, "but Grace could be with the protestors."

Anne and Kyle exchanged glances.

"Not *with* them," I clarified. "Confronting them. Maybe she finally got fed up."

"No way," Kyle said. "She gave us strict orders to ignore them. She's not going to be out there."

"It can't hurt to check." I gazed at Anne, hoping she'd offer to join me.

"Sorry, Mara," she said. "I can't deal with their negative energy today."

I set off alone, my own energy far from positive.

SPIRES' CREW WAS protesting on a dead patch of grass next to Parking Ramp 1 instead of by the main entrance. Either the ramp cut the sharp October wind, or Spires had decided it was bad PR to impede the sick and infirm. His group was chanting, but their words were muffled by the hospital's fountain and a fleet of idling cars. I couldn't spot Grace or Spires among the signs. His daughter Celia held one that read "Real Women Don't Buy Sperm." A tired-looking teenager held a sign with an equally tired phrase, "Family Values." A little boy sucked his thumb, and a man hid behind a placard, "My Manhood Is Not For Sell." (Good news, fella, nobody's gonna want it with those spelling genes.) Behind the botched sign, I noticed some short silver curls, but they weren't Grace's. They belonged to a woman with a sign that proclaimed "Family = Adam and Eve!" (Like that couple had done a banner job for humanity.) Next to her, an aging Princess Leia—humongous glasses, coiled braids like white pin cushions above each ear—grasped a sign with both hands, "Dads Not Deviance." A big man about my age held a sign that announced "The Wages of Sin is Death." This message wasn't half as unnerving as the tiny bald guy lurking at the edge of the group. He carried no sign, but he didn't need to. His darting eyes radiated hatred and contempt, and his wrestler's body looked ready to spring.

Seemingly oblivious on the ground nearby, a teenage girl made a new sign, her tongue curling over her top lip as she wielded a magic marker. I was about to retreat when the girl got up and headed toward Celia Spires. They had to be mother and daughter—same sprawling auburn hair, high forehead, and sharp chin. The girl offered the sign to Celia, who returned the favor with a tirade. The girl held her sign aloft— "Support Families. End Hunger." Celia offered her own sign to the girl, but the girl refused and waved her own more furiously. Then Celia grabbed her daughter's sign, the girl wrenched it away, and it tore.

"Sad, isn't it?" The woman I'd seen arguing with Celia Spires stood next to me. Her face was mapped with smile and laugh lines, but her eyes and voice were worn. "Why can't they build fathers up without tearing everyone else down?"

She didn't seem to expect an answer, but I gave her one anyway. "They like to tear things down. Reverend Leo Spires enjoys sowing hate."

"You're wrong. About him at least."

I studied her tie-dyed shirt, the peace sign on her chest. "Do you know him?" I asked.

"Once," she said, "I thought I did." Then she walked away.

THE CLOCK IN Grace's office said 1:34. As I gazed at the note I'd flung on her desk, Anne contemplated photos of Grace's grandchildren and asked their names. All I could remember was that one started with the letter *C* and that the boy wanted a dragon tattoo.

"I can't believe Sophie and Esther still haven't named their little girl," Anne said. "How can you see your baby — hold her in your arms — and not..." She fell silent as a gangly girl in dark scrubs pushed a cart toward the lab's entrance.

"Excuse me," the girl mumbled, keeping her eyes fixed on the cart. Her scrubs were at least a size too big, and her hair, pulled back in a loose ponytail, was redder than my own.

"We're looking for Dr. Everest," I said.

The girl stopped. Her blue eyes opened wide, round like her face and the small beauty mark below her mouth.

"Have you seen her?" Anne asked.

The girl edged closer to her cart.

"The doc is tiny," I prompted. "Short curly silver hair. Glasses on a chain around her neck."

"I haven't seen her," the girl said. "Not today."

"How long have you been here?" I asked.

"I'm new." She released her grip on the cart. Her hands were flawlessly manicured, a ring on every finger.

"Today," I clarified. "How long have you been here today?"

She twisted one of her rings and shrugged. "Hope you find her," she said. "I got another lab to clean." A wayward wheel made her cart veer to the right as she pushed it out of the lab.

"Talk about child labor," I whispered.

Anne leaned against the door frame and sighed. "She's probably in college. Or grad school."

We're both thirty-seven. Old for a university town. Geriatric if you're trying to conceive your first child.

"Come on," I said, "we need some lunch. I'll write Grace another note, and then we're outta here."

A seahorse zigzagged across Grace's computer screen. A half-eaten roll of Tums lay next to her keyboard. The desk itself was covered with Therapeutic Insemination Donor reports. Grace had shown me a blank report the last time I interviewed her, and she'd explained that it had to be filled out and signed each time the lab prepped a batch of sperm.

"What are you looking at?" Anne asked.

Some of the reports were for Anne herself. Her signature was easy to spot — the *A* pointy like a teepee, the broad loop of the final *g* in Golding, its tail rising up and arcing back over her last name. I pushed Anne's reports aside and saw names of other women I'd interviewed for my series on AI.

Anne leaned toward me and glanced at the documents. "Those are private."

I shuffled through a few more. There was another for Anne and one for Sophie. "This isn't right," I said.

"So quit looking at them, and let's—" Anne stopped. Her deepening frown told me that we'd reached the same conclusion. A dedicated lab director—especially a consummately professional and anal-retentive one like Grace—would never leave patient information on her desk. Not with her office door wide open. Not if she were leaving the lab.

"You look across the hall," I said, suddenly frantic. "I'll take this side."

I ran into the main office, then the prep room next to it. I pushed aside a wheeled stool and darted between two black counters lined with microscopes and test tubes. "Grace!" I called, "Grace!" I took two right turns. Cupboards towered over me. There were more stools. More microscopes. Bio-waste signs. Then, near the door, a bright orange light on the base of a hot plate.

Grace had halted in front of it when she gave me my tour, and she'd chewed out a hapless lab tech for leaving it on. What was it she'd said? The hot plate should be used only for diagnostics, something about testing the lab's equipment or chemicals. The one thing I'd understood was that the hot plate should be on only when the lab was fully staffed. Never on weekends. Never unattended.

"Mara?" Anne's voice sounded far away.

Had Grace used the hot plate to run some test of her own? And then what had happened? Aneurism, stroke, heart attack?

Anne tugged at my arm. I let her pull me into the hall, and I headed for the one room I hadn't checked. The cryo room.

I cracked the door open and squinted through the darkness. When Grace had shown me the room, I'd been creeped out by the metal canisters, some of them nearly my height. The freezer that held the sperm looked like a giant cauldron, especially when Grace opened its lid and liquid nitrogen smoked into the air. "So cold it burns," she had said.

I pushed the door open a few more inches. Light from the hall-way illuminated rows of perfectly aligned canisters. They were not an evil metallic army or a stainless steel coven, I told myself, just evidence of Grace's desire for order. I opened the door the rest of the way. Anne gasped, and after that, I heard nothing but my own blood thrumming through my ears. I saw nothing but Grace, surrounded by the canisters she'd tended for so many years, crumpled on the concrete floor.

Chapter Three

I SAT IN the waiting room outside of Grace's lab, trying to focus on the boyish cop across from me. But I was bombarded with flashbacks of the cryo room, and I ached for Anne's presence. She and I had huddled together waiting for the cops, but when they arrived, they promptly separated us. Alone with the young cop, I felt helpless, sealed off from Anne and the bustling I sensed on the other side of the door.

"Ma'am," he prompted. "I need you to tell me what you saw."

I closed my eyes and forced myself to speak. "There was a chain around her neck—a huge chain." Bile rose in my throat as I remembered Grace's waxy skin and empty eyes.

"Ma'am?"

The cop's badge was slightly crooked, and his words drifted away from me as if he were at the far end of a long, dark tunnel. My head tingled, and the tunnel started swaying before its darkness swallowed me.

I FOUND MYSELF lying on a small couch, my feet propped up on the armrest.

"You fainted," said a voice. It was warm and gentle, the long, sweet vowels definitely not Iowan.

I moved my arm from underneath a mound of blankets and nudged my glasses up the bridge of my nose. Seated across from me was an ample woman with a thicket of cinnamon-colored spirals that fell to her jaw. She was older than me, maybe by a decade, and completely at home in her business attire, a cranberry-colored blouse and a herringbone suit with a badge on its lapel.

A police badge.

Then it hit me. Grace on the floor. Cops everywhere. I started trembling.

The woman opened a can of Coke and held it out to me. "I'm Detective Dallas Henry."

I eased myself into a sitting position and accepted the pop. It shook in my hand, so I set it on a pile of magazines. I was still in the same waiting room where the boyish cop had questioned me. Across the room was a table with a blank computer screen and a small shelf of brochures about sperm counts, fertility drugs, and in-vitro fertilization. One of the brochures was splayed open on the seat of a chair.

"I know you've already answered a lot of questions, but I need to ask you a few more."

I couldn't stop shaking. I planted my feet on the floor and tucked my arms back underneath the blankets.

"Have some soda."

I took a long swallow. Then another. The can felt cold and solid in my hands, something to hang onto as Detective Henry began asking questions. When did you arrive at the lab? How long were you alone there? What is your relationship with the victim? Why were you meeting her? Who did you see? When did you find the body?

The body. How quickly Grace lost everything, even her name. My eyes burned with tears.

"Anne Golding went to the lab's main office and phoned 911," Detective Henry reminded me, "and you remained with the body."

"Grace," I said. "Her name is Grace."

Detective Henry blinked. "Did you remain with her?"

I nodded.

"Did you touch anything?"

Her dropped *g*'s and honeyed vowels seemed at odds with her matter-of-fact questions.

"Did you?" she repeated.

I shook my head.

She sat back and consulted her notes. "You had a 1:00 p.m. appointment with the doctor, and you arrived at 1:05."

I winced.

"You couldn't find her," she continued, "so you went back to the lobby and found your friend. You both came back up around 1:30, and that's when you found the—" She stopped herself. "That's when you found Dr. Everest."

I nodded miserably.

"What else can you tell me?" she asked.

"Grace was doing some controversial work." I swallowed. I wasn't ready to say *was* yet.

"Ms. Gilgannon?" she prompted.

I forced myself to forge ahead. Detective Henry's pen raced across her notebook as I explained Grace's endowment for low-income patients and Leo Spires' increased opposition. In my crowd, you mention Spires, you get a reaction, but this woman simply kept writing. "He's the minister who runs his own little town north of here," I said. "Spiresville. There's a cookie factory, called Sugar Spires, and a so-called church. Spires and his followers protest everything remotely related to homosexuality."

"Soldiers' funerals?" she asked. "Like that minister from Kansas?"

"No," I said, "but Spires and his crew have been picketing the hospital because of Grace's work. They were here this morning."

Detective Henry made a note, but she didn't seem impressed. She didn't seem to understand Spires' level of hatred.

"But Spires himself wasn't with the protestors when I saw them." I leaned forward.

No reaction.

"Neither was his daughter Celia." My God, did I have to connect *all* the dots for this woman?

She flipped a page in her notebook. "So you didn't actually *see* the reverend this morning."

Okay, so no one wants to believe that a man of the cloth — even a warped one — is capable of murder. But this woman seemed to dismiss Leo Spires without thinking. What else would she dismiss? "He and his people hate Grace," I insisted. "They'd do anything to shut down her lab."

Detective Henry looked at me. "Tell me about the history between Leo Spires and Dr. Everest."

And so I did. I described the legendary battles Grace won back when I was still a wannabe actress at the university. She had the courage to take on Spires — and the hospital attorney and its ethics board — so that her lab could work with lesbian couples and single women. The more she accomplished, the more Spires protested.

"Has the reverend ever threatened Dr. Everest with violence?"

"He calls her the devil," I said, "the destroyer of fatherhood and family."

Detective Henry recorded a lot more than I said. Just like when Anne and I tried couples' counseling. I'd say yes or no or I'd shrug, and the shrink would write and write.

"Look," I said, "Spires doesn't advocate violence, not in so many words, but he's a hatemonger. If one of his followers killed Grace, he's responsible."

"Did she ever talk with you about any of the reverend's followers? Someone she was afraid of?"

"Grace wasn't afraid of anybody."

Voices rose and fell in the hallway. I listened for Anne's as the detective kept scribbling. I stared at her badge and tried to summon her first name. Dallas. Dallas Henry. Her first name made me think of Grace's strange belief that babies shouldn't be named after places. "People always wonder if that's where the child was conceived," she'd say.

The voices in the hall grew louder. Then something thudded on the other side of the wall.

"Stay here," Detective Henry commanded, and she was out the door.

"Let me see her," the man shouted. He thudded against the wall again, presumably courtesy of a cop or two. "You can't keep me out."

I stood and tentatively peeked out the door. Sure enough, two cops pinned a large man against the wall. I recognized his scrawny silver ponytail, and I caught his tear-filled eyes. Roger Lipinski, Grace's longtime office manager. Detective Henry attempted to reason with him, but Roger kept yelling about his right to see Grace. He kept struggling against the cops who were holding him. When he finally wound down, they released him, and he doubled over, weeping. After they guided him away, the hall was empty.

I stepped back into the waiting room and sank into the couch. I stared across the room at a watercolor of Iowa cornfields, a lump forming in my throat. Grace hadn't liked watercolors. "Soft-focus for painters," she scoffed. Anything that failed to match her own boldness evoked her scorn. But because she was so difficult to please, if she liked you, you felt special.

I thought back to the first interview I did with Grace. I was early and was shown into this exact waiting room. As I sat there, I heard Grace in the hallway talking. "I have to do an interview," she said. "Damn things are like eating bran. I only do it because I have to." Not wanting to be linked with a disgusting breakfast food, I had worked hard to make the interview fun. When we finished, Grace announced that she was going to ask me a question. "Do you hope that your children will have red hair like your own?" I hadn't expected her to turn the tables. How could I tell her the truth, this woman who'd devoted her life to helping others become parents? "Ah," she said, reading my face before I had a chance to speak, "you don't want children, do you, kiddo? It's not just that you lack the desire for them. You're determined to avoid motherhood." I was used to her proclamations from our book club, but I was stunned that she saw me so clearly. I tried to tell her that I still respected her work, but she cut me off. "Even bakers know that some people don't like bread." I got her point, but, really, what kind of person doesn't like bread?

I was crying when Detective Henry returned. She handed me some Kleenex and remained silent during my nose blowing. "Do you know Roger Lipinski?" she asked.

"Not really. He scheduled Grace's interviews with me. He was real protective of her time." But he hadn't protected her today. No one had. I made myself look the detective in the eyes. "If I'd found her earlier, would she still have..." I struggled to finish the sentence.

"There's nothing anyone could have done." Detective Henry's face was soft and gentle like her vowels.

"But if I'd found her sooner and tried CPR. Maybe she wasn't all the way..." I couldn't bring myself to say strangled. "Whoever killed her is going to have scratches all over," I continued. "Grace would have fought. She wouldn't have gone quietly." I paused, trying to make sense of what had happened. "The killer must have been really strong because Grace would have—"

"She was struck on the back of the head first," Detective Henry interrupted.

I felt like I'd been struck myself. My Aunt Glad had died from a blow to her head. She too had been struck down while doing work she loved. And, I reminded myself, I found her killer. I took a steadying breath. "So Grace never saw her attacker," I said.

Detective Henry nodded. "The killer surprised her. Anyone could have done it, no matter their size." She raked her eyes over me. "There wouldn't be a mark on them."

"Was that what killed her? The blow?"

"We won't know for sure until the autopsy."

"What was she hit with?" I asked.

Detective Henry wrote something in her notebook.

"What was Grace hit with?" I repeated.

More writing.

I can do the silent treatment as well as the next girl. It gives you a chance to think. And think, I would. My emotions would not get the better of me. Since the killer relied on surprise, he was patient and calculating. And a coward. Since he hit Grace first and then used the chain, he really wanted to make sure she was dead. Or he was enraged, out of control.

A wave of nausea swept over me. The nearest trash can was across the room.

"Tell me more about this radio series you and Dr. Everest were working on."

Were. I swallowed the lump in my throat and explained. *Trying Times* was about Grace and the controversy surrounding her work. It was also about the people who used her lab—single women, lesbian couples, gay male couples and their surrogates, and straight couples (including a pair who'd taken out a second mortgage to finance their treatment). I was interviewing all these people, and many of them were also keeping audio diaries for me. KICI, the university radio station where I work, had recently aired some of the segments that featured single women, and Spires had protested in front of our building.

"Did your show cause Spires to escalate his protests at the hospital?"

"Maybe, but it was Grace's new endow—"

"How did Dr. Everest feel about the increase in the protests?"

"She never said." I moved to the edge of the sofa.

"Did you sense her losing enthusiasm for your project?"

"It was *our* project. Her idea. In the beginning, I was just going to help publicize some fundraisers for the endowment, maybe interview a big donor or two. But then Grace said I should be more ambitious—interview some of her patients and pitch the whole thing to NPR." What I didn't say was that Grace and I constantly fought about the nature of the series. She wanted an upbeat story about technological advances and growing families. I was fine with that, but I also wanted to include the lab's enemies, Grace's struggles, and the struggles of women like Anne.

"The interview today," Detective Henry said, "who initiated that?"

"Initiating interviews is my job. Grace was happy to do it." Not exactly happy, I thought, but willing.

"Did you have disagreements about the series?"

Her voice was pure candy, but it didn't fool me. I shook my head.

"Someone overheard the two of you fighting about it."

"We had different visions," I said. "We negotiated."

"You were yelling."

Uh oh. Someone, maybe Roger, must have eavesdropped on our big blowup in the lab last week. It was the only time we'd ever raised our voices to each other.

"You were accusing each other of ruining the series. Dr. Everest said that you'd never understand the importance of her work and that she wanted out of the project."

Even third-hand, those words stung. "She didn't mean it," I said, "she was angry."

"What about you?" Detective Henry asked. "Did you mean it when you said Dr. Everest didn't understand your work? When you said she didn't give a damn about anything except her own agenda?"

"I was exaggerating. We were both angry, but we resolved the issue the next day after we cooled down."

"Tell me about it."

"It has nothing to do with her death."

Detective Henry simply waited, pen poised over her notebook.

I explained that Grace wanted to exclude an interview I'd done with a couple who hadn't been able to conceive, even after using her lab. They went on to adopt, but it took years. I thought their discussion of the two processes would add layers of complexity and emotion to the series. Grace thought their story would play into the hands of people who favored adoption over AI. She was afraid the interview would turn off financial donors.

When Detective Henry quit writing, she tilted her head as if she were waiting for more.

"In a way," I said, "we were both right."

"Who won?" she asked.

"I agreed to use the interview for a different project."

The detective smiled faintly and shut her notebook.

"We compromised on other things," I said. "We were friends."

"Good to know," she drawled. "Otherwise I might entertain the possibility that you'd argued with her again today while Ms. Golding was in the lobby."

Chapter Four

"DO YOU REALLY think she suspects you?" Anne asked.

"Let's hope not." I tried to sound confident. I downed the last of my Corona, my second, and set the bottle on the table too hard.

Anne was still working on the tea I'd given her when we first arrived at my place. Actually, I'd given her hot water. She has her own tea, herbal stuff that's supposed to make you fertile. It smelled like cherries, or at least something did. Maybe it was the remains of Vince's Pop-Tart on the kitchen table. I removed the plate, pulled another beer from the fridge, and asked Anne if she needed anything.

She didn't respond. Her face, half-hidden by bangs, was drawn. I wondered if she felt as lost and numb as I did. I turned from her and opened my beer. Its cap landed in the kitchen sink with a muted clang. Light faded behind the pines in the backyard. Anne had been so excited about those trees when we discovered this place together — our home. I took a long swallow of beer and returned to the table.

Anne stirred her tea.

Vince's Persian, Norma Desmond, sauntered in and plaintively demanded her dinner. Anne reached down to pet her, but Norma slunk away and leapt onto my lap. The only other time she'd deigned to occupy a lap was three years ago — swear to God — the very day my Aunt Glad was killed. I stroked Norma and hoped she wasn't predicting more grief. Even without any new tragedies, I could barely imagine making it through the next few days. In fact, I had no idea how I'd navigate the next few hours. I pictured Anne returning to an empty house and me remaining in one if Vince spent the night with his default date, Richard.

"You should stay here tonight," I said to Anne. "Vince cleared his wig collection out of the guest room. It's all yours. The guest room, that is."

She gave me a small smile, so I could tell she was tempted. Then her cell phone bleated. She looked at the incoming number and told me it was Orchid.

I took the hint and hefted Norma into the living room. Incensed by the indignity, she kicked my chest and thumped to the carpet. I thought about calling my own girlfriend, but I didn't want to tell her about Grace over the phone. I wanted Bridget to hold me, stroke me, kiss away my pain. But Bridget wasn't in town. When we first got together, about a year ago, I was really turned on by being with an assistant coach for the University of Iowa women's basketball team.

Bookworm gets jock. Little did I know that Bridget spends half her life visiting potential recruits.

I sank into my favorite chair, a cushioned rocker from Goodwill, and Norma returned to my lap. She stared at me as if uncertain of her next move. I could relate. But hesitation was a mortal sin in Grace's book. Bridget's too. Once Grace invited us to go cross-country skiing, and the two of them forged the path, stabbing at the snow with their poles, Bridget a stocky point-guard of old, and Grace a mere wraith. Forward. Forward. Forward. No stopping in the snowy woods...

But someone had stopped Grace forever. All that purpose and energy, vanished like a snowflake.

I called Bridget and got her voicemail — her voice ice cream, velvet, and the low riffs of jazz clarinets. I couldn't bring myself to speak.

The kitchen was quiet, but that didn't mean Anne was off the phone, not with Orchid on the other end. Norma kneaded my legs, poking her claws through my Levis. As I pushed the cat off my lap, Anne appeared in the kitchen doorway, her face twisted with anger. "Orchid thinks I should quit using the lab until the killer is found."

For once, I thought Orchid was right, but I knew better than to say so.

"Her energy is absolutely toxic."

True enough, I thought.

"She's been waiting for an excuse to get me to stop." Anne's lip quivered.

I headed toward her, and I was about to hug her when the front door opened. In whooshed Vince, bringing with him the October chill and a skinny chick who was all legs and eyeliner.

"Mar-Bar!" Vince bellowed. "The play is cast. You're looking at the newest stars of Oscar Wilde's immortal classic, *The Importance of Being Earnest*." He curtsied deeply and fanned out his fingers on his chest. "I am Lady Bracknell. And this," he gestured elaborately toward his companion, "is Miss Fairfax."

The skinny chick raised her chin in haughty defiance and assumed a remarkably good English accent. "My ideal has always been to love someone of the name of Ernest."

The four of us stood in an awkward tableau — comedy meets tragedy.

"What's wrong?" Vince asked.

I explained about Grace.

"Get out!" Miss Fairfax said. "My boss was murdered?"

Her boss?

Vince stepped away from her. "Oh, Mar-Bar, how awful." He barely knew Grace — or Lady Sperm, as he called her — but he knew how much she meant to me. With hugs, hand-pattings, and sympathetic clucks, he mother-henned Anne and me to the couch, offered us tea and a sympathetic ear. He wanted to comfort us, he really did, but he also wanted details. If there's one thing Vince can't stand, it's being out of the know.

He would have to wait, however, until Miss Fairfax vacated the premises. I glared at her, willing her to leave, but she plopped onto a chair, clearly not planning to depart any time soon.

Vince introduced Justine Nissen, who, it turned out, was a tech at Grace's lab. She rifled through a buckle-laden purse that probably cost more than my monthly mortgage payment and pulled out a pack of menthols.

"Not in here," I said.

She shoved her smokes back in the bag and clasped it to her chest with taloned fingers. Her purse dwarfed her torso, and she seemed off-kilter in other ways too—her flared jeans and clunky shoes too big for her toothpick legs, her bottle-blond head too heavy for her tiny rounded shoulders.

"This is crazy." She glanced at her oversized watch. "Crazy."

As an actress, she might have had the decency to feign a little sorrow. "How long have you worked at the lab?" I asked.

"Like two months?"

So that's why I couldn't place her. I'd toured the lab before she started there.

She whirled toward Vince. "It would be crazy if the lab were closed tomorrow. I could totally start learning my lines."

"Was Dr. Everest bothered by any particular patients?" I asked. "Or by any issues in the lab?"

Justine shook her head.

Norma Desmond mewed at Vince's feet, and he picked her up.

I kept pressing. "Did your boss ever seem distressed about Leo Spires and his protests?"

Justine slowly shook her head. "Crazy."

I couldn't tell whether she meant Spires' protests, Grace's silence, or Vince's willingness to let Norma groom his goatee. "Had she seemed extra tense about anything?"

"Mar-Bar," Vince interrupted, "there's no need to grill our guest."

Justine gave him a fake smile. "It's all good."

I wanted to tell her it wasn't, not by a long shot, but Anne joined the conversation. "You work with Kyle Bremmer, right?"

"He trained me." Justine narrowed her eyes until they were mere slits of flint.

I thought about Anne sharing her secrets with the frat boy. "You don't like him?" I asked Justine.

She shrugged. "He's all work and no play."

"What about Dr. Everest? How did she feel about him?"

"She was all like he should go to grad school and follow in her footsteps. It was crazy."

"How did *you* get along with her?"

Vince shot me a dirty look.

"I like my day job," Justine said. "You look in the microscope, and there's like this whole other world that's totally beyond your control."

Why had Grace hired this girl? I wouldn't trust her to prep an omelet, let alone a sperm sample. "Did you like Dr. Everest?" I asked.

Again, the shrug.

"What about her office assistant?"

"What about him?"

Finally, a chink in the apathy. "Were they close?"

Justine hugged her purse tightly.

"He was sobbing and shrieking when he found out about her death," I said.

"How do *you* know?"

"I saw him at the hospital."

"This morning?"

I nodded.

"Crazy," Justine murmured. But this time, her nonchalance rang false.

Chapter Five

I SAT IN the middle of my bed, door closed, ready to call Bridget again, but I was distracted by footsteps in the hallway. Anne's footsteps. She was going to sleep a mere two doors down from me in the guest room of what used to be her home. I gazed at the quilt underneath me. Anne used to lie right there, extend her arms over her head, and stretch, her back slightly arched. I'd tell her she was the only person in the whole world who stretched *before* falling asleep. "Their loss," she'd say, smiling, her face inches from mine. Too many nights, I'd taken that sweet ritual for granted, leaving her to fall asleep alone while I partied. Maybe that's what she meant when she said I was emotionally unavailable.

My phone rang, and I flinched. My muscles were so tight I felt like one giant fist.

"Hey babe," Bridget's voice was uncharacteristically quiet. "I heard about Grace. I'm so sorry."

Bridget always listened to NPR during her daily run. I pictured her stopping when she heard the bad news, her handsome face pink with chill and exertion as she gazed at the sky. She should have heard about Grace from me instead of some announcer.

"You okay?" she asked.

"I wish you were here."

"Me too." Her voice was as warm and smooth as Irish whiskey.

"When are you coming home?" I asked.

"Tuesday afternoon."

No earlier than originally planned.

"I wish I could get back sooner," Bridget said. "My freshman point guard is real torn up about Grace's death."

"She's not the only one."

The line crackled. "Babe, I know you and Grace were close, but we're talking about a kid. Grace was her god-mother."

Grace never told me she had a god-kid.

"Liz Lipinski," Bridget continued. "The guard from West High."

I tried to picture the player. Since it was pre-season, I hadn't yet seen any of the freshmen in action. Bridget had shown me a tape, but that was months ago.

"The one with the rainbow three," Bridget said.

"A stocky white girl?" I asked. "Blond with corn rows?"

"That's Lipinski."

Lipinski. "Roger's daughter?" I asked.

"Yeah," Bridget said. "You know him?"

"He's Grace's office manager," I said. "God, he was hysterical at the lab this morning —"

Bridget cut me off. "You were there?"

"Yeah," I said. "I found her."

Bridget was silent.

I love a woman who knows when words aren't gonna cut it.

"Is Vince with you?" she asked.

"Down the hall."

"Good."

She probably wouldn't think it was good if I told her Anne was down the hall too.

"If I was there," she said, "I'd hold you all night long."

I thought of Bridget spooning me, resting her hand on my hip.

"Do you feel like talking about it?" she asked.

Her hopeful tone suggested that *she* did. Who could blame her? If I were in her shoes, I'd have a million questions.

"You probably already talked about it with the cops," she said.

"Pretty much all afternoon," I acknowledged.

"Did they interview Roger? Was he really hysterical?" Bridget didn't give me time to answer. "Maybe I should call Liz again."

I was expecting a question about how Grace had died or whether she had suffered. But everything was always about Bridget's players. We got involved because of her desire to shield them from a high-profile murder investigation. Dave DeVoster, a star Hawkeye hoopster, had raped one of her players and then gotten himself murdered. The police were convinced that the killer lurked in Bridget's roster. At the time, I'd recently bested my hometown cops by finding my aunt's murderer, so Bridget had asked me to sleuth.

"I just hope Roger isn't in trouble." Bridget's voice crackled over the phone.

"Why would he be?"

"You know cops," Bridget said. "They suspect everybody."

"Is Liz worried that the police might suspect her father?"

"Of course not."

Bridget's answer was too insistent. I knew from experience that she would lie to protect her girls.

"Mara," Bridget said. "Liz doesn't know anything about what happened to Grace."

"You don't know that."

"She's already upset. She doesn't need you grilling her."

"What about what I need?" I asked. "What about Grace?"

"AN OCCASIONAL BOUT of insomnia is a gift." So Grace once said. She used the time to shop online and read *Middlemarch*. Once, she actually baked brownies in the middle of the night. But I had no idea what to do with my "gift." Besides brood about her. Or Bridget.

Or Anne. The uncompromisingly square red numbers of the bath-room clock said 3:33. In the mirror, my eyes and nose were swollen. My face, paler than usual, seemed to host new galaxies of freckles, and my hair threatened to go Medusa.

Someone knocked on the door. "Mar-Bar, are you okay?" Vince asked. "You've been in there a while."

This from a guy who spends over an hour on his morning ablu-tions.

"Mar-Bar?"

"Ssh," I said. "You'll wake Anne." My mouth felt like I'd gar-gled with sand.

"I bought some lovely lavender bath beads," he said. "You should try them. They'll help you sleep."

I opened the door and glared at him. "Maybe a nice facial will take my mind off the fact that my friend was just murdered."

Vince tightened the sash on his red silk dressing gown. "I was just trying to help," he said. "If you're going to stay up, I'll make you something to eat."

Never in the umpteen years I'd known him, since we were fresh-men at the U, had I ever heard him offer to cook anyone anything.

"Slack-jawed is not a good look for you, Mar-Bar." He placed his hands on his hips. "Freshen up. I'll be in the kitchen."

I continued to gape.

"What can I say?" He curtsied. "I am your faithful Watson, your George and Bess, your Rachel Ray—all in one adorable package."

IT TURNED OUT, however, that Vince was mostly in Oprah mode, serving scrambled eggs with a hefty side of questions about my feelings. I had the stomach for neither, but I forced myself to sip some orange juice as I pondered my next move. The surest way I could honor Grace's memory was to finish *Trying Times*. But that meant I'd have to edit my interviews with her. I'd have to listen to the tapes.

Vince handed me a napkin, and I realized I was crying. Then his chair was next to mine and his arm was around me. "Let it all out," he whispered.

When I finished crying, the shoulder of his dressing gown was worse for the wear and so was I. My nose was stuffed, and my dig-nity gone. I figured I might as well ask if Vince would come to my office with me.

"Now?" he asked. "You should try to sleep."

I didn't want to argue, and I didn't want to beg. But I couldn't ignore the combination of need and dread that mushroomed inside me when I thought about Grace's tapes. "Please," I said. "I just want to get it over with—listening to her voice on tape for the first time—

and I don't want to be alone."

Vince rubbed his goatee and ran his fingers through his bed-head. "Have you considered the fact that some of this is really about your aunt?"

I hate it when people declare that something you're upset about is really about something else. But Vince was probably right. Before Aunt Glad was murdered, she owned and managed a radio station with her beloved partner, my Aunt Zee (my biological aunt, or my *real* aunt, as my mother would say). After Aunt Glad's death, I'd taken some shifts at their station, and I heard her voice over and over on ads, station IDs, and public service announcements. There is nothing sadder than hearing a recording of someone's voice for the first time after they've died.

VINCE INSISTED ON driving. Even though ours was the only car on the road, we sat dutifully at every red light. As my patience grew thin, I stewed over my interviews with Grace. She'd interrupted nearly every one with a complaint. I was focusing too much on her lab's challenges, not enough on its successes. Too much on her, not enough on her work. If I so much as mentioned Reverend Leo Spires or other critics of her lab, I was giving free publicity to imbeciles. Once, when I was fed up with her objections, I told her she needed a more pliable journalist. "And miss all this fun?" she said. "You're my only friend who has the courage to argue with me."

I wished someone had overheard *that* conversation.

"Mar-Bar," Vince said, "is Anne going to spend another night in the guest room?"

I shrugged, pretending I didn't care.

"I hope you know what you're doing."

"I'm not doing anything except being there for a friend."

Vince sighed. We passed an apartment complex with only one lit room in the whole place.

"She's going through a rough time," I said.

"So are you. Why make it worse?" He launched into his time-to-move-on-for-good spiel.

I tuned him out, but I couldn't tune out my own memory. I couldn't escape Grace's words. "Mara, it's time to stop dithering." The day she had said those words she'd been getting ready for a birthday party, scrutinizing her dining room table, making sure it met her expectations before the other guests arrived. There was an intricately decorated cake, rows of cookies, and a tart with a complex mosaic of fruit.

"What's on your mind?" Grace had asked. The sun glinted off her heavy agate necklace, off her glasses. Her shrewd eyes seemed to glow. She picked up a spoon, held it near her face, and frowned.

Before I knew it, I was seated next to her at a marble kitchen island, helping polish her silver. As I ran a cloth over the smooth curve of a spoon, I imagined the arc that Anne's emotions took every month. After each insemination, she nurtured the belief that this would be the one. For two weeks, this faith was her carefully guarded treasure. Then it vanished, and she had to sift through her disappointment. And who knew what else? Grief? Guilt? Shame? She had to claw through all of them to find one nugget of hope so she could try again.

I stared at my upside-down reflection in the spoon. "Do you understand the women who use your lab? Why they're willing to put themselves through so much pain when there's so little chance of..."

Grace stopped polishing as I sought the right word. She set her spoon down. "Kiddo, if you have to ask the question, you'll never understand the answer."

I hadn't expected condescension. My cheeks burned.

"This is about Anne, isn't it?" She waited until I met her gaze. "You've never wanted anything as much as she wants a baby."

I started to tell her she was wrong, but the words died in my throat.

She reached across the spoons and squeezed my hand. "Mara," she said. "It's time to stop dithering."

I wasn't sure what she meant—Was I too devoted to Anne? Not devoted enough to anything else?—and I was afraid to ask.

Chapter Six

SOMEONE HAD TRASHED my office. I stood in the doorway, unbelieving, Vince behind me. The place looked like it had been hit by a tempest straight out of *King Lear*—my shelves emptied, my books splayed in jagged rows on the floor, the top of my desk smothered with the contents of my file cabinet.

"Whoever did this could still be here," Vince said.

"Not if he knows what's good for him." I strode toward my desk and nearly slipped on the papers that blanketed the floor.

"Careful, Mar-Bar." He grabbed my arm.

I wrenched away and shuffled forward, accidentally kicking my clock. Its face was cracked, but its second hand ticked steadily. 5:17. I gazed at the wall where it had hung. Nothing was there anymore except for a photo of my two nieces riding a carousel. Their joyous innocence made me want to cry, but I squelched my tears and pawed through the papers on my desk.

"You're disturbing a crime scene," Vince said.

I kept pawing, searching for my laptop.

"I'm calling the police," he announced.

My laptop wasn't on my desk. In a burst of fury, I swept all the papers from it. Then I rooted through the mess on the floor, praying that my laptop had simply been moved, not stolen.

"What are you doing?" Vince asked.

On all fours, I pushed aside a heap of papers and jammed my finger on a paperweight. Dimly, I heard Vince phoning the cops. I checked under my desk. No laptop. No regular office computer either.

When I saw that my decade-old Dell was gone, I knew there was no use searching for my nearly brand new laptop. The vandal had stolen both my computers. I stood and forced myself to think. Someone wanted to intimidate me. That much was clear. But you don't steal an ancient computer if you're simply trying to scare someone. The vandal wanted to impede my work at the station. My work with Grace on *Trying Times*.

Little did he know, I always back up my computer files, and most of the time, I take notes longhand before typing them up. I could make do without my computers. But as I studied my desk, my cockiness turned to dread. I kept nearly all my handwritten notes for *Trying Times*, along with tapes of the interviews themselves, in my bottom desk drawer. I knew what I'd find before I opened it. The drawer was empty.

DETECTIVE DALLAS HENRY arrived shortly after the first cops established that the announcer on the graveyard shift hadn't noticed anything while my office was being ransacked. I told her it didn't matter because I knew that Reverend Leo Spires or one of his minions had done it.

Vince nodded. "Who else would steal Mara's research about Grace's lab—all her tapes and notes?"

"I'm going to need to interview you two separately." Detective Henry sounded tired.

"Ladies first," Vince said.

Detective Henry took me to Orchid's office, across the hall from mine. She shut the door and seated herself at Orchid's desk. I stood next to a wall that featured a huge photo of Anne and Orchid smiling together in front of the Golden Gate Bridge.

She nodded toward the picture. "Isn't that the woman you were with when—"

"Yes. She's my boss' partner." I used the word *partner* on purpose. Unlike most lesbian couples I know in Iowa, Anne and Orchid hadn't seized the opportunity to make it legal. My theory was that Anne didn't want to commit to Orchid until she was sure of Orchid's commitment to motherhood. And okay, sure, I'll admit it. Sometimes I entertained one other theory—more of a hope, really—that deep down, way deep down, Anne still had feelings for me.

"Ms. Golding is a patient at the lab where Dr. Everest was killed," Detective Henry said, "so I assume they're trying to start a family."

Did she disapprove of lesbians attempting to conceive, or was she simply trying to get her facts straight? I decided to take charge of the interview. "Leo Spires protests at the Women's Center Anne directs."

Detective Henry undid a couple buttons on her jacket and opened her notebook. "Has he ever vandalized it?"

I shook my head.

"Has he or members of his group ever vandalized anything?"

I didn't bother with her rhetorical question.

"He's never been charged with a crime, nor has his daughter," she said. "Neither of them has even been stopped for speeding."

"Have you done background checks on all their followers?" I asked.

Detective Henry flushed slightly and changed the subject. "Were any of your interviewees reluctant, Ms. Gilgannon?"

It would take more than an abrupt topic shift to fluster me. "If they changed their minds about participating, all they'd have to do is tell me. They wouldn't need to steal my research or wreck my office."

Detective Henry wrote as if her pen were possessed by a whirling dervish. Then she halted, pen poised, ready for another attack. "Where did you go after you left the hospital yesterday?"

As I summarized my evening, I edged closer to see what she was writing.

She rolled her chair back from the desk, taking the notebook with her. "How long were you alone when your friends were sleeping?"

"I didn't trash my own office."

Detective Henry removed her jacket, the same herringbone she'd worn when we first met some sixteen hours ago. Same cranberry-colored blouse too. She was working around the clock, but little good it would do if I was her prime suspect. "I've never been charged with anything either," I said. I did have speeding tickets, but why mention them?

Voices rumbled in the hall. I heard my colleague Dave explain that he was there for his 6:00 a.m. shift. "Holy shit," he exclaimed. "What happened to Mara's office?"

I felt a new surge of fury. "Whoever did this wanted to sabotage my series about Grace's lab," I said. "They took all my tapes and notes."

"You don't have copies?"

"Not of my notes."

"But the interviews?"

I nodded. There were copies in my bedroom closet in the box that also held my Aunt Glad's postcard collection.

"Will you be able to finish your project without Dr. Everest?"

I tried swallowing the lump in my throat. "I'll have to reconstruct my notes."

"Will that be difficult?" she asked.

"I'll manage."

"I suppose you will." She eyed me thoughtfully. "Now you'll be able to do the series your way."

"No," I said, fighting to keep my voice even. "My way was to create the series with Grace."

"Even so, if you complete the project, you'll really ramp up your career."

This time, I ignored her baiting.

She closed her notebook and set it on the desk. "I imagine there will be lots of interest in it, given Dr. Everest's murder and this robbery."

That was one drawling insinuation too many. I headed for the door.

"I know you've helped solve some murders," she said.

I stopped and turned toward her.

"If you weren't in shock, you'd see that the reverend and his followers make lousy suspects."

Out in the hall, I could hear Vince telling Dave an embellished story about finding my office trashed.

"Whoever stole your tapes probably assumed you had copies," Detective Henry continued. "And unless they were incredibly stupid, they had to figure that the theft—following on the heels of Dr. Everest's murder—would increase your story's appeal."

"You're assuming someone rational did all this," I said. "What if one of Spires' minions went berserk? They don't call it the lunatic fringe for nothing."

"I'm going to need copies of those tapes," Detective Henry said.

Even though Grace and I had made them for thousands of listeners, I didn't like the idea of this woman scrutinizing our words. But then I felt a shot of adrenaline. "Do you think they might contain a clue about her death?"

Detective Henry reached for her notebook.

"Do you have any suspects?" I asked. "Besides me?"

Detective Henry's penciled eyebrows squeezed together. "We're pursuing several angles."

I took that as an invitation to join the pursuit. I was about to describe Justine's odd reaction to her boss's death when the detective asked me another question. "That photo on your wall—are they your kids?"

"Nieces." What was this? She'd all but accused me of murder and now she was making small talk?

"Do you have children?" she asked.

"Nope. Never wanted them."

She chuckled. "But you're doing a story about motherhood and pregnancy?"

I didn't like being laughed at. "Do you have kids?"

"One daughter. And grandchildren. Three of them." She grinned. "All evil as their mama when she was a girl."

Detective Dallas Henry, a grandmother? A woman who handled a time-gobbling career? A woman not much older than me?

Someone rapped on the door. "Sorry to interrupt," said a grim-faced cop. "There's been a development."

I headed for the hall, but he blocked my exit.

Detective Henry hurried toward him and ordered me to wait.

"I'm the one who was robbed," I protested. "I have a right to know what's going on."

"Just stay put," she snapped.

As soon as she closed the door behind her, I pressed my ear to its surface, but all I could hear was Vince touting his own detective prowess. When Detective Henry returned, she gripped her notebook tight. "The hospital says no one was scheduled to clean the lab the morning Dr. Everest was murdered, and they don't have an employee that matches your description of the woman you saw."

I thought I was being accused of fabricating a custodian, but then Detective Henry explained that Anne and I would need to work with a police artist to create a sketch. A concrete way to help Grace and a chance to team up with Anne. Things were looking up.

A LITTLE LATER, at my kitchen table, Vince regaled Anne and me with a tale about his heroic stint as a witness. As I sipped my coffee, I studied the faint halo of Anne's bed-head and thought about how I used to see it every day.

Vince jabbed my arm and offered me a Pop-Tart. "What do you think? A female version of the-butler-did-it?"

It took me a second to realize he was talking about the girl in Grace's lab. "She could be a member of Spires' church," I said, "a loyal citizen of Spiresville."

"Maybe the reverend's love child," Vince speculated.

Anne gazed at her tea. "There *was* something off about her energy."

I hate it when Anne talks energy—sometimes I blame the New Age for our breakup—but that fake custodian had seemed nervous. And I should have noticed that she wore way too many rings for someone who supposedly scrubbed toilets.

"What if she was the killer," Anne said, "and we were talking to her right after she did it?"

There went the possibility of breakfast. Even Vince stopped eating.

The newspaper thumped against the front door, and we all flinched. None of us moved to get it. I couldn't bear the thought of Grace's death—her murder—transformed into one-inch columns of print. I didn't want her reduced to "an esteemed, yet controversial, member of the medical community." I didn't want to be "one of two university employees who found the body." I didn't want to read about the cops' inability to "release information." And I sure didn't want to start crying again, but there I was, right on the verge. My solution? Flee to the coffee pot.

"One thing is for sure," Vince said, "whoever trashed Mar-Bar's office doesn't know her very well. He thought he could scare her off and keep her from investigating Grace's death."

It felt weird to be talked about in third-person. I freshened my coffee and gazed at the birdless pines in the backyard.

"Little does the culprit know," Vince continued, "he has incurred the intrepid sleuth's wrath and increased her determination to bring his scumbag ass to justice."

I turned toward him. "Damn straight," I said with just a quaver in my voice. I headed to the front door, suddenly intent on combing the pages of *The Daily Iowan* for a clue. Such steely resolve proved unnecessary.

As I rolled off the rubber band and unfolded the newspaper, Reverend Leo Spires stared up at me. The caption beneath his huge photo read "Leo Spires takes a break from protesting lab where doctor was murdered." The photographer had captured Spires just as he was entering the hospital lobby. Apparently, the usually-publicity-hungry Spires was none too happy to have this "break" chronicled. He was lifting his arm, half-covering his face, and his expensive watch poked out of his designer shirt cuff. The watch hands clearly read 11:30. Spires had entered the hospital a full two hours before Anne and I had found Grace.

Chapter Seven

YOU HAVE LOTS of time to think when you work with a police artist. As he redid the "custodian's" beauty mark for the fifth time, I wondered how he'd come to make his living creating faces of people he'd never seen, clicking on a computer menu until he found just the right cheekbones. I imagined him as a boy, crayon in hand, scrawling curvy trees and magnificent beasts on the walls of his mother's newly painted hallway. And later as a teenager, daydreaming about his work enthralling the art world.

"Here?" he asked, leaning back so I could see the repositioned birthmark.

It was slightly to the left, below the small smile he'd given the girl. I was so hungry I was tempted to proclaim the birthmark perfect, but I thought about Grace and told him it was a little high. As he redid the mark, I wondered what Grace had daydreamed about when she was a teenager. I wondered where she got her fiery sense of purpose, her desire to help women conceive. Her youngest sister hadn't been able to. Was she the source of Grace's vision and determination? Is it other people who trigger our dreams? When I was a kid, I wanted to be an Olympic gold medalist, a best-selling novelist, and a co-star in a Jodie Foster movie. But most of all, I wanted to be like my lesbian aunts, living with my best friend in a house full of books. They took me in when I was a baby dyke warring with my parents, they offered me a weekend job at their radio station, they showed me the ropes, and voila, I was still wielding a mike. And I was still waiting for someone besides Vince to join me permanently in my house full of books.

"How's the angle of the jaw?"

I studied the computer screen. "It needs to be a little rounder."

The artist wanted to work with Anne and me separately. Anne had gone first and then left for the Women's Center. If we described the same girl, it would be a miracle. This was no simple indulgence in postmodern angst about differing perspectives. Sadly, if there was a truth that could be counted on lately, it was that Anne and I see things differently. When we realized that Grace's lab would be closed for a couple days while the cops finished processing it, Anne was distressed about the women who would miss their inseminations. Me, I was thinking about the lab's employees and the extra hours they would have to answer my questions.

BY THE TIME the sketch was done and I'd convinced the artist to give me a copy, I was starving. Find-me-the-nearest-vending-machine starving. The artist told me I'd find one at the bottom of the stairs. "You can't miss it," he said. But apparently I could. I strode down a long hallway lined with closed doors and metal chairs with vinyl upholstery from the seventies. I passed a bulletin board plastered with pictures of missing children, and then I finally discovered another set of stairs and the vending machine itself. But who stood between me and a roll of chocolate donuts? Reverend Leo Spires. He was thumping the machine and uttering the Lord's name in a distinctly un-ministerial fashion.

"Have you lost something," I asked, "besides your temper?"

He whirled toward me, his face red as the ribbon in an old-style Bible. Much less telegenic than his daughter Celia, Spires had wildly sprouting rust-colored sideburns, the mother of all overbites, and a nose that looked like someone had taken a wad of Silly Putty and pinched the hell out of it. Basketball-tall and praying-mantis thin, he always leaned forward, the better to be in your face. He and his followers had been in my face a lot lately, protesting the station and the lab, but this was the first time I'd ever been alone with him.

"Miss Gilgannon." He said my name as if it was a virulent disease, but his voice sounded like a virtuoso bassoon—I had to give him that.

A cop strolled by and nodded toward the machine. "Don't bother. Hasn't worked in weeks."

"A sign would be nice," Spires said, but he was talking to the guy's back.

"What brings you here?" I kept my voice casual and light.

"I'm rendering unto Caesar what is Caesar's."

I took that to mean that the cops had summoned him for questioning, but he seemed to interpret my silence as an inability to process his sophisticated Biblical allusion. "I'm here," he said, "to cast light on the good doctor's death."

The good doctor—that's what he always called Grace right before cataloging the "evil" she promoted. I wanted to say that no circle of hell was low enough for him, that I'd never known the meaning of abomination until I'd encountered his mildewed doctrines. But I needed information, so I couldn't risk increasing his animosity. "What's your theory?" I asked.

Spires straightened his tie. "If you're truly seeking edification, you can read my theory, as you call it, on my web site."

Right, I thought, www.charlatan.com. "How about a preview?" The man could no more resist an audience than I could pass up cake.

"Off the record," he insisted. "No tape recorder. I know how you reporters love to take words out of context."

This from a man who regularly pilfered the Bible to justify his special brand of hatred. "No taping," I agreed. But as we headed down the hallway and seated ourselves, I quickly reached into my jacket pocket and flicked on the mini tape recorder I always carry. As a journalist, I couldn't use his words on the air, not after he'd gone off the record, but I could share his words with Detective Dallas Henry if he said anything incriminating.

"It's clear what happened," he said. "The good doctor was a victim of her own hubris. If you play God, eventually, you get punished."

I should have seen this coming. He was going to use Grace's death to intensify his attack on her work. On her dreams.

"She was probably killed by one of her own customers."

"Patients," I said.

"She leads them on, promising miracles."

He'd obviously never set foot in her waiting room, never seen the brochures that detailed the success rates for artificial insemination. They weren't odds you'd bet on.

"And the sperm banks," he continued. "They're even worse. Step right up and order yourself a perfect baby." He adopted the tone of a carnival barker. "Eye color, height, musical talent, mathematical aptitude, sunny disposition."

This was a gross exaggeration, but it reminded me of the jokes Vince and I made about "dream donors." Vince's would demonstrate a fondness for stray cats, musical theatre, and evening gowns. Mine would be a well-traveled Midwestern bookworm with a keen sense of irony and 20/20 vision. My stomach clenched at the thought of having anything in common with Spires. "The Center for Advanced Reproductive Care is not a sperm bank," I said.

"It used to be before AIDS."

If he launched into his usual gay-bashing, there'd be no keeping my cool. I focused on the rhythm of a copy machine from a nearby office and started counting to myself.

"But that's beside the point," he said. "Labs like hers keep sperm banks in business." He smiled and steepled his fingers. "Let's say a parent or a potential parent is disappointed in their result."

I started to protest, but he cut me off. "Or perhaps there's a long-ago donor who comes to his senses. He's horrified at having a precious part of him marketed like cheap cologne. Or maybe he wants to know the children he's fathered. Imagine his anger when Dr. Everest tells him he's out of luck."

"Do you know someone like that?"

"Donor regret is very real."

"But do you personally know any donors who are that angry?"

"Not their names, but their stories, their suffering."

"Grace is the victim here." I fought to keep my voice even.

"Hardly," Spires said.

I stepped back, stunned by his coldness, his dismissal of Grace's murder.

"What about the children?" he asked. "The offspring of these unholy inseminations? They're a lost generation. They have no idea who their fathers are — who *they* are. Most of them have no way of finding out. They're desperate, frustrated, furious. They lash out at the creator of their monstrous lives..."

His Frankenstein scenario ricocheted through my mind. Furious children. Desperate offspring. The girl I'd seen in the lab. Did Spires know her? Would he admit it if he did?

I showed him the sketch, and he fell mercifully silent.

"Is she a member of your church?" I asked.

He studied the picture, his face unreadable. "She doesn't look familiar, but I have a large and growing flock." He smiled smugly. "Who is she?"

I didn't want to reveal her presence in the lab — not to this guy. "She was at the hospital when Dr. Everest was murdered. Maybe you saw her there."

His face reddened slightly. "No," he said, "but the hospital is a big place, and I was busy ministering to the sick."

In other words, he had hospitalized followers who were ready and eager to say whatever it took to provide him with an alibi.

"I always visit the hospital after our morning service."

His voice had an edge, and I figured he wouldn't answer many more of my questions. "Were you ministering near Grace's lab?"

He chuckled and gave me an eerie smile. "A God-fearing man need never stoop to violence."

"What about vandalism and theft?"

He looked puzzled.

But what could I expect? A full confession that he'd wrecked and robbed my office? I switched tacks. "I saw your daughter at the hospital that morning."

Spires' Adam's apple twitched. Then he smiled. "Celia was leading the protest."

"Not when I saw her."

There went the smile.

"She was arguing with some woman. Not far from the elevator that goes up to the lab."

His Adam's apple zipped up and down his throat. He made a show of checking his watch, but he seemed worried about something other than the time. His forehead was laddered with lines.

"Do you know Justine Nissen?" I asked.

"Is that who my daughter was arguing with?"

"No," I said. "Justine is a tech at the lab."

"I don't know anyone who works there," he said, "besides the good doctor herself."

There are two types of liars. Inexperienced ones can't meet your gaze, and experienced ones hold it too long. The reverend belonged to the second camp.

Chapter Eight

LATE THAT SAME morning, Vince and I pulled into the parking lot for Roger Lipinski's apartment building and parked near a shabby bike rack. It hadn't even been twenty-four hours since Anne and I had found Grace. As I reached for my coffee, Bridget called. I told Vince, and he nodded, reaching for his own beverage. "Some privacy would be good," I said.

He grabbed his coffee and slunk out of the car.

"Babe," Bridget said, "I'm sorry about last night."

"Me too." And that was all Bridget needed. Her apologies were miraculously quick. They came fast after the offense and required zero processing. With Anne, an apology was a psychological excavation. (Why had we fought? Not enough time together? Deeper issues? Mismatched auras? Badly aligned stars?) You ask me, love means never having to say *why* you're sorry.

"You hanging in there?" Bridget asked.

I told her about my office. She offered sympathy and unwanted advice. As in maybe I should sit this one out and let the cops handle it.

Vince rapped on my window and climbed back into the passenger seat.

"It's freezing," he stage-whispered.

"Tell Vince hi," Bridget said.

I gave him a glare instead.

"Babe, I know you two are investigating, so I've done you a favor. I talked to Roger Lipinski. The lab is closed today, so he's at home. And he's eager to answer your questions. He wants to do whatever he can to bring Grace's killer to justice. He'll tell you anything you need to know about Grace and her lab."

"That's great," I said. "Thanks." But I wondered about Roger's lavish offer. Did he think he could keep me from questioning his daughter Liz? Is that what Bridget wanted too? I wanted to believe she was more interested in helping me than in protecting her player, but I couldn't quite do it. I also couldn't quite bring myself to tell Bridget that I was already at Roger's, planning to interview him with or without an invitation.

ROGER'S APARTMENT WAS smaller than the one Vince and I shared during college, and it didn't suit him at all. One look at the man—his long silver hair, his stocky build, his penchant for large elaborate belt buckles—and you expected his décor to feature Navajo blankets, wildlife photos, and Grateful Dead memorabilia. Not pastel prints of flowers.

"My daughter." Roger tilted his head toward the offending florals. "She said the place needed some color." Those were his first words. He'd invited us in with a sweep of his arm and accepted our condolences with a slight nod. From my limited acquaintance with him, I knew that he liked to make grand productions out of the weather and the fate of the Hawkeyes. When he got excited, he morphed into a human thesaurus. "The hospital's new database would be a disaster, a debacle, a complete and total catastrophe." But who has words for a real catastrophe?

We stood awkwardly until Roger ushered us toward a shabby couch. As we sat, he blew his nose loudly and lumbered out of the room. When he returned, he handed me a framed photo. "That's us at an office party my first year with her."

I immediately recognized Grace, but I wouldn't have linked the smiling man with puffy-eyed Roger. The years had softened and blurred him.

"Who's the other woman?" Vince asked, pointing at the photo.

"My wife, Deb. We're separated." He took the photo from me and studied it. "Next month, it would have been twenty-five years for me and Grace."

I had expected him to say "me and Deb." But he was more broken up about the end of his relationship with Grace than the end of his marriage. I know death is worse than divorce, but his quick dismissal of his wife raised my antennae. And he hadn't just said how sad he was that Grace was gone. He'd talked about her like they were a couple.

Roger sank into an easy chair. "I was the first person she hired after she was named director. The very first."

He was obviously in love with his role as office manager and with his own self-importance, but that didn't mean he was in love with Grace. Did it?

"This is my fault," he said. "I was there yesterday morning, but I left. If I'd stayed…"

"Why were you at the lab on a Sunday?" I asked.

He appraised me with narrowed eyes. "The police had lots of questions about you."

"They're jealous," Vince said. "I'd pit Mar-Bar against their best any day."

"I didn't tell them anything," Roger said. "I couldn't. Grace didn't discuss your radio series with me."

Roger sounded bitter, and once again, I wondered if he'd eavesdropped on Grace and me when we fought. I also wondered why he'd dodged my question about being at the lab on a Sunday.

"Do you think she's their top suspect?" Vince asked.

Bass thudded from the stereo in the apartment above us, and Roger glanced at the ceiling. "I don't know," he said. "They had all sorts of questions. They wanted to know if Grace had been upset about anything."

"Had she?" I asked.

Roger was still holding the photo. He stared at it, and his chin started to quaver.

Vince and I exchanged glances. Whatever came next would probably be a half-truth at best.

Roger cleared his throat. "Her fundraising for the endowment was going slower than she'd hoped. But that was nothing new."

"What about Reverend Leo Spires or his daughter Celia?" I asked. "Was Grace upset about them?"

"She didn't give those crazies the time of day."

"And at the lab itself," I asked, "how were things there?"

"Fine," Roger said. "Superb. Perfect." His gaze fell to the photo again, and he traced its frame with his finger.

"What about the staff?" I asked. "When Justine Nissen found out about Grace's death, she didn't seem very sorry."

"Mar-Bar," Vince protested, "Justine is the dearest girl, an accomplished actress who—"

"Are you good friends?" Roger interrupted.

"The best," Vince said. "We've just been cast in *The Importance of Being Earnest*."

Hyperbole is Vince's *modus operandi*. Best friends with Justine? As far as I knew, he never laid eyes on the girl before callbacks. As my housemate launched into a plot synopsis, I wondered why Roger cared about Vince and Justine. I couldn't think of a graceful way to ask, so I opted for another question. "Do you think Justine might somehow be connected to Reverend Spires?"

Vince laughed. "That party girl wouldn't know a moral majority if it kicked her in the ass."

"I was asking Roger."

"We screen our employees," he said flatly. "Nobody at the lab had anything to do with Grace's death. We're like a family."

That's right, I thought, dysfunctional and laden with hidden resentments. "Maybe you could tell me about it," I said. "I'm hoping to talk to everybody who works there."

Roger scowled.

"Just in case they know something helpful," I added. "Bridget told me that you were eager to help find Grace's killer."

"I am," he said. "I can tell you everything you need to know. You don't need to bother the others."

So Roger didn't want me talking with his co-workers. What was that about? Was it just that he didn't like the idea of anyone knowing more about the lab or Grace than he did, or was he hiding something? "Since you've been with Grace since the beginning," I said, "you could tell me what each person is like. With your inside information, my interviews will be more productive."

I stroked his ego a few more times, and soon he was describing the clinical fellows, the residents, and the med students. But all I really learned was that Roger wanted to make the lab look good. Even though I pressed him, he had nothing but praise for every single employee, including Justine. He ended with a tribute to Kyle Bremmer. "Grace admired his smarts," Roger said. "She kept trying to get him to apply to grad school."

Grief surged through me as I thought about how Kyle and Anne and I had argued about Grace's whereabouts as she lay dead in the cryo room. "My friend who uses your lab absolutely loves Kyle," I said.

"He really cares about our patients." Roger frowned slightly. "The only problem is you can't trust everything he says about the other techs. He works a lot of extra shifts so he can help his grandma and his sister. His grandma raised him and his sister all by herself, and his sister has kids and a husband who's nothing but a burden. It's admirable, the way Kyle helps them. It's exemplary. But he looks down his nose at the other techs. He thinks they're slackers because they don't want to work weekends like he does."

"Why does anybody work weekends?" Vince asked.

"If a patient is ovulating, we have to be there." Roger said.

Vince screwed up his face. I guess he was sorry he asked.

"Someone has to prep the sperm before the client goes to ob-gyn for her insemination," Roger added.

"Does Kyle think Justine is a slacker?" I asked.

"Mar-Bar!" Vince protested.

I kept my focus on Roger. "Is there tension between them?"

"Tension is a strong word."

"Whatever you call it, was it bothering Grace?" I thought it unlikely that a rivalry between lab techs would result in murder, but stranger things have happened.

"Kyle is a very decent guy," Roger said. "When my wife and I separated, he invited me to stay with him until I found this place. And when my son Jared came over—he's ten—Kyle always took the time to ask him about school and sports—stuff like that."

"Did Kyle talk with your daughter?" I asked.

Roger stiffened slightly. "Sure, he said hello and asked her about basketball. But Lizzie's shy."

"Grace was her god-mother, right?"

"Lizzie is real broken up over what happened. Devastated and crushed."

"So the two of them were close?"

"They hadn't seen a lot of each other lately," he said. "Basketball and college are keeping Lizzie on her toes."

"Top recruit for the Hawkeyes," Vince chimed in.

Roger beamed. Then his smile faded. "Either one of you have children?"

"Not yet," Vince said.

Not yet? What was *that* about?

"If you have kids," Roger said, "you want to protect them. Ease their way. So I'd appreciate it if you didn't ask Lizzie any questions about Grace. It would upset her for nothing. She doesn't know anything about Grace's death."

"We understand," Vince said.

But I didn't. If Liz really loved her god-mother, wouldn't she want to do all she could to help find her killer? What was up with Roger's over-protectiveness?

Vince's stomach growled, and I realized that it was past noon. I stood, and the men followed suit. "One last question." I reached into my backpack for the police sketch. "Do you recognize her?"

Roger examined the picture and nodded.

"Well," I said, "Who is she?"

"I can't say. It's private. Confidential."

When I explained that she was posing as a custodian in the lab yesterday morning, Roger dropped back into his chair, his face drained of color. He stared emptily into space, even after I squatted next to him right in his line of vision. I was about to get up again when he spoke. "Zoey Hargrove. She came to the lab last week. I swear I thought she was exaggerating. I thought it was emotions talking..." Roger trailed off, and I resisted the urge to prod him. "She told me she wanted to find her biological father. She asked for her donor's name, but he was a closed one so I couldn't give her any information. She said her mother had died, and her father, the one who raised her, had remarried. She needed to know her real dad."

My throat and stomach tightened. I flashed on Reverend Leo Spires' theories about donor offspring.

"Then what?" Vince asked.

"She started bargaining. She said all she wanted was her donor's ID number. I said labs aren't allowed to give any information to minors, but her father should have the number and he could tell her. She got all sullen, so I'm guessing she already tried that route." Roger sighed. "I felt sorry for her, real sorry. But what could I do? I repeated the rules, and then she refused to leave until she got to talk to Grace." Roger shook his head grimly. "I should have called security right away. But I took the girl to Grace's office. Grace tried to explain donor privacy rights, but the girl started crying and telling Grace she'd be sorry. When she grabbed some papers on Grace's desk, I started to call security, but Grace said no and asked Kyle and me to escort the girl to the elevator."

Roger stopped, but his haunted eyes told me that there was more to the story. I waited silently, squatting next to him, afraid that if Vince or I moved, we'd never hear the rest.

"When we showed her to the elevator, Kyle and me, she kept saying she'd make us sorry." Roger's voice caught. "She said it five or six times, but I didn't think she meant it."

Chapter Nine

WAS ZOEY HARGROVE Grace's murderer? Roger seemed to think Zoey had motive, and I was pretty sure she had opportunity. That left means. The murderer — whoever it was — could have struck Grace with something that was already in the cryo room. Maybe with a canister of liquid nitrogen. Many of them were small enough for a teenage girl to lift. And the chain around Grace's neck? My stomach churned, but I forced myself to think about what I'd seen during my tour of the lab. The largest canisters of liquid nitrogen were secured with chains, but there had also been a few spare chains coiled on a shelf.

"Mar-Bar?" Vince said. "Are you okay?"

We stood by my car in the lot next to Roger's apartment building. I'd been thinking so hard, I didn't remember getting there, and I barely registered Vince's words. "You drive," I said, tossing him my keys. They landed at his feet. Vince isn't particularly uncoordinated — he was probably just surprised. I usually make him beg before I let him drive. We were both quiet as he navigated out of Roger's lot.

"A teenager," I mused, "a girl whose life Grace made possible..." I couldn't bring myself to say more, but Vince seemed to know what I was thinking.

"Kids are impulsive," he said. "Some of them are violent."

"But Grace had information Zoey wanted," I argued. "Why would Zoey kill her?"

Vince slowed at an intersection. "Maybe she snapped."

Maybe. I still didn't know whether the killer had been enraged or calculating. Or both.

"You've got to admit," Vince said, "it doesn't sound like Zoey Hargrove has a tight rein on her emotions."

I thought about Zoey's face — the real one, not the sketch. Big blue eyes, stringy red hair in a ponytail, a few zits on her chin. In other words, me at the same age. And that's not where the similarities ended. We both had family trauma. Unlike Zoey, I knew my "sperm donor." I had issues with my dad, but I knew him. I'd lived in the same house with him until my sophomore year of high school when my mom discovered me kissing Susie Sorenson. After that, it quickly became clear that both my parents would be happier if I moved in with my aunts. Zoey had experienced even more upheaval. No one in my family had died, not when I was a teenager. Whatever Zoey did or didn't do at the hospital, she was a kid desperate to find at least one adult who cared about who she really was. I could relate.

I could also use another perspective. I consulted Vince, and we decided to pay Kyle a visit to get his take on Zoey's outburst at the lab.

We caught him working out, shirtless and sweating, hair perfectly spiked. But his eyes were weighed down by dark circles, and he'd lost much of his swagger. "Dr. Everest," he said slowly, as if he knew why we'd come.

I found that I couldn't speak. Kyle's shock and grief sharpened my own.

Vince broke the silence by offering condolences and introducing himself.

Kyle mumbled his own name, invited us in, and went to get a shirt.

Vince and I stepped over a couple barbells on the way to the sofa. While we waited for Kyle to return, I perused his book shelves. The ample supply of fiction endeared me to him, as did the framed calligraphed quotation on his middle shelf. *"The little things are infinitely the most important." – Sir Arthur Conan Doyle.* Maybe the Holmesian idea inspired Kyle as he fine-tuned his biceps or worked extra hours at the lab. Whoever did the calligraphy had lavished attention on it, making capital letters more intricate than lace. His grandmother? The photo next to the calligraphy was probably her, I decided. She looked familiar—large glasses from the eighties and white braids circling tightly atop her head—but I couldn't place her. Vince was no help.

Kyle returned, clad in sweats and full of questions. Could he get us something to drink? How was I holding up? How was Anne? Were Dr. Everest and I close?

I reached into my backpack, found the sketch of Zoey, and handed it to Kyle.

He recognized her instantly. "She pitched a fit in Dr. Everest's office a few days ago. Roger and I had to escort her out." He looked up from the drawing. "Why do you have this?"

"She was posing as a custodian at the lab yesterday morning," Vince said.

Kyle's eyes widened, and he threw out more questions. Did the police think she'd done it? Had they questioned her? Had she confessed? If she wasn't the killer, was she a witness? Had she taken anything? When he realized that we knew nothing more than he did, he stopped firing questions and studied the picture. "She's just a kid," he said.

"How old?" I asked.

He shrugged.

"Why did you have to escort her out?" I asked. "Was her fit that bad?"

"Did she seem unstable or dangerous?" Vince added.

"She was just letting off steam," Kyle said. "She wanted the scoop on her donor — her donor dad, she called him. And, of course, we couldn't give it to her. You can't blame her for being upset."

"But Roger saw her as a threat," I said.

"She seemed like all talk to me." Kyle worked his jaw, and then he asked, "What about that so-called minister?"

I felt a surge of adrenaline. "You think Leo Spires had something to do with Grace's death?"

"Don't you?" Kyle moved to the edge of his chair. "Talk about unstable and dangerous. That hateful piece of trash should be behind bars."

His vehemence seemed over-the-top. I wondered if that's how I sounded to Detective Henry. Maybe she was right to discount Spires as a suspect. Maybe he was too unlikable — too obvious. I asked Kyle if the minister had threatened Grace.

"He might have. She wouldn't have told anybody." Kyle's voice was bitter as he turned toward me. "You were her friend, right? You knew her a lot of years?"

I nodded.

"Did she ever share any worries with you? Ever show any fear?"

"Should she have been afraid of someone?" I asked. "Besides Spires? His daughter maybe?"

Kyle started trashing the minister again. Vince was transfixed by the rant even though it contained nothing we hadn't already heard or said ourselves. Of course, Vince would have been mesmerized by a handsome guy like Kyle even if he'd been describing oatmeal.

My attention drifted back to the photo of Kyle's grandmother. Her hideous glasses obscured her best feature, large brown eyes that sparkled with determination. Where had I seen her before? The only other photo in the room featured three kids and a woman. Kyle's sister, probably. Like Kyle and his grandmother, she had stunning dark eyes. I thought about Zoey. It would be hard not to know where your eyes had come from, where *you* had come from. I was glad Anne was using an open donor. When her kid turned eighteen, he or she could learn all about the donor and maybe even meet him.

There was a soft knock on the door, and Kyle went to answer it. "Toni." He sounded surprised. I couldn't tell whether he was pleased. I would have been if Toni was knocking on my door. Even in scrubs peppered with Winnie-the-Pooh characters, she was hot. Leggy like Anne with full lips and smoke-colored eyes. After Kyle gave her a quick kiss, Toni introduced herself. She'd just gotten off her shift in pediatrics and wanted to see how Kyle was doing after, you know, yesterday's tragedy.

Kyle explained that I was Dr. Everest's friend and that Vince and I were trying to find out what happened to her. He also noted that we were about to leave.

I ignored this hint and explained that I had some questions about his co-workers.

"Do you think someone at the lab did it?" Toni asked. She edged closer to Kyle.

"Mara suspects Justine," Vince said, "because she didn't weep like a Victorian heroine when she learned about the death."

I shot him a dirty look.

"Justine plays her cards close to her chest," Kyle said.

I'd expected him to badmouth Justine, so I gave him another chance. "How did she and Grace get along?"

He shrugged. "They were cool."

Vince headed toward the door, looking smug.

"Roger says you have issues with her," I said.

"Me? He's the one who's always riding her when she's late or makes a mistake."

"Does she make a lot of mistakes?"

"Mar-Bar—" Vince protested.

"Roger only criticized her—or any of us—when Dr. Everest was around. It was like he was performing. He had it big and bad for her, poor guy."

"Are you sure?" I asked.

Kyle nodded.

"Totally," said Toni. "When Roger lived here, all he talked about was Dr. Everest. I could hardly stand it."

I should have heeded my intuition about Roger's feelings for Grace. "Is that why Roger and his wife separated?" I asked.

"Dr. Everest never encouraged him," Kyle said. "At least not that I ever saw."

"Was there tension between them?"

"She didn't seem to notice how he felt." Kyle shook his head and smiled slightly. "But the rest of us did."

I wondered if Grace truly hadn't noticed or if she thought that ignoring Roger's infatuation would make it go away. "What about Roger's daughter, Liz? Did she know about it?"

Kyle shrugged.

"The basketball player?" Toni asked me.

I nodded.

"She and her dad fought about Dr. Everest in this very room." Toni glanced at Kyle. "I overheard them when Roger was staying with you."

"When was that?" I asked.

"Five or six months ago," Kyle said.

"Five," Toni declared. "He stayed almost two months."

"You heard him fighting with his daughter," I prompted.

"Their voices were so loud I could hear them from the hallway." Roger was saying it was natural for him to talk about Grace because she was his boss. His daughter said she never wanted to hear Grace's name again."

I turned to Kyle. "Do you think Liz blamed Grace for her parents' separation?"

He hesitated.

Toni gave him an exasperated smile. "Come on, Kyle, you know she'd want to blame someone besides her mom and dad."

Kyle edged away from Toni, but she didn't seem to notice. "When my parents split, I blamed my mom's best friend, my dad's boss, even the mailman. You have to blame someone," she said. "Otherwise it hurts too much. Of course Liz blames Dr. Everest."

As Toni spoke, Kyle's expression darkened, and when she stopped, he headed to the door, held it open, and smiled tightly at Vince and me. "You two must have other people you need to talk with," he said.

After the door shut behind us, Vince and I stood in the hallway, stunned by our quick dismissal. Then we heard Toni ask Kyle what was wrong with him. What indeed? Was he trying to protect Liz, or was he hiding something else?

Chapter Ten

ZOEY HARGROVE LIVED on a cul-de-sac lined with McMansions. My rusty Dodge Omni drew stares from children laden with backpacks and violins. "Welcome to the land of the bland," Vince said. I tried to picture gawky red-headed Zoey growing up in a neighborhood where color-coordination and hedge pruning reigned supreme. The only sign that real people lived at her address was a tiny bicycle sprawled near the front porch.

Finding Zoey's home had been easy. There was only one Hargrove in the Iowa City phone book, and when Vince called the number and asked for Zoey, a woman gave him Zoey's cell number, explaining that she herself was expecting an important call. I hoped Zoey was home. I wanted to talk to her in person. I wanted to watch her reaction as I asked her about Grace.

The doorbell echoed loudly. I rang it twice before a thirtyish woman answered. Delicate-boned and flaxen-haired, she laughed nervously when I asked if we could talk with Zoey.

"She isn't available right now." Again the laugh, followed by a forced smile. "Where are my manners?" She extended her hand. "I'm Zoey's step-mom, Natalie."

Vince introduced me as Zoey's English teacher, and himself, as her guidance counselor. I crossed my fingers, hoping that we were correct in our assumption that Natalie didn't know squat about her step-daughter's life.

"Oh sure," she said, "I've heard a lot about you, but I didn't know you made house calls."

I was about to offer some vague explanation for our presence when a little boy bounded into the room. He was, as my dad would say, "the spitting image" of Natalie. "Mommy," he yelled. "Is it more police?"

Natalie blushed and tried to quiet him.

"Are they taking Zoey away?" He began bouncing up and down.

"Don't be silly, Ethan. These nice people are her teachers."

He paused for a moment and gazed up at us. "Were you there when they came and got her? Did they put her in handcuffs?"

Natalie's blush deepened. "Ethan," she said, "why don't you go finish your tower. Mommy will come see it in a minute."

His face puckered. "I wanna hear about the handcuffs."

"What an imagination," she said. "The police needed to ask Zoey a few questions during school today, and Ethan thinks she's in trouble."

"Paul says she has an alibi," Ethan chimed in.

"You're supposed to call him Daddy Paul, remember, Sweetie?" She turned toward us. "I need to run an errand for my husband before he gets home. I'll tell Zoey you stopped by."

As she gestured toward the front door, I peered down the entryway. In a doorframe flanked by potted bonsai trees, Zoey looked back at me. I wondered if Natalie knew she was there and was trying to keep us from talking to her or if Natalie simply hadn't checked to see if Zoey was home. Neither option boded well for the girl.

Vince must have seen Zoey too because he asked to use the restroom. Seizing the opportunity to learn more about the family, I asked Natalie how many years were between Zoey and Ethan.

Natalie decided to play math teacher. "How old are you, Ethan?"

"Six," he proclaimed.

"How old is Zoey?"

Ethan raised his eyes to the ceiling as he thought. "Fifteen?"

I wondered how young Zoey had been when her mother died.

"What's fifteen minus six?" Natalie asked.

"How old is Paul?" Ethan asked abruptly.

Natalie's face reddened again. "Daddy Paul likes to keep his age private."

Ethan turned to me. "Paul puts people in jail," he explained somberly.

"Only sometimes." Natalie gently pulled the boy to her side. "Daddy Paul is a judge. We're all real proud of him, aren't we, Sweetie?"

The boy wrenched away from her and stomped out of the room, the lights on the heels of his tennis shoes blinking red.

VINCE AND I were back in the car, headed east on Melrose Avenue, as he described his tête-à-tête with Zoey. "I told her that we solved the Dave DeVoster murder, and I assured her that if she had done away with Dr. Everest, we would swiftly bring her to justice."

"That'll make her eager to talk with us."

"Mar-Bar, I realize that sarcasm is your native language, but you might occasionally try other modes of communication."

I cracked my window. "What did she say?"

"That she didn't do it. That she wasn't even there."

Big surprise, I thought, keeping my sarcasm to myself.

"She said she was with her father, Judge Hargrove."

"My word against a judge's."

"You've got Anne to back you up," Vince said. But he rubbed his goatee, so I knew something was bothering him.

"What?" I asked.

"She said that if we don't leave her alone, her father will make us sorry."

Visions of restraining orders and slander charges danced through my head.

"She must have learned the fine art of making threats from her old man," Vince said. "Score one for nurture."

I thought of Zoey staring past her step-mom and step-brother. The girl was probably not receiving a whole lot of nurture.

"Slow down!" Vince commanded.

I took my foot off the gas. We were in University Heights, home to Iowa City's biggest speed trap. Sure enough, a few blocks ahead, a cop waited on a dead end street. Riding my brakes to stay below the limit, I felt a surge of rage. How dare any police officer waste time on speeders a mere day after Grace had been murdered?

Tears blurred my vision as we passed through University Heights. Still on Melrose, we found ourselves in a long line of cars waiting for the light at Hawkins Drive to turn green. Ahead on our left were Kinnick Stadium and the UI Hospital. The hospital's sprawling parking ramps and new pavilions jutted harshly against the early twilight sky. I wanted to get past the place as soon as I could, but traffic barely moved even after the light turned. Once we got closer to the intersection, I could see why. Leo Spires and his minions were protesting on the sidewalk nearest the hospital. He'd moved from the hospital entrance and Parking Ramp 1 to a place where he'd attract more attention. Three or four little kids held signs that said "Daddies Matter." A woman with a baby strapped to her held a sign that read "Do the Math!!! Dad + Mom + Baby = Family." Celia Spires sported a fur-trimmed jacket and carried the same sign she'd had yesterday. "Real Women Don't Buy Sperm." The tiny bald signless guy was there too, looking ready to rush the cops who were talking with the reverend. Next to the police car, some white-haired women wielded a huge banner. It featured a photo of Grace with a red slash drawn through it.

How could people who claimed to treasure life celebrate death? How could they be so hateful?

"You suck!" shouted a guy from the car in front of me. He gave Leo Spires the finger.

A couple other drivers honked their horns — in agreement or impatience, I couldn't tell. The cops exchanged worried glances.

"Zealots-R-Us," Vince said. "Look at those kids learning their family values. And check out the grannies."

I studied the white-haired women. One of them was burdened with large unfashionable glasses and a braided mound atop her head. I had seen that woman's face a mere hour ago on Kyle Bremmer's bookshelf. And now I knew where else I'd seen her. On the day

Grace was killed, Kyle's grandmother had been protesting in front of the hospital.

WITHIN BLOCKS OF Kyle's apartment, Vince was still trying to dissuade me from visiting the young man twice in one day. "Just because Kyle's grandma is a Spires' groupie doesn't mean he is."

"You're absolutely right," I said, continuing toward Kyle's apartment.

"You should collect your thoughts before you talk to him again."

"I'm trying." As I pulled into the parking lot behind Kyle's apartment, Detective Dallas Henry emerged from a car and strode toward the building. I prayed that she wouldn't turn around and see us. We had just as much right to be there as she did, but I didn't care to explain our presence.

She disappeared into the building, and Vince heaved a dramatic sigh.

"She's probably here to talk with Kyle," I said. "We'll have to wait until she comes out."

"That could be hours."

"She's investigating a murder. She's not going to take her time chit-chatting."

"What if she sees us?"

I was about to bribe him with a trip to the Hamburg Inn, his favorite diner, when my phone rang. It was Anne, her voice wracked with sobs. Something terrible had happened, something she couldn't say over the phone.

Chapter Eleven

MY THOUGHTS CHURNED as I dropped Vince at Justine's and sped toward Anne's. Someone must have died or been horribly hurt. Anne's mother or Orchid. Or one of our friends. Oh God, not Bridget, please, not Bridget.

I opened Anne's front door without knocking and rushed to the chair where she was curled up, clutching the phone in both hands. Labrys, her golden retriever, stood guard beside her, whimpering. When the dog saw me, she barked and wagged her tail, but she didn't come greet me as usual. She never leaves the side of a hurting human.

"I'm here," I said softly.

Anne didn't budge, so I squatted next to her and Labrys. She still didn't acknowledge me, so I gently took the phone from her and held her hands in mine. Slowly, she looked up, her face raw and red. Without her glasses, she seemed exposed, incomplete. I asked her what happened, and her lower lip trembled as she tried to speak. I couldn't take much more. My pulse skittered crazily. I squeezed her hands.

She pulled away and straightened herself in the chair. She reached for her glasses on the end-table, and slipped them on. "My period started."

"What?" I exploded. "I thought someone was dead."

Anne went glacier. "I should have known you wouldn't understand."

"Me? You're the one who doesn't get it. I was investigating Grace's murder. I stopped what I was doing to come help you. You terrified me. Then you criticize my reaction?"

Labrys barked.

Anne dabbed beneath her glasses with a Kleenex.

I should have been nicer. I knew what the start of a period meant to Anne — another round of trying and hoping, wanting and waiting. But seriously, was she this distraught every month?

"I used our donor's last vial," she said.

I hadn't known that was a possibility. She hadn't said anything about it in her audio diary.

"Orchid wants us to take a break before we choose another one."

"How long?" I asked.

Anne's face tightened.

Again, I'd said the wrong thing.

"She's been waiting for an excuse to get me to stop trying. First she says she doesn't like what it's doing to me. Then it's too stressful for her. Now she says we need to find another lab because the university isn't safe." Anne yanked another Kleenex out of the box beside her. "Orchid thinks one lab is as good as another, but I've bonded with the staff at this lab. Roger always asks how I'm doing and Kyle always does my preps, even when I've needed to inseminate on a weekend."

I flashed on Kyle's grandmother protesting with Spires, but I pushed the image away. Right now I needed to focus on Anne.

She squeezed the Kleenex until it vanished in her fist. "I can't deal with finding a new donor and a new lab."

Labrys rested her head on Anne's lap and whimpered again.

"I just can't." Anne insisted.

I tried to think of something to say.

"Orchid doesn't get it," Anne said.

Outside, a car without a muffler growled past, and the wind buffeted bare trees.

Anne chewed on the inside of her lip. "I think this may break us up," she said quietly.

I'm ashamed to admit it, but I felt a jolt of elation. Then I saw a tear rolling down Anne's cheek. I wiped it away without thinking. She gazed at me, her eyes filled with pain and confusion.

"Annabelle," I said, using her nickname of old.

She looked away. I didn't want to say anything good about Orchid, but I knew I should. I was Anne's friend, and friends help each other through relationship troubles. "Orchid worships you," I said.

Anne turned back toward me.

"She'd do anything to make you happy," I added.

"That's not good enough," Anne said. "Don't you see?"

I didn't, not the least little bit.

"I don't want Orchid to do this *for me*," Anne said. "I want her to *want* a baby — our child — as much as I do."

Oh, Annabelle, I thought, nobody can meet that desire.

"But I shouldn't criticize her," Anne said. "That just creates bad energy."

I sat on the floor and stretched my legs in front of me. One of them had fallen asleep as I'd crouched next to Anne.

"I must be doing something wrong." She blew her nose. "Do you know how much money I cost us every month?" She pulled her knees toward her chest and hugged them. "I don't know what else to do. I've tried ovulation predictor kits, taking my basal body temperature, checking my cervical mucus."

Whoa, I thought, too much information.

"I've tried extra massages and affirmations," Anne continued. "New visualizations." She paused and bit her lip. "I've even tried Clomid."

Clomid is a fertility drug. That was something else Anne had left out of her audio diary—probably because she didn't believe in drugs. Not even Advil or cough drops. I thought hard before I spoke. "That must have been a tough decision."

"It's been a waste."

Anne tucked her hair behind her ear, and I saw that she was wearing the gold heart-shaped earrings I'd given her our first Christmas together. I'd kissed each ear after she put them in. My throat tightened at the memory, and I forced myself back to the present. "Tell me about the donor," I said. "I want to know what he was like." It felt strange to use past tense on a guy who was probably alive and well, but he was gone from Anne's world. And that's what mattered.

She gave me a quizzical look, then a hesitant smile. "You want to see his profile?"

I nodded, and she slipped sock-footed out of the room, Labrys trailing after. I was glad Anne was up and moving, and I was happy to follow suit. Hardwood floors and hemp rugs are more inviting to the eye than to the rear. I wandered into the kitchen, started some water for tea, and savored my first quiet moment of the day. It wasn't meant to last. Just as the tea kettle started rumbling, my phone rang.

"Hey, babe," Bridget said. "I'm home. When can you come over?"

I'd forgotten all about her homecoming. "I'm not sure," I said, "I'm kind of in the middle of something."

"Oh. Okay." Bridget sounded surprised.

We hadn't made any specific plans, but I always came over after she'd been on the road. I was about to explain that Anne was having a rough time when Bridget asked about my sleuthing. I gave her an abbreviated account, omitting what I'd learned about her point guard. I wanted to ask about Liz's relationship with Grace, but I was in no mood to fight.

"We're going to get that 6'6" center from Minneapolis," Bridget said. "A real banger."

"That's great." I tried to sound enthused, but I was thinking that Grace wouldn't be in the stands to see the new Hawkeye superstar. Before my thoughts snowballed with all the moments Grace was going to miss, Bridget asked about arrangements. She wasn't prone to euphemism, so it took me a moment to realize she was asking about the funeral. "I don't know anything yet," I said, "but there's going to be some sort of tribute at the Women's Center. Anne's planning it." Bridget hadn't asked about Anne. Maybe she didn't know that Anne was with me when I found Grace.

"You must be wiped out," Bridget said. "What do you say we both crash tonight and see each other tomorrow?"

I agreed, but Bridget's flexibility irritated me. Wasn't she the least bit disappointed to postpone our reunion? Was there something she wasn't telling me? I seethed for a moment and then I realized I had no right to be angry with Bridget. There was plenty I wasn't telling her.

As the tea kettle screeched, I wrenched it off the burner, battling a Catholic flashback. Sister Mary Frances stood in front of a chalkboard, tapping her ruler against a yellow cursive phrase, "Sins of Omission." These sins, she explained, were just as serious as sins of commission. The idea petrified me. You didn't have to be a math whiz to see that sins of omission doubled your chances for dying with mortal sin on your soul. You were literally damned if you did, and damned if you didn't. With Bridget, I'd just committed two sins of omission. I hadn't mentioned my discovery about Liz Lipinski, and I hadn't revealed that I was with Anne. But maybe I was being over-scrupulous about the Anne thing. After all, I was simply comforting a friend.

WHEN ANNE RETURNED to the kitchen, she had washed her face, combed her hair, and donned a sweater. She handed me one too, explaining that they hadn't turned the heat on yet. My hair crackled with electricity as I pulled the bulky cable-knit over my head. Anne set a manila file folder on the table next to me and sipped her tea.

"Tell me about him first," I said.

"He was perfect. We both thought so."

I couldn't imagine Orchid using the words *perfect* and *man* in the same sentence.

"No, really," Anne insisted. "Orchid read the profiles before I did, and she said there was one that she thought was perfect and that I'd know it when I saw it. She was right. We didn't have to negotiate or anything." Anne's face clouded. "The only problem was the limited supply, but I told myself I'd get pregnant long before it ran out." She shook her head. "Stupid."

I didn't want her to beat herself up again. "What did you like about him?"

"He had Orchid's coloring." She opened the folder. "Look at his baby picture."

There, sitting on the beach next to a sandcastle, was a blue-eyed toddler with dark hair. He held a seashell toward the camera.

"Doesn't his energy seem great?" Anne said. "Creative and in tune with nature."

What I noticed about the lad was his wiriness, not a trait you'd associate with Orchid.

"Several women who purchased his sperm have reported pregnancies. You can't buy it if you live in San Francisco or LA."

That meant his little guys had generated so many children in those cities that the sperm bank was worried about half-siblings accidentally hooking up.

"He graduated summa cum laude from Berkeley," Anne said, "and now he's a civil rights attorney."

"Impressive," I said.

"He's also a vegetarian Unitarian who practices mindfulness, meditation, and supports the Green Party."

I'm no scientist, but I'm pretty sure you can't inherit things like dietary habits and political affiliations. "What about his parents and grandparents?" I asked.

"That's the best part. His mom is a lesbian—that's why he wanted to be a donor. Here—" She flipped to the last page. "Read his essay."

The "essay" consisted of short answers to four questions, a sort of Baltimore Catechism for sperm shoppers. Anne pointed to his third answer. "My mother and father taught me everything I know about love, respect, and courage. Mom is a lesbian who came out late in life, but women who come out early also deserve the opportunity to build families. I do this to honor my beautiful mother."

Okay, that made *me* want his sperm. According to Grace, a lot of donors just want extra cash for med school. That, or they worship their own genes. "Too bad we can't breed out arrogance," she'd said.

"Well?" Anne asked.

I proclaimed him perfect and tried to think of a tactful way to phrase my condolences. I'm sorry that his sperm is gone? I'm sorry you won't be able to use him? Where was the Hallmark card for this situation?

"Look at the rest," Anne said.

I was glad to oblige. I'd studied plenty of short profiles online preparing for my radio series, but I hadn't seen many long ones. And I was happy that Anne was sharing something important with me.

As Anne filled a soup pot with water and removed vegetables from the fridge, I read about donor 1763. His Meyers-Briggs type was ENTJ. He spoke four languages, including Japanese, and played three musical instruments. His favorite color was blue. His favorite animal, the tiger. His favorite movie, *Casablanca*. It didn't ask about his favorite book. A right-handed gentleman, he had no tattoos, piercings, or military service. And, of course, no health problems or vices except for drinking four ounces of alcohol per week. Presumably, he enjoyed measuring almost as much as the folks at the sperm bank. In inches, they listed the measurements of Donor 1763's neck, chest, inseam, waist, sleeve, wrist, shoe size, and hat size.

You could know your sperm donor better than your partner—better than yourself! What was the circumference of my wrist? How many years of piano lessons had I endured?

"It's a lot to take in, isn't it?" Anne said.

I nodded.

She was chopping a carrot, her cutting board surrounded by an army of vegetables. Broccoli, onions, celery, and something I didn't recognize. The rhythm of her chopping soothed me, and the scent of cooking rice made me think of lazy Sunday afternoons when she'd make huge batches of soup and we'd make love while it simmered.

I turned my attention back to the profile. After the donor's information, you got the skinny on his father, mother, siblings, aunts, uncles, and grandparents. All college educated and multi-lingual except for an underachieving aunt. All musically or athletically talented. All healthy and long-lived. That last part was par for the course with sperm donors, but—call me cynical—isn't so much good luck bound to run out sooner or later?

I closed the profile and went to help Anne. "I'll do the onions," I said. "You've had enough tears for one night."

She set the knife down, but didn't move away from the cutting board. "What am I going to do?"

I guided her toward the table. "Relax while I finish dinner. Then after we eat, you'll take a long hot bath."

"Come on," she said. "You know what I mean."

Lapsed Catholic or not, I sent up a prayer that I'd say the right thing. "You'll find another donor. Your first one set the bar high, but he helped you know what you want, right?"

She nodded and sat down.

I sat next to her. "You're surrounded by great energy."

She started to protest, but I cut her off.

"You've got all your friends," I said. "You've got me." You've always got me, I thought. More than anything, I wanted to lean over and kiss her, make her forget everything except how good we were together. But we wouldn't be good if I took advantage of her, so once again I reminded myself to behave like a friend, like a decent human being. "Orchid is in shock over the murder," I said. "We all are. She has her parents' move to deal with, and she's away from you." I made myself continue. "She'll come around."

"What if she doesn't?" Anne picked up her donor's profile and held it with both hands.

I wanted to say that Anne herself might come around, might realize that she and Orchid could use a break from their quest to conceive. But I kept quiet. The last thing Anne needed was an argument with me.

Labrys sauntered into the kitchen and slurped some water, but Anne had eyes only for the profile. I felt far away, helpless, and— yes, I'll admit it—sad that she'd never asked me to help her create a child when we were together. Sadder still, knowing I would have denied her.

Chapter Twelve

THE NEXT MORNING I once again faced my trashed office, frantic and furious because I was scheduled to interview a novelist right after lunch. I hadn't cracked his book's spine, and now I had no idea where the damn thing even was. As I squatted on the floor and rifled through files and papers, I thought about the person who'd scattered them there, maybe the same person who'd killed Grace. But I had no time for fear. After my author interview, I needed to investigate Kyle's potential connection with Spires, and then I wanted to check on Anne.

It had been close to midnight when I'd crashed on her couch, and now not even a double espresso could revive me. I grabbed a pile of papers on my desk and gave myself a paper cut. Hoping it wasn't an omen, I gazed at the only thing left on the wall, the photo of my nieces on a carousel. I shivered at the thought of the robber—the killer—studying their smiling faces. For once, I was glad they lived in Florida.

The phone rang and made my heart skitter. After two more rings, I found the receiver under some papers.

"Mara," the station's longtime office manager said, "I'm sorry to disturb you."

My anxiety ratcheted up a notch. I had asked Noreen to hold my calls, and since she hadn't, there must be an emergency.

"There's a young woman who insists on seeing you. She's looming over my desk." Noreen said the word *looming* as if it were a Class A felony.

I fought to keep the irritation out of my voice. "Get her contact information, and tell her I'll get back to her as soon as I can."

"She says you want to talk to her. A Miss Zoey Hargrove."

Zoey was indeed looming over poor Noreen's desk although, given Zoey's gangly awkwardness, the sight was more comical than menacing. With her hair down, Zoey looked even younger than she had at the hospital, and her standard teen-wear, layered shirts and flared jeans, added to the effect. Shoulders hunched, she folded her arms over her chest and fixed her eyes on me.

I once again asked Noreen to hold my calls, and I ushered Zoey into Orchid's office. Ignoring my invitation to sit, Zoey stood right next to Orchid's desk, no doubt mistaking it for mine, and she raked her eyes over the contents. A prism-shaped paperweight, a Tupperware container filled with granola, and a block of sticky notes that said "Take Back the Night." Zoey could loom over Orchid's desk all she wanted. I would simply wait. Often, the best interview strategy is keeping your mouth shut."

Zoey glanced at me, then back at the desk.

Orchid's clock ticked, and someone laughed in the hall.

Zoey screwed up her face as if she were getting ready to bench press her entire weight. Then she spoke. "Your friend Vince says you're good at finding out the truth."

I tilted my head in acknowledgement.

"I want you to help me find my donor dad," Zoey said. "My birth father."

I remained quiet, this time out of surprise.

"Vince says you want to find out who killed that doctor," Zoey continued. "Well, I can help. I overheard some stuff when I was at the hospital, but I haven't told the police. My father, Judge Hargrove, said not to admit I was there."

"What did you hear?"

"First you gotta promise to help me find my donor dad." Zoey looked at me, her blue eyes wide.

I wondered how Grace had felt when Zoey confronted her, demanding to know her donor's identity. Grace favored open donors, yet she respected the privacy of closed ones because the system depended on them. She'd devoted her life to that system — possibly given her life for it. Would she want me to muck with it in order to increase my odds of finding her killer?

"I'm not gonna ask him for money or mess up his life. I just want to know who he is."

"The doctor who was murdered was my good friend," I said. "You're obstructing justice. You could be arrested for withholding information."

"Not gonna happen." Zoey squared her shoulders and stood taller. "You say you saw me at the hospital, but the judge says I was home with him."

"Since you two are so close, why do you want to find your donor?"

She looked like I'd slapped her. Given what I knew about her family, my question was cruel, but I was angry. "Remember the woman I was with at the hospital?" I asked. I stepped away from the wall so Zoey could see the large photo of Anne and Orchid at the Golden Gate Bridge. I pointed to Anne. "She and I each met with a police artist. Separately. And both times, the result was an easily recognizable picture of you."

Zoey twisted one of her many rings. Then another.

"You had motive for killing Dr. Everest," I continued. "She wouldn't give you the information you wanted, and several witnesses heard you threaten her."

"I didn't think she'd be at the lab," Zoey said. "It was a Sunday. I just wanted to look at her files."

"Maybe so. But she interrupted you. She threatened to call the police. You panicked, and then you—"

"No," Zoey said. "The doctor never saw me. I hid. As soon as I heard someone enter the lab, I squeezed under the closest desk." Zoey lifted her chin defiantly.

I wasn't sure what to believe. The girl had a temper. She could have easily lost it and killed Grace. But Zoey was also persistent. She could have hid, hoping to continue her search after Grace left.

"I was in the main office right next to the doctor's," Zoey said, "and I heard some very interesting stuff." Her face was slightly flushed.

I wanted to believe Zoey. I wanted her to be innocent. I wanted her to offer me a nugget of information that would help me find Grace's killer.

"Do we have a deal or don't we?" Zoey asked.

"Tell me what you heard," I said, "and we'll see."

"Once I tell, you'll have no reason to help me."

"If you can't trust me, why would you want me to?"

She twisted another ring and studied me. "Promise not to tell the police."

Great. Then I'd be obstructing justice. Or worse, helping Grace's killer.

"If you do, I'll deny it." Zoey's voice quavered.

I had to give the kid her props. She knew what she wanted, and she was determined to get it. I asked her to have a seat, and this time, she did. Pulling up a chair next to her, I explained that my first priority was finding Grace's killer. The donor search would come second.

Zoey started to protest, but I cut her off. "Take it or leave it."

She nodded sullenly, and I reminded myself that she was only fifteen. "I'm not a private investigator," I said gently. "I've never tried to locate a sperm donor. We might not find him."

"I know."

I didn't want to squash her dreams, just ease her disappointment if we failed. "But you have my word," I said, "I'll give it a good shot."

"Your best shot."

"My best," I agreed, "after I—"

"Got it," she said. "The doctor comes first." She extended her hand to me, stiffly. I'd never made such a pact before, and as we shook, I hoped I wouldn't regret it.

Zoey's eyes darted around the room. "Like I said, I wanted to look at the doctor's files so I could find my donor dad. I didn't think anyone would be in the lab on a Sunday, but still, I thought I should have a disguise. My boyfriend's mom is a custodian at the hospital, and he borrowed her uniform for me."

"Borrowed?" I asked.

"Whatever."

"Where did you get the cleaning cart?"

"He gave me her keys too."

What kind of guy steals from his mom to help his girlfriend commit a crime?

Zoey seemed to read my thoughts. "It was my idea," she said.

I wondered if Judge Hargrove knew about his young daughter's helpful boyfriend.

"Anyway," Zoey said, "I parked the cart in the main office because I think that's where most of the files are. I tried to open some of the file cabinets, but they were locked. I was about to try another one when I heard footsteps. There was no place to hide except under the desk, so that's where I went. I barely fit."

I imagined Zoey scrunching her long limbs under Roger's desk.

"It was dusty too, and I was afraid I was gonna sneeze. In the room right next to me—"

"Doctor Everest's office?" I asked.

Zoey nodded. "Someone—the doctor, I guess—was shuffling papers around and sighing."

"What time was this?"

Zoey rolled her eyes. "I couldn't look at my watch. I was trapped under the desk, remember? My legs were completely asleep when I heard more footsteps." Zoey paused dramatically. "Then voices from the doctor's office. At first I couldn't make them out, but then they got louder. The doctor goes, 'Roger, I have no choice but to fire Justine.'"

My pulse quickened. "Are you sure about those names?" I asked.

Zoey nodded. "I couldn't hear what Roger said. His voice was too low. Then the doctor goes, 'Don't be daft, Roger. Justine is the worst tech we've ever had. I was a fool to hire her.'" Zoey smiled proudly. "I could hear the doctor clear as day."

Grace almost always spoke loudly. I attributed this volume both to her hearing problem and to her staunch belief in her own pronouncements.

Zoey glanced at me and continued. "Then Roger goes, 'Please, just give her one more chance.'"

I wondered if Justine had known that Grace was going to can her, and I wondered why Roger was pleading her case. If Justine was so inept, wouldn't her departure make his job easier?

"I think he was crying," Zoey said, "because she goes 'Roger, for God's sake, get some help,' and then someone blew their nose super hard like a guy would. Then he goes, 'If you fire her, you'll destroy my family.' And she goes, 'You've done that yourself. One more incident and you're out of here too.'"

Zoey studied me expectantly. "Good stuff, huh?"

It sure was, although I had no idea what to make of it. How could firing Justine ruin Roger's family? How had he ruined his own family? All I could imagine was that Roger and Justine were sleeping together. But that hardly seemed possible. It sure didn't mesh with what Kyle had told me about Roger's feelings for Grace. And even if Kyle was wrong, it was hard to imagine Justine wanting Roger. And if Roger had been sexually harassing Justine, Grace would have fired him.

"The doctor was seriously pissed off," Zoey added. "She told Roger that he was pathetic."

I thought about Roger's hysteria the day Grace died. Had it stemmed from genuine pain? Or from fury or guilt?

"Then she got a phone call," Zoey said. "From her grandkids, I think, because she was asking them ten million questions about school and soccer and that kind of crap." Zoey's voice had an edge.

Maybe she never got such questions from her dad and step-mom. "Did you hear Roger leave?" I asked.

Zoey shook her head.

"What else did you hear?"

"The doctor was on the phone forever, but she stopped for a second to say, 'Good morning, Kyle.' He said 'hey' back, and she thanked him for working on a Sunday. Then she went back to the grandkid talk. Something about apple-picking."

Each fall, Grace took her grandkids to Wilson's Orchard, and then they made everything you could possibly make out of apples — not just pies and cakes, but edible sculptures and puppets. I'd been in the audience for many a performance featuring the adventures of the Amazing Applehead. I fought the urge to cry, and I refocused on Zoey.

"A few minutes after the doctor hung up, I heard Kyle talking across the hall."

"Was he in one of the prep rooms?" I asked.

Zoey shrugged. "He sounded like he was in the room right across the hall from where I was."

"That's a prep room," I said.

"Whatever. He was talking to a woman. Not the doctor. This woman had a super soft voice, and I think she had been trying to get pregnant for a really long time because Kyle goes, 'You never know when it will be the one.' And he told her a story about a woman who was almost ready to give up when she got pregnant. I hope someone super nice like that worked with my mom." Zoey hung her head and fiddled with more rings.

"I'm sorry," I said.

She didn't respond, and I was about to reach over and touch her arm when she started up again. "He offered to walk her somewhere, and I guess he must have because I didn't hear any more from them."

"Did the woman say anything to Dr. Everest?" I asked.

Zoey shook her head.

"Did you catch the woman's name?"

"Just her first. Felicity. Felicity who sounded sad. That's why I remember." Zoey complained about parents giving their kids names that could turn ironic, but I was only half listening. Felicity Cheng's insemination reports had been among the ones on Grace's desk. She was a sculptor who'd been trying even longer than Anne. I knew this because Felicity and I frequented the same potlucks and she let me interview her for *Trying Times*. "After Felicity left, did you hear anything else?"

"Some papers rustling in the doctor's office. Some footsteps."

"Heavy or soft?"

Zoey gave me an apologetic look and shrugged. "I waited a super long time because I couldn't tell whether the doctor was still in her office. Or even if Roger was. My back was really starting to hurt, so I slid out from underneath the desk. But I stayed on the floor just in case there was still someone else in the lab." Zoey frowned. "Besides, I had to get the feeling back in my legs. I was about to try standing when I heard more footsteps. And I scooted back under the desk with not a second to spare. A woman came into the room where I was. She walked right around to the side of the desk where I was hiding. Her feet were three inches from my hands. I almost peed myself."

"What did she look like?"

"She had alligator stilettos and skinny legs."

Celia Spires, I thought. "What else?"

Zoey looked sheepish. "I closed my eyes. I was afraid she'd feel me looking at her and find me. But I heard her try to open ten million file cabinets."

Celia hadn't trashed that office. She'd simply searched for something. But Celia wouldn't have searched the lab's main office if Grace had been in her own office right next door. Celia wouldn't have tried to open file cabinets unless she believed she was alone in the lab. My stomach mutinied. What if Grace had already been killed by the time Celia arrived? If the murder had taken place in the cryo room, where Grace's body was found, Zoey wouldn't have heard anything. And when Celia arrived, she would have assumed she had the lab to herself. Unless Celia had killed Grace.

"I was sure the alligator woman was gonna find me," Zoey said, "but she left. I waited a while to be sure, and just as I was gonna get out of there, you came in and called out Grace's name."

"Did you hear the entrance to the lab open before you heard my voice?"

Zoey shrugged.

"Think," I urged. "It's important."

She tugged at the ring on her pointer finger. Then she shook her head.

"Did you ever hear the door to the lab open or close?" I pushed.

"No." Zoey's eyes slowly widened. "Omygod. Anyone could have come and gone and I wouldn't have known if they didn't say anything or come into the office where I was hiding. I let her die."

I battled more queasiness. Grace had been killed while Zoey was hiding under Roger's desk.

"I let her die." Zoey's voice flattened. "She might have known my real father, and I let her die."

This time I didn't hesitate. I put both my hands on her shoulders, gently but firmly. "Listen," I said. "There is no way this is your fault."

But a minute later when I was heading down the hall toward the Coke machine, I wondered if I really meant it. I didn't doubt that Zoey had told the truth about what she'd heard, but I wondered if it was the whole truth. After the Roger/Justine soap opera, Zoey could have confronted Grace and lost control of her emotions. But then why would Zoey have remained in the lab? That was a good, logical question. What wasn't logical was my desire to believe in Zoey's innocence, to believe in Zoey herself. One Coke in hand, I tried to get the pop machine to accept another dollar bill, and I told myself that detective work is not a time to play sentimental favorites. I couldn't afford to rule out Zoey.

But I was glad she wasn't my only suspect. Roger, Kyle, and Celia had all been in the lab that morning. Leo Spires had been at the hospital, and for all I knew, so had Justine. She and Kyle, however, didn't have very strong motives. Kyle had none at all unless he shared his grandmother's devotion to Reverend Leo Spires. And it was hard to imagine Justine killing just to keep her day job.

The exact-change light shone on the machine. I had a huge supply of quarters in my top desk drawer. If the vandal had left them.

The vandal.

Zoey could be in a lot of danger. Even though she was officially denying her presence at the hospital, the cops were no doubt showing her picture around. I myself had shown it to Leo Spires, Roger, and Kyle. The killer would wonder what Zoey had witnessed.

I dashed back to the office and handed her the Coke. "I'm sorry I gave you a rough time about lying to the police. Your dad may have a point."

Zoey looked puzzled.

"I don't condone lying," I added, "but there's no need to advertise the fact that you were there. You should be careful."

Her eyes glazed over. There I was, another adult assuming she couldn't handle herself.

I don't like scaring young people, but sometimes you don't have a choice. I took her across the hall and showed her my office.

"Wow," she said, "you need to seriously work on your organizational skills."

"The killer did it," I snapped.

"Really?" Zoey asked. "Why?"

I had no answer for her, but as she gaped at the carnage, I spied the novel I'd been searching for — in plain sight, of course, on top of a file cabinet.

Zoey stepped away from my office, hugging her arms to her chest. As she headed back to her seat across the hall, I spelled out the reasons why I was worried about her safety, and I told her to avoid spending time alone.

"My boyfriend's got my back," she said.

"Right," I countered. "He sounds really responsible, stealing from his mother."

Zoey glared at me, and footsteps sounded in the hallway.

"Well, well, well," drawled Detective Dallas Henry. "Look who's as close as two peas in a pod." She stood arms akimbo. Her suit matched her saccharine peach lipstick.

I froze, but Zoey gave the detective a smile. "My father, Judge Hargrove, discovered that Mara was one of the people who claimed to see me at the hospital. I wanted to introduce myself so she could see her mistake."

Smooth, I thought. Too smooth. Maybe I was wrong to trust Zoey.

"How thoughtful," Detective Henry said, "but it's a shame you're missing school. How about I give you a ride?" With her sweet tone and her no-nonsense pumps, she might have been Zoey's social studies teacher.

"My father says police can't interview minors unless their parent or guardian is present."

"No interview," the detective promised. "We'll just listen to the radio." Then she turned her attention to me. "I'll be in touch, Ms. Gilgannon."

Chapter Thirteen

WHY HAD DETECTIVE Henry come to the station, and what had she made of seeing me with Zoey? These questions niggled at me as I prepped my author interview. After the interview itself was done, I decided to use some sick leave so I could spend the rest of the afternoon sleuthing. I phoned Roger and told him I had more questions. Since the lab was still closed and he was eager to do anything he could for Grace, he agreed to meet me at the downtown Java House. I purposefully picked a public place in case Roger turned homicidal. But if he did, I was on my own. The students at the back of the shop had ears only for their iPods and eyes only for their laptops.

Wedged between the back wall and a tiny table, Roger looked extra beefy. He tried to smile, but his lips twisted into a grimace. As he gave me the details about Grace's visitation and funeral, sorrow welled up inside me. I wanted nothing more than to flee, to sink into my couch and cry the afternoon away. Instead, I sipped my coffee and thought about the ground I wanted to cover with Roger. It was a lot of ground, and it would require a lot of indirection and flattery. "The lab must generate a lot of paperwork," I said.

"You can't imagine." Roger gestured expansively. "Patient histories, billing, personnel records, supply orders, correspondence—mostly about insurance. Of course, we track most of that electronically as well."

"And you handle it all?"

Roger smiled. "Me, myself, and I."

"Did you file anything related to Grace's work with me?"

Roger's smile faded as he shook his head.

"What about the endowment?"

His smile returned. "I handle most of the correspondence related to it."

I thought about the papers on Grace's desk. "Insemination reports?" I asked.

"Those go in patient files. Hard copies. The patient has to sign them."

"It seems like a lot of people might be interested in those."

"Only the patients and the staff get to see them."

"Yeah," I said, "but lots of other people would probably like to. Kids looking for their donor dads, closed donors with a change of heart, people looking for ammunition to shut down the lab." As I continued, Roger's expression darkened. "If Leo Spires had access to those reports, he could track down the donors or the kids and try to get them worked up. Somebody like that would be a great poster-child for his cause."

Roger shook his head. "They'd never have access to the records."

I let a beat go by. "Celia Spires was in your office the morning Grace was killed."

Roger's eyebrows shot up.

"Yeah," I said. "The police told me." By police, I meant Zoey. Maybe her fibbing was rubbing off on me.

Roger slid back from the table. "They never said anything to me about it."

"Well, she was there," I insisted, "and she was searching for something. Any idea what?"

An espresso machine whirred. Roger gazed grimly at his coffee.

I decided to try another approach. "What do you know about Kyle Bremmer's religious background?"

Roger sighed, and I quickly explained that I'd seen Kyle's grandmother protesting at the hospital with Leo Spires. Roger frowned briefly, then rallied. "You agree with your granny on every-thing?"

I didn't answer, and Roger's frown returned. "Kyle hates Spires. In fact, he has a real beef with religion. He thinks ministers are wind-bags."

I drank some more coffee.

"Look, Kyle's a good guy, and like I told you the other day, we screen our employees carefully. We ask them all sorts of questions about their moral beliefs."

"What if he lied?"

"Don't forget—I lived with him after my wife and I separated. There were no revival meetings in Kyle's living room. When he wasn't working, the only place he went on Sunday mornings was the bagel shop."

"Not every religious nut goes to church," I said.

Roger stayed firm. "Kyle had nothing to gain from Grace's death. Everything to lose. She would have given him a glowing refer-ence for grad school, a new job, whatever he wanted. He was her favorite." Roger stopped, then sat up straighter and smiled. "Among the lab techs," he added.

Clearly Roger was her favorite among the whole staff, at least in his own imagination. But I hoped his view of Kyle was accurate. For Anne's sake, I wanted Kyle to be just what he seemed, a diligent young scientist who liked helping people.

Roger stole a glance at his watch, but I didn't take the hint. I had a lot more questions. "I know you and Grace were really close." I let Roger preen a moment. "But how did your daughter feel about her?"

"No particular way," Roger said. "I mean, Lizzie likes every-body."

"Not according to Kyle's girlfriend," I said.

"What do you mean?"

"She said you and your daughter argued about Grace."

"I don't recall that." Roger stirred his drink. His wedding band was large and ornate like one of his belt buckles.

"She said your daughter never wanted to hear Grace's name again."

Roger wrapped both hands around his mug. "Lizzie is still a teenager. She says things she doesn't mean. She's been under a lot of stress. Her first year of college. Her mom and me living apart."

"What does that have to do with Grace?"

"Nothing."

"So why do you think she said it?"

"You analyze everything your teenager says, you go crazy."

I smiled at Roger so he'd think I agreed. He released the hold he had on his drink, and I shifted gears. "I heard Grace wanted to fire Justine Nissen."

"News to me," Roger said brightly. His eyes shifted away from mine.

"I also heard she was planning to fire you."

Roger's chair screeched as he jumped to his feet. "That's a lie. Absolutely false. Slanderous."

A man on a cell phone edged past our table, and Roger lowered his voice. "Who told you that?"

I kept silent.

"Whoever it was is a malicious gossip. A trouble causer, a snake." And with that burst of thesaurial venom, Roger exited the coffee shop.

I FOLLOWED ROGER'S car to Bloomington Street, and I parked as he pounded on Justine's door. I knew it was her door because he was braying her name as if he were auditioning for *A Streetcar Named Desire*, and he kept braying long after it was clear no one was home, at least no one willing to talk with him. Then Roger sat on Justine's front porch steps, stewing. Maybe the two of them were having an affair. How else do you explain the braying?

I hunched down in case Roger happened to look my way, but he seemed absorbed in his own thoughts. They couldn't have been pleasant if he'd risked his marriage, his job, his friendship with Grace—all for a fling with a girl who looked like a Bratz doll.

A squirrel skittered down the orange maple in Justine's front yard. Roger scowled at it and pulled out his cell. I cracked my window so I could hear, and the breeze cooled my face. All I learned, however, was that he wanted Justine to call him ASAP. As he headed back to his car, I hunkered down in my seat even further and waited until I heard him pull away.

Roger's next stop was Zoey's. He'd probably looked up her address after I'd shown him her picture and told him that she'd been in the lab the morning Grace had been killed. Nice job, Mara. I parked on the opposite side of the street a couple houses down and tried to assuage my guilt. I told myself that Roger probably just wanted to get a sense of what Zoey had witnessed the morning Grace died. Maybe he too was trying to find Grace's killer. Or maybe he wanted to know if Zoey had overheard his argument with Grace and if she had told the police about it. But what if he had something worse to hide? What if he was the killer?

As he headed toward Zoey's front door, his silver ponytail sliced the middle of his leather jacket. He rang the doorbell twice, shifting back and forth impatiently. I squeezed my steering wheel and held my breath. Then someone knocked on my passenger window. Heart thumping, I turned and faced a freckled boy barely tall enough to peek in the window. He smiled and wiggled his fingers. I waved back, feeling foolish about my jumpiness, and returned my attention to Roger.

Another knock on my window.

I leaned over and rolled it down.

"Why are you parked in front of my house?" the boy asked.

"Haven't your parents told you not to talk to strangers?"

"Yes." The rhetorical question sailed right over his head. "What are you doing?" he asked.

"Waiting." I rolled the window halfway up.

"What for?"

"Ryan, is everything okay?" This from a nine- or ten-year-old girl on a pink bike. She turned to me. "Why are you talking to my brother?"

"Ask him," I said, glancing toward Zoey's. Her step-mother answered the door, her son not far behind. I was right in their line of sight. "Look," I said, "I'm busy. Why don't you two move along?"

Zoey's step-mom rested her hand on her son's head.

"Hey, what's going on?" A helmeted girl on a scooter joined us. Zoey's step-mom would have to be completely oblivious not to notice the small crowd I'd drawn.

"This lady is waiting." The boy seemed proud to know something the girls didn't.

"What for?" the sister asked. Like her brother, she was freckled and fond of questions.

"A friend," I said. Zoey's step-mom eased away from the door. It wouldn't be long before Roger turned to face me. "Maybe you three can do me a favor," I said. "See if you can find a woman waiting in a car nearby in case I'm at the wrong address."

The boy gave his sister a Can-we? look, and she frowned.

"Please," I said, "my cell phone is dead."

Still the frown.

"I'll give you five dollars if you can find her."

"Ten," said the sister.

The three took off just as Zoey's step-mom closed the door on Roger. As he stepped off the front porch, I slid down in my seat. Either Zoey wasn't home, or Roger had received the same song and dance I had.

Zoey was safe. For the moment.

ROGER PICKED UP a six-pack at Handi-Mart and headed home. As I sat in his parking lot, I left a message on Zoey's cell, telling her that he'd stopped at her house and urging her to avoid him. I called directory assistance for Liz Lipinski's number, but it was unlisted. I could try getting it from Bridget, but there had to be an easier way. Liz's mother? I didn't know her name. If I called Kyle, he might mention my request to Roger. Bridget's other players might mention it to Bridget. Then she'd think I'd gone behind her back, and she'd be right. We were destined to butt heads over Liz Lipinski, but the better part of valor is procrastination.

A guy strolled past my car, guzzling a Coke. Roger was no doubt on his couch with his six-pack while I sat in my car with nary a bottle of water.

I coaxed my car into starting, cranking the ignition twice and patting the dashboard. Then I went back to Justine's. There was a light on in the front room, so I retraced Roger's steps and knocked on the front door. It was answered by a young man who looked like Justine's polar opposite. Pudgy, wholesome, and conventional—complete with chinos and a button-down shirt. A gold nametag suggested that Derek had just gotten off work at Hills Bank. When I asked for Justine, he clenched his jaw. "She doesn't live here anymore."

Now what? I couldn't very well explain that I'd been tailing a man who just minutes earlier had sought Justine at this exact same residence. "Are you sure?"

"I asked her to leave myself." His tone was matter of fact, but his eyes looked sad.

"Do you know where I can find her?"

"Sorry," he said. "She a friend?"

I was too tired to lie, so I explained that I wanted to ask her some questions about her boss's murder.

"Teeney's boss was murdered?" He seemed much more upset about it than Justine had been.

"Did she ever talk about work?" I asked.

"Not really."

"Did she complain about her boss?"

"Who doesn't?" Derek said. "And Teeney, she complains about anybody who wants her to behave like a responsible adult."

I remained silent, hoping for more dirt.

But he simply pulled his wallet out of his back pocket and handed me his business card. "If you find her, will you email me? Just so I know she's okay."

"Why wouldn't she be?" And if you care so much, I thought, why did you kick her out?

Derek dropped his gaze to his loafers and sighed.

"Don't worry," I said. "She's fine. She's in a play with my house-mate."

"Are they friends?"

"They haven't known each other long," I said, "but Vince makes friends quickly, especially if he's cast with somebody."

Derek frowned. "Tell him not to loan her anything. Teeney's a great girl, but she has solvency issues."

I remembered Justine's expensive handbag and jeans. "Does she owe you?"

He nodded grimly.

This could be a clue. Someone up to her eyeballs in debt might do some pretty unsavory things for money. "Is that why you kicked her out?"

"I gave her lots of chances," he said. "I offered to help her make a budget, but I couldn't keep covering her share of the rent and utilities while she maxed out her Visa. I kept thinking she'd turn it around, but then I found out she also owed this guy at work."

"Do you remember his name?"

"Roger somebody."

I pictured Roger's humble apartment, his worn couch, the sad pastel prints that Liz got for him. I thought about his estranged wife and young son. Why would Roger loan money to anyone, let alone Justine?

Chapter Fourteen

WHAT'S WORSE THAN discovering that your housemate has befriended a spendthrift murder suspect? Finding her in your living room, that's what. Justine was curled up in my favorite chair, doing her nails. Bottles, files, and clippers perched atop my most recent *New Yorker*. "Hey," she said, opening a bottle of polish remover.

Its smell stung my nose and eyes.

"Do you have any cotton balls?" she asked. "I checked the bathroom, but I didn't find any."

"Where's Vince?" I said.

She shrugged, and I imagined her prowling our place unsupervised.

"I've had a crazy day." Justine closed the polish remover. "My housemate kicked me out. Vince said I could crash here."

I was entertaining some serious thoughts about kicking my own housemate out. "This isn't the Holiday Inn," I said.

My phone rang, and I held up a hand to halt Justine's protest.

It was Bridget. "Something wrong, babe? You sound funny."

I didn't want to talk in front of Justine, but I didn't want to turn my back on her either.

"Babe? You there?"

I retreated to the kitchen. If I talked softly, I'd have some privacy, and I'd be able to hear what Justine was up to.

"How about you come over for dinner?" Bridget said. "Then we can head to Sophie and Esther's."

What? I was counting on a quiet, romantic evening. Just Bridget and me.

"Sophie and Esther's baby-naming ceremony," Bridget said. "Remember?"

"They didn't postpone?" I was horrified. They wouldn't even have a baby if it wasn't for Grace. The least they could do was show a little respect.

"Esther's mom has to head back to New York tomorrow."

I leaned against the counter and noticed an empty package of Chips Ahoy on the table. Someone had finished my cookies.

"Esther's brother needs to get back to work too," Bridget continued.

"What's the baby's name?" I asked.

"The moms are keeping it secret until the ceremony."

There was a thud and some rustling in the living room.

"How about 6:00?" Bridget asked.

I moved to the doorway. Justine had knocked a pile of my books to the floor. Norma Desmond was hissing at her, tail bristling. Good old Norma.

Bridget tried to entice me with a new lager.

"I can't," I said. Then I raised my voice and stared at Justine. "I need to evict someone."

Justine's eyes widened, but she quickly recovered her usual coolness and picked up the books.

"Did you and Vince fight?" Bridget asked.

"Not yet."

"You sure you're okay?"

Justine flipped through one of my books.

"I've been better."

"You want a ride to the ceremony?"

I did want some alone time with Bridget—even if it was just ten minutes en route to an obligatory social event—but I wasn't sure how long it would take to get rid of Justine. "I'm going to have to meet you there," I said. "Sorry."

Our line crackled with static as Bridget spoke. "Roger Lipinski says you interviewed him again."

What? Bridget asks Roger to help with my investigation, so he runs to her after I ask him a couple tough questions?

"Roger is a good man," Bridget continued. "A terrific father. Liz worships him."

The kind of dad, I thought, who'd do anything to protect his kid. Anything to keep her from knowing that he was somehow embroiled with a co-worker, a woman not much older than Liz herself. I didn't want to discover anything about him that would hurt Liz or mire Bridget's team in yet another controversy, but I couldn't ignore my suspicions.

"Let's talk about him later," I said. "I still have an eviction to handle." I gave Justine a pointed look and told Bridget I'd see her at the ceremony.

The phone crackled again as she told me good-bye.

Before I could say word one to Justine, her phone rang. She checked her caller ID, turned the ringer off, and shoved the phone in her purse. Since etiquette wasn't high on her list of priorities, and since she hadn't seized the opportunity to postpone our confrontation, I could only assume she had serious issues with her caller. Visa? The cops? Roger? It occurred to me that I was seeing the glass half empty. Sure, I was in an annoying and possibly dangerous situation, all alone with a vapid young woman who might have committed murder. But it was the perfect opportunity to grill her, especially since she needed to get on my good side. "I'm sorry about before," I said.

Justine shrugged. "It's all good."

I resisted the urge to throttle her and invited her to sit. She plopped into my favorite chair and crossed her legs, swinging the top one back and forth, a frenetic pendulum.

"Here's the deal." I sat on the futon across from her. "You can spend a couple nights here, but only if you answer my questions."

She averted her gaze to Norma Desmond. The cat was circling her purse.

"What do you know about Kyle Bremmer's religious beliefs?" I asked.

"Nothing," Justine said. "He never talks about church."

"I heard he has a connection to Leo Spires."

"Are you kidding? The nicest thing he's ever said about that guy is that he needs to get a life. This one day, I was upset about the picketing, and he goes, 'They're wasting their time, don't let them waste ours as well,' and I'm like 'excuuuse me.'"

For someone who didn't want to waste time on the reverend, Kyle Bremmer sure spent a lot of time complaining about him. Doth the lab tech protest too much?

Norma Desmond swatted at a buckle on Justine's purse and launched herself atop it. When Justine tried to rescue the handbag, Norma scratched her. I suppressed a smile and asked about Roger. Justine kept her eyes firmly on her besieged purse. "We don't talk much."

A half-truth if ever there was one. "Where were you the morning Grace was killed?"

"I don't have to answer that."

"If you want to stay here, you do."

Justine scowled. "With a guy."

"What's his name?"

She shrugged. "We met at a party. It was crazy."

"Where does he live?"

"We hooked up at the party."

That was believable enough. But how convenient—an alibi that couldn't be checked. "Where was the party?"

"You can't treat me like a criminal just because I need a place to stay. I'll go thirdsies on everything."

"Really? Before or after you pay back Derek and Roger?"

Justine stood. "Derek's been telling lies about me because I won't sleep with him. That's why he kicked me out."

I imagined her giving Vince a tearful account and asking him for a twenty, just to tide her over until pay day. I imagined him delighting in her offer to pay a third of the mortgage and utilities, the bogus windfall good as spent. I imagined me picking up the slack. "What about Grace?" I asked. "Why did *she* want you out? Why did she want to fire you?"

Justine opened her mouth and snapped it shut. Then she gave me a long, evil look and flounced out the front door.

Make a dramatic exit, and you're bound to forget something. Justine had left her purse at Norma's mercy. The fierce feline pounced, strewing the contents of the bag across the rug. Amidst the flotsam — lipsticks, raffle tickets, Tylenol — were several empty plastic vials not much bigger than the end of my thumb. They looked exactly like the ones Grace's lab used to store sperm.

Chapter Fifteen

I ENTERED THE animal shelter ready to tear Vince a new one, but he was talking with a young couple who were looking for a puppy. The guy was already smitten with the mutt in his arms. It was smaller than his girlfriend's purse. "What do you say, hon?" he said to her.

She shrugged.

The dog tried to kiss the guy's five o'clock shadow.

"Hey!" he protested, grinning and hugging the dog closer.

The girl shifted from one skinny jean-clad leg to another. She reminded me of Justine.

"Ginger is one of our most affectionate dogs," Vince said. "She has a darling temperament."

"Darling is just what we want," said the guy. "Right, hon?"

"I don't know. I was hoping for a dog with one of those super-cute names. Like a puggle or a labradoodle. Or like Jessica Simpson has. A maltipoo."

Vince stiffened. "Designer dogs cost thousands of dollars," he said.

"How much is Ginger?" asked the guy.

"Just a thirty-five dollar fee to cover her spaying and vaccinations."

The guy nodded appreciatively and held the dog toward the girl. "What do you say to our little budget buddy?"

The girl wrinkled her nose.

Vince caught my eye.

I gave him a thumbs-up. Sure, I was furious with him, but I still wanted him to create a happily-ever-after for this guy and his new best friend.

"Paris Hilton's dog looks supercute on her," the girl said. "What kind does she have?"

"A chihuahua," Vince said. "But a dog is not a fashion accessory."

"You don't need a dog to look good, hon," the guy said. "Let's get this one. She's cute."

"And well-trained," Vince added. "Ginger has been at the Center for months. She's ready for a loving home."

"Come on," the guy said. "Please."

"Daddy says you should always get your dog from a breeder. Then you know exactly what you're getting."

Vince gave her a huge fake smile. I knew he wanted to tell her that breeding dogs was irresponsible when thousands of them lived and died in shelters every year. I wanted to tell her that myself. But Vince kept his focus on the one dog in front of him, and he kept his mouth shut.

"We know what we're getting with this dog," the guy said. "She's right here." He thrust Ginger into the girl's arms. The dog pulled out all the stops. Looking right at the girl, Ginger cocked her head and perked her ears. Who could resist? The girl extended a single finger and tentatively petted Ginger.

Vince excused himself and asked a volunteer to help the couple.

"We need to talk," I said. "You invited a total stranger to live with us. When were you planning to run the idea past me?"

His back and face stiffened. "It was an emergency."

"Do you know a single thing about Justine Nissen?"

Ginger yipped, and the girl holding her glanced our way.

I lowered my voice. "Do you know why she got kicked out of her place?"

Vince shook his head. "She's a divine actress."

"I don't care if she's Meryl-freaking-Streep. I don't want her in my home." I told him everything I'd learned about Justine.

"Those could be lies," he said.

"They could also be the truth. That's the point. Neither one of us knows Justine Nissen, yet she's living with us."

Vince sighed. "I've got to leave for rehearsal, Mar-Bar. Let's finish this later."

"Finish it at rehearsal," I said. "Tell her she's out." But I was talking to my housemate's back.

At least things seemed to be going well for Ginger. As the couple completed their paperwork, the dog wagged her tail jubilantly.

NO ONE SAW me slip through the shadows and hide beneath the bleachers at the community theatre. Fighting the urge to sneeze, I stood amidst an army of dust bunnies and peered through a tiny crack between two levels of seats. Richard, Vince's default date, was onstage with some new guy, muffing the opening scene of Wilde's comedy. Richard looked the part of a dandy, but he had the comic timing of a water buffalo. Vince and Justine, I assumed, were backstage awaiting their entrance.

I could have observed the rehearsal openly—after teching God knows how many productions, I had a right to be there—but I didn't want another confrontation with either housemate, legitimate or spurious. I didn't want condolences or questions. What did I want? What did I hope to gain from my hyper-allergenic vantage point? Surely, I didn't expect to witness Vince giving Justine a firm deadline for vacating our premises. I knew better than that.

As I tried to get a different view of the stage, cobwebs caught in my face and hair. I swiped at them and stifled another sneeze. If there were spiders, I hoped I hadn't disturbed them. I hoped they weren't poisonous.

Richard/Algernon proclaimed, "The truth is rarely pure and never simple."

I'd said that to Grace the last time I'd seen her. She hadn't wanted to do an interview with Anne. "If you must interview me with someone else," Grace said, "why not someone my lab has actually helped?"

"Anne's helping you," I argued. "She's helping you fundraise. You two will be great on the air together."

Grace shook her head. "The truth is you'll do anything to spend time with Anne Golding."

That was when I laid the Oscar Wilde on her. Grace had rolled her eyes and snorted.

Onstage, Lane the butler announced Lady Bracknell and Miss Fairfax. Vince used his script as a fan, peeking over it coyly and delivering his first bon mot. In full drag, he would steal the show. But he wouldn't have an easy time of it, not with Justine next to him. Her acting skills were, to use her own limited vocabulary, crazy. Gone was the spoiled, shallow slacker, she of the eyeliner and talons. In its place was a creature of poise, elegance, and simmering vitality. Even when other characters spoke, even when Justine stood motionless, she had me. A tilt of the head, and I was hers forever.

Then she spoke. "I am always smart, aren't I, Mr. Worthing?"

It was what, their second rehearsal? Already, her English accent flowed over me, pulled me into its crisp and sultry depths.

Mr. Worthing blinked and checked his script.

As she glided across the stage, delivering her next line, I wasn't thinking of Oscar Wilde, but his countryman, William Butler Yeats and his famous line, "A terrible beauty is born." You needed poetry to describe acting skills like Justine's. Combine those skills with zero moral fiber, and you had one dangerous girl.

Somebody with a wide ass sat on the bleachers right above me, obliterating my view. Next to the view-blocker was a sandwich laden with onions and sausage. The odor made me queasy, and I couldn't mouth-breathe because of the dust. A hand reached for the sandwich, and I was treated to a small groan and a series of lip-smackings. I moved away from the noisy eater and returned my attention to Justine. If she continued crashing with Vince and me, I'd have to keep a close eye on my credit cards, but I could also keep a close eye on her.

After Justine exited the stage, she joined the hoagie-eater above me. I was about to exit myself when a third person tromped up the bleachers and stood next to Justine. "You haven't returned my calls." The tromper sounded like a young woman. She wore leather high tops.

"Are you crazy?" Justine said. "I'm rehearsing."

"You're not onstage now," High Tops said.

Justine sighed and stood. The bleachers creaked as she and High Tops made their way to the floor. I looked on both sides of the hoagie-eater, trying to find them. The director sat in the opposite bleachers, twirling his glasses in the air and scribbling in a notebook. Leftover flats were propped against the back bleachers. The top one, from *Hairspray*, was fuchsia. Onstage, Jack Worthing explained that he'd been found in a handbag, and Lady Bracknell gasped.

Justine and High Tops appeared near the flats. At first, I couldn't see their faces, but I could tell that High Tops was stockier than Justine. I hunched down and looked through the cracks between lower—and dustier—bleachers until I could see the girls' faces. Justine and a blonde with corn rows. Liz Lipinski.

What did Bridget's player, an apple-pie Iowan with an Energizer Bunny work ethic, want with Justine? I was dying to hear what they were saying, but my bleachers weren't connected to the back ones so there was no way to get closer without blowing my cover.

Liz spoke rapidly, her face pink. Justine shushed her, but Liz continued, gesturing wildly.

My phone vibrated, and the noisy eater above me paused. I glanced at the incoming number. Bridget. Probably at the baby-naming ceremony, wondering where I was. I shoved the phone deep into my back pack. Above me, the chewing and smacking resumed.

Liz put her hands on her hips and glowered at Justine. Justine shrugged. Then Liz shook her head furiously and strode off.

I scooted away from the front seats, eager to follow her, and headed toward the open end of the bleachers. It was blocked by Richard and a woman running lines. As Liz zipped past them and their scripts, there was nothing I could do but stand silently in the dust and darkness.

Chapter Sixteen

GET TOO MANY lesbians in one room, and you're bound to OD on words like *affirm* and *process*. I mused on this vocabulary as I rang Sophie and Esther's doorbell. Much to my surprise, Anne answered it. Her smile was hyper-bright above the mauve scarf she always donned when she needed extra strength. It once belonged to her Grandma Betty, who'd survived two World Wars, four tornadoes, and three husbands. Anne hurried me in, stepping away as I was about to hug her. Then she played tour guide. Gifts went in the dining room. Food and drinks were there too. Sophie and Esther were in the living room, and last Anne had seen, Bridget was in the kitchen. Before I knew it, Anne was halfway down the hall with my jacket in tow. Gone before I could offer a shred of support.

Not that I blamed her for keeping busy. The living room was a veritable baby shrine. Sophie and Esther were enthroned on the couch, glowing as their friends took turns holding their new bundle of unnamed joy. A woman with Esther's angular cheekbones and jaw worked the crowded room with an inch-thick stack of baby photos. Before she could target me, I headed to the kitchen.

Its entrance was clogged by a group of older lesbians. "Things sure have changed," one of them said. "I remember a time when we mothers were second-class citizens."

"Especially if you had a son," added the woman next to her. "It's like you were a traitor."

"Yeah," said another. "Just try getting into Michigan with a male child. Even in diapers, he was still the enemy." They chuckled about the Women's Music Festival.

A man and a woman near the fridge were doing a cost-benefit analysis of organic baby food. Then the woman lowered her voice. She didn't want to judge, but she thought that fostering and adoption were the way to go. Her comment was out of line at Sophie and Esther's, but truth be told, I used to think the same thing. I thought that kids were like dogs at Vince's shelter. Why go to the trouble and expense of creating new ones when there were already so many who needed homes? But then Anne started trying, and I began collaborating with Grace. I learned that adoption usually took more time and money than AI. I witnessed Grace's passion for her work and Anne's quest to conceive and give birth. I tried not to judge a desire I'd never experienced, but when I saw Anne hurting, it wasn't easy.

The couple near the fridge drifted toward the stove, where the topic was sperm, as in "good sperm is hard to find." Good conversation was also hard to come by, and Bridget was nowhere in sight. At the far end of the kitchen, a cluster of women eyed me and fell silent. Felicity Cheng was the only one I knew well, so I greeted her. We quickly found ourselves standing alone.

She studied me from behind her tortoise shell glasses, her face solemn. "Dr. Everest's death is hard for us all. Really hard." Felicity had a slight accent, so when she said "hard," it sounded like "heart." "I know you were her good friend, but the policewoman doesn't. She's been asking everybody about you and Dr. Everest—did you get along, have fights, stuff like that."

Great. Now I'd have an extra hard time getting anyone to talk about the real suspects. Given the speed with which the kitchen cleared, I'd have a rough time getting anybody to talk, period.

"I'm sorry," Felicity said, "but I thought you should know." She gave me a small smile. "Don't worry. I told the policewoman all good things about you." Then Felicity's expression turned somber. "I was there that day when Dr. Everest was killed. And I told the policewoman I never saw you."

How could I have forgotten that Felicity had been in the lab with Kyle the morning Grace died? "What did you see?" I asked. "Anything unusual?"

Felicity's mouth twisted to one side. "Most of the time I'm very observant, but when I'm at the lab, I'm only thinking about the baby I want so much."

"Did you notice anything different, anything at all out of the ordinary?"

"You sound like the policewoman."

For a second, I worried that I was scaring off the one person at the party who would talk to me, but I forged ahead anyway. "Did you see anything strange?"

Felicity reached for a cup on the counter behind her. "I never saw Dr. Everest there on a weekend before. Just the lab tech."

"Which one?" I asked.

"Kyle Bremmer."

"Was there tension between Kyle and Grace?"

Felicity shrugged. "The doctor said hello, but they didn't have a conversation. She was on the phone."

So far, Felicity's account of that morning matched Zoey's. "What about Kyle? How did he seem?"

"Same as always. Super nice and affirming. Full of pep talk. He walked me to the ob-gyn." Felicity held her cup close to her lips, but didn't drink. She set it down, her face drawn. "Maybe it happened after we left."

Or maybe, I thought, Kyle had returned. But if I wanted dirt on him I'd need to get it from someone other than the women he helped. "Do you know any of the other lab techs?"

Felicity shook her head.

"How about Justine Nissen?" I prompted.

Felicity shook her head again and shivered. "The killer might have been in the lab when I was there," she said.

I felt bad for upsetting her, so I asked how she was doing.

"I'm not liking my odds."

Her answer threw me off. I'd been wondering how she was handling Grace's murder.

"I thought I was smart, starting before I was thirty," Felicity said. "It's supposed to happen faster then. That's what the numbers say, but they're not working for me. I've tried three different kinds of fertility drugs, and my bank account is empty. Sometimes I feel like giving up."

This was not the Felicity I knew, the sculptor who constantly battled bureaucratic goliaths in order to launch outdoor art projects. Trying to have a baby had zapped her confidence, reduced her, muted her. That's what was happening to Anne too.

"I had no idea it would be so hard," Felicity said. "I did plenty of research, but you can't know what it's like until you try."

There it was. Another reminder that I could never understand Anne. "Tonight must be difficult," I said.

Felicity nodded. "But I need to see the baby. I need to see that it can really happen."

I WENT INTO the dining room to look for Bridget, but she wasn't there. The room was filled with pre-schoolers who were making quick work of the gender-neutral party decorations. Tearing at the pale green and yellow crepe paper, they swatted the matching balloons and chased each other around the overburdened gift table, pausing only for a second as I added my present—a book called *Shakespearean Tales for Toddlers*.

"I wanna present," proclaimed a gray-eyed girl.

"Me too," cried a boy. "The biggest one." He tried to point, but he had nearly mummified himself with crepe paper.

There was a chorus of me-toos, some pushing and shoving, and I was surrounded. Night of the Living Toddlers! "These presents are for the new baby," I said to the pint-sized mob.

The mini-demons ignored the voice of reason and pressed closer to the table. Any second, those gifts were gonna come a-tumblin' down. My stomach growled, and inspiration struck. "Look!" I pointed at the refreshments. "Let's see if there's candy."

They stampeded across the room and stood eye-level with some pâté. "That looks like poo," said a girl. She rubbed a balloon against her hair, which was already live with static, a blond dandelion puff.

"Where's the candy?" demanded the mummy.

Some sage adult had placed the sweets on the far side of the table. "I'll get everyone a cookie," I said, as if I were in control.

"I'm not supposed to have peanuts," said Static Girl.

"Me neither," said the mummy. "I'm also allergic to wheat and milk."

The boy next to him announced that he couldn't have chocolate. The girl next to him declared eggs off-limits.

I studied the sugar cookie in my hand. It looked innocent enough — pastel frosting that matched the decimated decorations. "Go find your parents," I said. "Ask them what you can have."

Much to my surprise and relief, the kidlets drifted away, but then I faced an even scarier situation. Orchid was headed straight for me, her jowls red with cold. She stopped, silent, when she spotted me. Her face was grim. I wondered if she knew that Anne had told me about their fights or that I'd spent the previous night on their couch.

Orchid ran her hand over her silver buzz cut. "I'm sorry about Dr. Everest," she said. "I know you were fond of her."

I was still in that place where every condolence made me want to cry, so I simply nodded in acknowledgment.

Orchid helped herself to some cider. "I wish Anne hadn't been with you when you found the doctor's body."

"Me too," I said curtly. Truth be told, Orchid wished that Anne would never be with me. Period.

From the living room, I could hear Vince ask if the baby was ready for her close-up.

Orchid waddled off. I closed my eyes and took a bite of cookie. I tried to focus on the butter cream frosting, the hint of almond and vanilla.

"Lemme tell you whose sperm I want."

My eyes flew open. There was Lindsey Hoover, one of the many women who'd been waiting to visit the new baby at the hospital the day Grace was murdered. Now Lindsey stood at the other end of the food table addressing the newest Women's Studies professor at the university. Tamar Thomas was a cute thirty-something. Butch in a nerdy sort of way. I'd been attracted to her until I heard her talk. The woman couldn't string together two sentences without mentioning Princeton. Occasionally, for variety, she'd complain about Iowa. "The people here are so nice," she'd say, as if being nice were a crime against nature.

"I'd take Kyle Bremmer's sperm any day," Lindsey announced. "He's got it all. Looks, smarts, personality. And he's gay-friendly."

"You can tell all that from meeting him once?" Tamar asked.

"I've also heard good stuff about him," Lindsey said.

If Kyle shared his grandmother's right-wing beliefs, he was sure fooling lots of people. I finished my cookie and helped myself to some chocolate cake so Lindsey and Tamar wouldn't think I was eavesdropping.

"Kyle has been the tech for lots of lesbians," Lindsey continued, "and once he knows you, he takes a personal interest. He comes in on the weekends if that's what you need."

I froze over the vegetable tray. What if Kyle, at the behest of Leo Spires, was tampering with sperm—lesbian sperm? What if that's why Anne and Felicity hadn't conceived? I thought of the insemination reports on Grace's desk. I thought of her bemoaning the delicacy of sperm. "Nothing is harder to store or easier to kill."

But then again, Kyle had been Sophie's tech, and there we were, celebrating her brand-new baby. Had Kyle been the tech for any other lesbians who'd gotten pregnant? I couldn't think of anyone, but I didn't know every lesbian in Iowa City even though it felt like it sometimes. And I still didn't know whether Kyle had a motive for sperm tampering. Hopefully, I'd find out the next day. Vince and I were planning to go sleuthing in Spiresville. Maybe even talk to Kyle's grandmother if we could keep from gagging while doing so.

Even though I wanted to find Grace's killer, and I wanted to do it soon, I hoped it wasn't Kyle. I couldn't bear the thought of Grace and Anne being betrayed by someone they admired and trusted so deeply. Besides, if anyone was capable of a grand deception, it was Justine—thespian extraordinaire. She was the one with sperm vials in her purse. And she was the one Grace wanted to fire.

"Excuse me." A guy with a thin mustache edged in between me and the vegetable tray. I took a bite of cake and returned my attention to Lindsey and Tamar.

"I'm still having a really hard time choosing a donor," Tamar said. "There's a guy who's almost perfect. He's tall, he plays the mandolin, and he has a Ph.D. from Princeton. But he's allergic to cats."

"Is that a deal breaker?" Lindsey asked.

A very pregnant young woman joined them. Was she a lesbian? Had she used Grace's lab?

"He also gets headaches," Tamar said.

I thought about my sister's husband, the father of my charming nieces. Phil talked way too much about mutual funds, but he was a good, decent man. Poor thing would never make it as a sperm donor because he had an overbite and hangnails.

"Why mess with a lab?" the newcomer asked. "You must have pals who are willing to donate to the cause." She patted her belly.

Lindsey and Tamar exchanged glances.

"Why pay for something you can get for free?" the pregnant woman asked.

"When Renee and I processed that issue, we realized that we wanted more than our friends could offer." Lindsey spoke as if she were addressing a recalcitrant toddler. "The donor we chose has Renee's exact coloring. He shares some of her interests and some of mine. Our values too. Our choice validates our partnership."

The mother-to-be grabbed a canapé and exited.

"Does he like dogs?" Tamar asked.

Lindsey nodded smugly.

Talk about irony. There I was—hoping Kyle didn't take after the grandmother who raised him—surrounded by women who believed they could determine whether their child would be a dog- or a cat-person.

Chapter Seventeen

I FINALLY FOUND Bridget in the living room. She was holding the baby-of-honor, surrounded by a third of the adult guests, including Anne and Orchid. Rocking gently, Bridget smiled at the bundle in her arms, as did everyone around her. How they focused on the kid instead of Bridget was beyond me. I stayed on the other side of the room, mesmerized by her swaying Levis, her powerful arms, the soft waves in her short dark hair.

"Better watch out, Mar-Bar," Vince said. "Bridget looks pretty happy with that baby." He smiled rakishly and fussed with his pink and blue feather boa.

"What are you doing here?" I hissed.

"Rehearsal finished early." He leaned toward me. "You have something in your hair. Cobwebs?"

I smoothed my hands over my head.

Bridget spotted me, grinned and winked. Her eyes reminded me of a vacation sky.

"Seriously, Mar-Bar," Vince said. "Your girlfriend looks positively maternal."

"She's the oldest of seven. She's used to holding babies. It doesn't mean she wants her own." Did it? I hadn't actually asked her. But she was 100% devoted to her players. Surely that would satisfy any maternal urges.

"You should see your face," Vince said. "It's all Hamlet-sees-the-ghost-of-his-father."

I punched him in the arm.

"Macbeth sees the slain Banquo!" As he raised his voice, Orchid shot him a dirty look.

I punched him again. Harder.

"Ow! You know I bruise like a peach."

"And you know I already have plenty to worry about."

"Let's just relax and enjoy the show," Vince said.

Everything was a show to Vince, even a christening. I scowled and started to punch him again. But just then Bridget handed the baby to Anne. I paused, my half-clenched fist still raised. Anne didn't smile as she took the child. She didn't sway or rock. It was as if a beautiful wild bird had landed next to Anne and she didn't want to scare it away.

The spell was broken by a Buddhist chime. All heads turned toward the rippling ping, toward a woman in a rainbow stole and lavender robe. I'd come a long way from Aldoburg, Iowa, where guitar Masses were viewed with suspicion.

"Come," the woman intoned, "let us quiet ourselves and cele-brate the new life among us." A New Jersey accent worked its way to the surface of her ethereal voice. Amidst the ebb and flow of her words, crepe paper rustled, and a small boy whined about his sister pinching him.

The minister repeated the summons, louder this time, and Bridget swept to my side. We hugged, and I squeezed her close. I kissed her neck and breathed in the scent of sandalwood. She placed her hands on my hips, gently pushed me away, and kissed me on the lips.

"Get a room," Vince murmured.

Nearby, I could hear Tamar chattering about a christening she attended at Princeton.

The minister rang the chime again. Somehow the crowd parted, and Esther's mom brought an empty bowl and placed it on a make-shift altar—a card table covered with white linen centered in front of a large picture window. The moon or a streetlight shone on the altar as the guests formed a sort of horseshoe around it. On one side, Vince, Bridget, and I were sardined between a bookshelf and a group of people with lots of kids. On the other side, Anne and Orchid looked equally squished. Even more folks squeezed into the back of the room straight across from the altar. Some huddled on the couch, and some wedged between it and the piano.

Not far behind Sophie's mom, Sophie's dad carried a pitcher. His eyes were fixed on his granddaughter, who was now in Sophie's arms near the altar. I had missed the handing off, Anne to Sophie, and I was glad.

As Grandpa set the pitcher on the altar, Vince jabbed my arm. "If that's full," he whispered, "it's an accident waiting to happen."

I hushed him, but sure enough, Diego Sanchez-Smith trundled toward it, pudgy arms outstretched. Both his mothers reached for him at once, sweeping him away just in time. He whimpered and strained against them.

Reason 859, I thought, continuing an inward tally of the reasons to remain child-free. I glanced at Orchid, and she smiled faintly. Before she and Anne started trying, my boss and I used to keep score together. Toddler running willy-nilly in our reception area, reason 754. Child demanding nachos, ice cream, and caramel corn at a ball game, reason 755. Said child dumping ice cream in his mom's lap, 756.

As the minister rang the chime again, I noticed that she was in her twenties. Authority figures—priests, doctors, news anchors—were getting younger every year. The minister closed her eyes and extended her arms, revealing a Celtic tattoo on one forearm and a yin/yang symbol on the other. I wondered if there was a cross or a dove on her shoulder, a Buddha on her ankle, and a seminary somewhere that specialized in inter-faith tattoos.

"We gather here tonight, Beloved One, to thank you for bringing a new life into our midst and to dedicate ourselves to teaching her the ways of peace and hope." The minister lowered her arms and gently laid a hand on each new mother. "We gather here tonight to celebrate with Sophie and Esther, who had the vision and the desire to bring a child into their family."

Grace flashed into my mind, she with her own vision and desire to help people like Sophie and Esther. Her belief that every woman deserved the opportunity to conceive and bear a child. I swallowed a lump in my throat and tried to concentrate on the ceremony. Grace would have wanted me—all of us—to focus on the baby, on new life. "Dwell in possibility," she would say. She had flung Emily Dickinson's words at me whenever she'd had enough of my brooding.

Bridget stroked my back. The minister said something about the circle of life and asked us to bow our heads and take a moment of silence to honor the life of Dr. Grace Everest. I gazed at the baby in Sophie's arms and wondered if Grace had the chance to see her. I thought about Grace's collection of baby photos and letters from women and couples thanking her for making their dreams come true. She called it her hyper-extended family album, laughing at her own medical pun. The lump returned to my throat. If I let myself think much more about Grace, I wouldn't be able to make it through the ceremony. I moved my arm from Bridget's waist and squeezed her hand. Tight.

She returned the squeeze, but kept her eyes closed and her head bowed. A quick check of the room revealed similarly bowed heads. The unnamed baby and I were the only ones with eyes wide open. The child's plentiful hair was dark like Sophie's, and Sophie had obviously gotten her amazingly thick locks from her dad. Three generations tangibly linked.

Anne's hair hid her face, but I could feel her grief, her longing for the child she carried in her dreams and heart. A child who would, perhaps, echo parts of her.

Next to Anne and Orchid were Lindsey and Renee. Then Michael, a sweet guy I'd interviewed for *Trying Times*. One of his arms was draped around his wife, Penny, and the other held their daughter, a flaxen-haired cutie on the verge of sleep. With Michael in his tie and Penny in her pearls, they looked like a poster-family for Leo Spires. He would never guess that Michael was a Wiccan accountant for Planned Parenthood and that Penny was a bi activist who wrote erotic vampire fiction. Behind Penny and Michael were Dave and Ted. They'd fostered over a dozen kids and adopted one. Then there were Danielle and Latisha who'd developed the unfortunate habit of dressing alike, usually in chinos. A few months ago, there'd been a rumor that Latisha was expecting twins, but it turned out to be just that — a rumor. Wishful thinking, maybe, by her many friends who were also visiting Grace's lab every month. There were single women like Felicity Cheng and like Henna Perkins, who'd given me the evil eye in the kitchen. And there were couples who'd been together forever — Madeline and Corky, Nancy and Georgia, Lynx and Jill — gathered now at the back of the room by the piano. All trying and all childless.

Once again, the idea of sperm tampering niggled at me. It had been a while since my circle of friends had celebrated an actual birth. Last month, Serena and Carrie adopted Jamal, a sweet five-year-old with severe asthma, and a few months before that, Wendy and Camille started fostering twin girls. But how long had it been since anybody — any lesbians — besides Sophie had given birth? I studied Diego, the little boy who'd gone after the pitcher. Spiderman T-shirt, fidgets, cow-licks. He was three. That's a long time between conceptions, even in the unpredictable world of AI.

The minister raised her head. "And now," she said, "let us create a bowl of blessings for the new life among us. First, Sophie and Esther will pour some water into the bowl and offer their daughter a blessing. Then they invite the rest of you, their family and friends, to do likewise. Please offer your own blessing, a prayer of thanksgiving, a wish for their daughter, or some other petition. When the bowl is full, we will use this sacred water to christen her."

Sophie handed the baby to Grandpa. Then she and Esther grasped the pitcher together.

"I wanna pour it!" Diego squawked.

His mothers shushed him, and Sophie and Esther held the pitcher above the bowl and poured some water into it. Sophie spoke first. "We name our daughter Stormy Grace."

"An oxymoron if ever there was one," Vince whispered.

I didn't dare acknowledge him. I was feeling oxymoronic myself — torn between laughing and crying, afraid of marring the ceremony with an inappropriate outburst.

"We name her Stormy," Esther continued, "because she was conceived during a huge storm full of furious wind and swirling snow."

"Good thing they didn't name her Blizzard," Vince murmured.

"We want her to be strong and beautiful like that storm. We want her to understand that no obstacle is insurmountable."

I glanced at Anne. Orchid whispered something in her ear. Whatever it was made Anne tense and pull away.

Then Sophie spoke. "We call our daughter Grace to honor the memory of Dr. Grace Everest. Her work has helped so many of us in this room. She too was a storm of a woman." Sophie's voice broke, and my eyes burned with tears.

She and Esther stepped back from the bowl, and there was a moment of silence before Sophie's dad stepped forward. His hand shook slightly as he poured the water. "A big thanks to this magnificent family that has gathered to support my daughters and granddaughter."

His words made me even more teary-eyed, and I felt a twinge of envy. Even though I'd been out since junior high, my parents barely tolerated my "lifestyle."

Then Michael stepped forward. "In thanksgiving for all the many people who help create queer families."

I flicked my eyes toward Orchid. She hated the word *queer*, and was none too fond of guys either. She and Anne stood next to each other, but somehow apart, eyes on the floor and arms folded across their chests.

Michael continued. "For all the men who generously share parts of themselves."

Vince jabbed me.

"He means sperm donors," I said.

"For justice-minded scientists like Grace Everest." Several people nodded in agreement. "For her friendly staff. For Kyle Bremmer and Roger Lipinski." Several more people nodded, including Anne. She gave Orchid a defiant look.

"For supportive friends and family."

Again, I thought of Grace. "Sometimes it takes a village to *make* a child." She always winked when she said it. I swallowed and swallowed, but still a tear worked its way onto my cheek. I quickly wiped it away, hoping no one would notice. Both Bridget and Vince put their arms around me.

A carefully coached five- or six-year-old struggled through a prayer, glancing at her mom and dad for approval as she neared the end. Diego gleefully poured half the pitcher's contents into the bowl and told Stormy Grace that he hoped she would have fun opening her presents. As the group laughed, Bridget made her way to the pitcher and asked God to grant Stormy Grace a life filled with play and friendly competition.

"And a great jump shot," someone called out.

There was more laughter and some riffs on girl-power. Then Vince stepped toward the pitcher. "I wish Stormy Grace a life rich in friendship." He smiled slyly. "And tasteful accessories." Everyone chuckled as he poured some water. Dave and Ted's little boy — Liam, the one they adopted — burst from the crowd and launched himself into "Uncle Vince's" arms. Vince smiled at the toddler and ruffled his hair.

Orchid stepped toward the altar and grasped the pitcher with both hands. "Goddess," she said, "grant Stormy Grace the serenity to accept the things she cannot change, the courage to change the things she can, and —" Orchid's eyes darted toward Anne — "the wisdom to know the difference."

Anne's cheeks flushed.

Orchid poured some water, and returned to Anne's side. Anne fixed her eyes on the new baby.

Tamar hoped that Stormy Grace would have a healthy body image. Lindsey urged the baby to embrace peace, and others spoke up for faith, justice, and love. Amid all these words, I watched Anne, wondering if she would acknowledge Orchid or offer a blessing, but she didn't budge.

Chapter Eighteen

MY CELL PHONE jolted me awake. The ringtone insisted that girls just wanna have fun, but this girl wanted a good night's sleep in the arms of her beloved. Bridget's water bed sloshed as I rolled away from her and groped the nightstand for my glasses. I always wear them when I talk on the phone. Call me crazy, but they help me hear better. And they give me confidence. Without them, I feel naked. Although come to think of it, I was naked.

"Are you getting that?" Bridget asked.

I flipped on a lamp, and she pulled a pillow over her head. I located my specs and stood shivering, scanning the room for my phone. A few more bars of Cyndi Lauper, and I found it under my discarded clothes.

"Mara Gilgannon?"

The voice was familiar, but I couldn't quite place it.

"This is Zoey Hargrove. You're finding my sperm donor."

"Not right now, I'm not. I'm trying to sleep."

"You gotta check your email."

"You gotta check your watch," I countered. Bridget's alarm clock said 10:45. After the baby-naming ceremony, Bridget and I had made love and fallen asleep in each other's arms.

"Seriously," Zoey said. "Check your email. I sent you a photo."

A low voice on her end mumbled something about intimidating.

"Are you okay?" I asked.

"It's incriminating," Zoey said.

Whoever she was with mumbled again.

"Shut it, dude," Zoey said. "I know what incriminating means."

"What are you talking about?" I asked.

"Babe," Bridget groaned from beneath her pillow.

I took the hint and left her in peace, closing the door behind me on my way to the living room.

"You know that guy who works at the lab?" Zoey asked. "The one who was there that morning? Me and my boyfriend, we're following him. We found out where he lives and we went there to see if he'd help me find my donor dad, but he was leaving so we followed him instead and—"

"You're following Kyle Bremmer?" I shivered—and not just from the cold.

"He drove and drove. It took forever and ever, and Reed—he's my boyfriend—he wanted to bag it, but I go, 'No way, dude.'"

I grabbed an afghan from Bridget's couch and draped it over my shoulders. It was scratchy, but at least it was warm.

"So we follow Kyle to the total boonies, and he finally pulls over at some bulldozed lot. We park down the road and walk back and hide behind this monster pile of dirt. It's freaking cold. Reed is ragging on me, and Kyle is just sitting in his car when this other car drives up and pulls around to face Kyle's car. The cars are just sitting there like they're trying to blind each other with their headlights. The driver's door opens — not Kyle's — the other guy's — and a super tall skinny guy gets out. He's in a hoodie and a baseball cap. Like he's trying to hide his face."

Who could that have been? Who was tall and skinny? Spires, that's who. Just like his name. "Do you know what Leo Spires looks like?" I asked. "Do you think it was him?"

"I don't know," Zoey said, "like I told you. He was wearing —"

I cut her off. "What happened next?"

"The hoodie guy just stood by his car for a minute. Kyle didn't move, and Reed goes, 'This is a waste.' But I get out my phone and get ready to take a picture, you know, just in case they do something incriminating. Then the hoodie guy opens his back door and reaches in. He pulls out a briefcase, and then he stands there some more. Finally, Kyle gets out. He stands facing the other guy, like in the old west. It's completely retro and creepy. Then the hoodie guy walks over to Kyle and hands him the briefcase. Me and Reed think it's filled with money. Why else meet out in the boonies all cloak and dagger? I got a picture of the handoff, and I emailed it to you with directions to the place. Maybe this will help you find whoever killed your friend, and then you can find my donor dad."

My thoughts raced faster than Zoey's words. If Spires was indeed the hoodie guy, and if he had given Kyle Bremmer a briefcase full of cash, what did it mean? Was the reverend paying his faithful follower for services rendered — sabotaging the lab? Killing Grace? Or was Spires buying the young man's silence?

"The photo's a little dark," Zoey said, "but I'll try again if there's another handoff. Kyle is almost back to Iowa City. We're still following him."

"What about the hoodie guy?"

"I know, right? We had to pick one, and I said the hoodie guy, and Reed said the lab guy, and then I go, 'We already know who the lab guy is. He's the lab guy!' But Reed goes, 'I'm driving and I want to see what's in the briefcase,' and I go —"

"Never mind," I said. "Did you see the hoodie guy's license plate?"

Zoey's brief silence gave me my answer. As my phone crackled, I thought I heard Reed say ouch.

"We forgot to check the license plate, Reed." Zoey's voice cut in and out.

"What about the car?" I asked. "What type was it?"

"A big white SUV. After it drove off, Kyle stood there looking around for a super long time, and Reed goes, 'He's seen us,' but I go, 'No way.'" Zoey's next words were swallowed in static.

I told her my phone was dying, and I started to give her Bridget's number so she could call me back. But then I remembered that Bridget's internet connection was dicey and that what really mattered right now was accessing my email and seeing the photo. So I asked Zoey to wait a few minutes and call me back at my place.

"Kyle is pulling over," she said.

I tried to tell her to be careful, but my phone died.

Crap! What if Kyle noticed he was being followed? Was Zoey still planning to talk to him? Was she in danger? I couldn't call her back on Bridget's phone because I didn't have her number, and I couldn't very well call "the judge" and ask for it. All I could do was give my girlfriend a quick kiss, head home, and hope that Zoey phoned sooner rather than later.

BACK AT MY place—I use the phrase loosely—Vince and Justine were on the computer. They sat side by side, a pajama-clad wall blocking the screen. Justine's hand covered the mouse. The entire living room smelled of menthols.

"I need to check my email," I said. "It's urgent."

Vince swiveled in his chair. "Did you have a fight with Bridget?"

I glared at him and my unwanted houseguest until she lifted her lacquered talons and released the mouse. "Vince was helping me update my profile on Match.com," she said.

How hard could that be? Straight white female seeks gullible male for leeching. Must enjoy secondhand smoke.

"Call me Cupid," Vince said.

I had other names in mind, but I kept them to myself. My body was pulsing with adrenaline. I wanted to see that photo. I wanted the phone to ring. And I wanted Zoey to be okay.

"What I need," Justine said, "is a guy who is not earnest."

"Someone who will drive you wild," Vince said. "W-i-l-d-e."

They laughed at each other's stupid jokes and drifted toward the couch. Justine's pajama bottoms said "Angel" right across her ass. Nothing like ironic lounge wear.

Conveying my irritation with each sharp key stroke, I opened my inbox, and there, atop a tower of spam, was Zoey's email. I clicked on it and glanced at her Hotmail address, 94seeker. The photo took forever to open, and it wasn't worth the wait. All I could see was Kyle Bremmer's face floating in darkness. The hoodie guy wasn't even in the picture.

"Mar-Bar," Vince said, "what's wrong?"

I closed the screen. Despite Zoey's sleuthing, I had no evidence linking Kyle and Reverend Spires. Truth be told, I had no evidence of any kind against anyone who had motive or means to kill Grace. Zoey, for all I knew, was playing me. A little Photoshop, a little imagination, a little less suspicion headed Zoey's way.

"You alright?" Vince asked.

But if Zoey was telling the truth, she could be in big trouble.

"Do you need to talk?" Vince said. "I could help Teeney with her profile some other time."

"Thanks for the offer, but I'm expecting a call." I got up and went to my front window. "The computer is all yours."

Headlights flashed, and a car drove past, a beater like a high school kid would have. I hoped Zoey's boyfriend had a safe car. I hoped he was a good driver. Why didn't she call?

I turned and gazed at the phone. It was flanked by Pop-Tarts and nail polish.

"Maybe we should just crash," Justine said to Vince.

"Go ahead, Teeney. You do have work tomorrow."

"The lab's open?" I asked. That was a good thing, surely. Grace would want it to go on without her. Yet to turn her place of death back into a place of business seemed wrong. It hadn't been three full days since she'd been killed. We hadn't even had her funeral. The visitation wasn't until tomorrow evening.

"Roger called with the news," Vince said.

I studied Justine, but she kept her face blank. "Back in the saddle for you," I said.

She grabbed a magazine and slowly turned a couple pages. Then she made a show of settling into the couch and gave me a big smile. She was deliberately trying to keep me from talking to Vince.

He studied us, stroking his goatee.

Then the phone rang, and, thank God, it was Zoey. As I asked where she was, Vince and Justine both watched me, so I took the cordless and headed upstairs to my room.

"First Kyle went to Hy-Vee," Zoey said, breathless. "But he didn't buy anything. Not even milk. Then he went to Walmart, and Reed started ragging on me again. He was all uptight about needing to study his calculus."

How old did you have to be to study that? Was Zoey's boyfriend way older than her or just a math geek? I closed my bedroom door behind me and sat on my bed. "What about the briefcase?" I said.

"Why are you whispering?" she asked.

"Long story," I whispered back.

"Whatever," Zoey said. "The briefcase is in Kyle's car."

I heard two pairs of feet padding up my stairs. One moment of privacy — was that too much to ask? I told Zoey to hang on, and I listened for doors closing before opening my own. Then I crept back down the stairs, avoiding the two that creaked, amused at the thought of Justine eavesdropping on an empty room. "Where are you now?" I asked.

"I told you," Zoey said impatiently. "Walmart. I made Reed follow Kyle in, and then I went to his car to see what was in the briefcase, but it was locked. The car, I mean."

What if Kyle had caught her there? "Are you back in Reed's car? Have you locked it?"

"You don't need to go all maternal."

Maternal? Me?

"If I lock the doors, I'll just have to unlock them when Reed gets back."

"How far are you from Kyle's car?"

Zoey heaved a sigh, and I realized that I'd asked another mom question. What was happening to me? I would have done the exact same thing she'd done, so why was I giving her grief? Because I'm thirty-seven, and she's fifteen—that's why. Mathematic epiphany, I was old enough to be Zoey's mother. And we weren't talking teen motherhood.

"Did you see the briefcase?" I asked.

"No. He probably stuck it under the seat. Who wouldn't?"

"Did you see anything?"

"Oh yeah," she said proudly. "The car's parked under a super bright light, so I could see part of a photo on the front seat. A boy in a hospital bed. I snapped it and emailed it to you."

I went back to the computer and logged onto my email, hoping this photo turned out better than the other one Zoey sent. "How old was the boy?" I asked.

"Open your email."

"I'm working on it." Vince and I really needed to spring for a faster internet connection.

"It's super clear for a photo of a photo," Zoey said.

Once it finished loading, I saw that she was right. The boy was five or six years old, a scrawny carrot-top. I couldn't remember any red-headed kids among the photos at Kyle's place, so this child was probably not his nephew. The way the boy leaned forward slightly in the hospital bed reminded me of somebody, but not Kyle. Someone was with the boy, touching his shoulder, but all I could see was a sweater-clad arm. I couldn't even tell if it belonged to a male or a female.

"Here they come!" Zoey said. "It doesn't look like Kyle bought anything here either, but Reed will know."

I heard Reed—presumably—open and shut the driver's door and start the engine. Music from the car radio pulsed through the phone.

"Come on, dude," Zoey said to Reed. "You don't have to stop at every stop sign in the parking lot."

I resisted the urge to comment on traffic safety, and I heard Reed's voice though I couldn't make out his words.

"Kyle bought gift cards." Zoey sounded disappointed. Then there was more murmuring punctuated with several "dudes" from Zoey. "Five hundred dollars' worth," she said, her voice triumphant again. "He paid with cash. Which means there was cash in the briefcase. Nobody carries that kind of green."

A horn blared.

"Dude," Zoey said. "You don't honk at your friends when you're tailing somebody."

They bickered, and I tried to make sense of Kyle's bizarre late night shopping spree. The gift cards could be for his grandma and sister. But wouldn't it be simpler and nicer for him to give them money? Why force his flesh and blood to support Sam Walton's evil empire?

"Kyle's heading toward his apartment," Zoey said. "I bet he's gonna count his money, but we'll hang out in his parking lot in case he goes somewhere else."

Reed offered no argument. Why would he? He'd just been handed the opportunity to park with his girlfriend. "I doubt Kyle will go out again," I said. "He has to work tomorrow morning. The lab has reopened."

"You never know," Zoey said.

"He might see you."

"We'll be careful."

"I thought Reed had to study calculus."

"That was just an excuse," she said. "He hates spending money on gas. He's a complete tightwad."

Reed protested, but I couldn't understand what he said. Nor could I stop "going maternal" when I thought about Zoey parking with a guy who might be older and more experienced than she was. A guy who might try to take advantage of all the chaos in her life. Then I told myself to get a grip. Zoey was more than capable of speaking her mind to Reed. Yet I couldn't help but remember the time my mom fixed me up with her best friend's nephew. Even after I told the hapless lad that I liked girls, he tried to unhook my bra.

"We're closing in on Kyle's place," Zoey said.

"I wouldn't waste too much time there."

"We won't."

"When you see that Kyle is in for the night, you should have Reed take you home."

"Right," Zoey said, "because it's a school night and I need my sleep."

I had no response to her sarcasm. Vince would have relished the moment.

"I'm a big girl," Zoey said. "The only thing I need from you is help finding my donor dad."

After she hung up, I kept the phone to my ear, hoping she was right. Reason 757, I told myself, but my heart wasn't in the counting.

Chapter Nineteen

I HAD SET my alarm an hour early to avoid Justine, but when I came downstairs the next morning, she was tapping away at my computer. "Maxing out another credit card?" I asked.

She ignored me. Without pounds of eyeliner, she looked young and sort of sweet, but then I remembered her virtuoso performance as Gwendolen Fairfax. For all I knew, her slacker-girl thing was an act too, designed to mask a calculating killer. Whoever the real Justine was, I couldn't face her without caffeine. I followed the scent of coffee to the kitchen and poured us both a cup. Hers I set near the mouse so I could glance at the computer screen. Match.com. Justine's profile looked like an instant message from e.e. cummings. I'm no grammar snob, but I do appreciate an occasional comma.

Justine reached for her coffee and raised her eyebrows at me.

I mumbled a sorry and stepped away.

"What the hell, it'll be online anyway. Knock yourself out." She stood. "You got any cream or sugar?"

"Skim milk," I said, "but it might be bad."

Justine nodded toward the computer. "Vince says I sound too demanding. I need a second opinion."

Fortifying myself with more caffeine, I scrolled to the top of Justine's profile. In her photo, she suggestively straddled a guitar. I wondered if she really played or if it was just a prop. "wyldgrrl84 seeks good times no strings attached." Maybe she was going for a pun.

In the kitchen, wyldgrrl opened and closed cupboards, probably seeking food. In her profile, she identified her eyes as her best feature and admitted to a "strategically positioned" tattoo. Her favorite things? Theatre, partying, shopping—not necessarily in that order. Truth-in-advertising points, I'd give her those. "Top or bottom," she'd written, "it's all good i like to be spoiled but not smothered no babytalk no judging no clinging no talking about the relationship." So much for pina coladas and getting caught in the rain.

"What do you think?" Justine asked, strolling back into the room and opening a package of Lorna Doones.

I liked her *so* much better as Gwendolen Fairfax. "I'm no expert," I said, "but it does seem a little negative."

Justine handed me the cookies and slipped back in front of the screen. "I've already edited it like three times."

"How about emphasizing what you want instead of what you don't? Think about the guys you've..." I floundered. The word *dated* didn't seem right. "Think about the guys you've enjoyed. What did you like about them?"

"I like guys who are really ripped, like Kyle at the lab, but not all obsessed with their own muscles. And not all about getting me to live in the gym. And not—"

"You went out with Kyle?"

"No," she said. "We just hit the bars a couple times when I first started at the lab. He's practically got a live-in. They're all about monogamy." Justine rolled her eyes. "She can have him. He got like all in my face whenever I wanted more than two drinks." Justine sipped her coffee. "It was crazy."

It seemed to me that Justine had lots of "crazy" relationships with people who were connected to Grace. Kyle and Roger at the lab, and Roger's daughter, Liz, who had confronted her at the theatre. I hadn't poked around about Liz out of respect for Bridget, but maybe it was time to start. I was about to ask Justine about Liz when the phone rang. Justine and I gazed at each other wide-eyed. A call at 6:00 in the morning seldom brings good news.

It was Orchid. "I need a favor," she said. "You're taking today off, right?" Before I could answer, she asked if I could take Labrys.

My boss calls before sunrise for a dog sitter? "Are you okay?" I asked. "Is Anne alright?"

Justine peered at me over her coffee cup.

"We've had a break-in. They drugged Labrys."

I sank into the nearest chair.

"The vet says she'll be okay, but we don't want to leave her alone," Orchid said. "Can you take her?"

"Sure. But if you want me to handle things at work so you can stay—"

"Thanks," Orchid said, "but we just want out of here."

"How's Anne?"

"Shaken up. They took the tapes she was making for you—for your show, I mean. That's the worst part. Besides Labrys."

I tried to fathom Anne's losses. The baby she'd imagined into being, the donor she'd painstakingly chosen. Her story of choosing and trying.

"They broke one of our brand-new back windows," Orchid continued. "That's how they got in. Sometime during the baby-naming ceremony."

"They?" I asked.

"The robber," Orchid said, exasperated. "Whoever did this."

I had no idea where Reverend Leo Spires had been last night before he met Kyle. If he met Kyle. Of course, Spires or his daughter Celia could have masterminded the break-ins. The thief could be their minion. The tiny bald guy at the protests looked mean enough to drug a dog. Kyle could have done it before Zoey and her boyfriend started following him. Of course, Zoey herself could have done the deed, but as far as I could tell, she had no reason to. Nor did Roger or his daughter. Justine would have had the opportunity after rehearsal, but again, it was hard to figure a motive. Unless it had been a personal fundraiser staged to mimic the break-in at my office. If she hadn't done that deed, she could have gotten the details from Vince. "What else is missing?" I asked.

Justine's shoulders tensed. Her hand froze on the mouse. She appeared to be concentrating on the screen, but I knew she was eavesdropping.

"We're still checking," Orchid said, "but lots of Anne's journals and notebooks are gone."

"Your computers?"

"Mine was in my car. Anne's was at work."

"What about valuables?"

Orchid was silent.

"Besides Anne's things," I added.

"Some cash," Orchid said, "although we don't leave a lot lying around. But you know what's really weird? Our Tupperware is missing."

"Tupperware? Are you serious?"

Justine gave me a tense smile and scurried up the stairs. Her sudden exit was almost as bizarre as the Tupperware theft.

"Some of our other kitchen containers are gone too."

"What did the cops say?"

"About the Tupperware?"

"About anything."

"Well," Orchid said, "they asked about you."

"Me? I have my own Tupperware." I joked, but inside I was seething. The police were wasting their time on me when the real thief was still out there.

"I told them you have a key to our place and no reason to break in. And I told them that you adore Labrys and would never drug her, but they had no interest in the truth." Orchid's voice pulsed with anger. "All they wanted to talk about was you and Grace and *Trying Times*. They even had the nerve to ask how the station would benefit if your project did well, and I told them to quit blaming the victim and take a look at Leo Spires and his so-called church." She paused for air. "Patriarchal dupes."

I'd need to leave the house soon unless I wanted another tête-à-tête with Iowa City's finest.

"I'll be honest," Orchid said. "I wasn't thrilled about *Trying Times* when you first started working on it. I thought you were blindly reinforcing the patriarchy's valorization of birth and motherhood, but now I'm behind you one hundred percent. No Tupperware thief or misogynist police force is going to influence the shows my station produces."

Justine thumped around upstairs. I hoped she wasn't a bathroom hog.

"You are planning to finish the series, aren't you?" Orchid asked.

"Of course." If my other audio-diarists didn't bail once I warned them about the thief.

Chapter Twenty

A FEW HOURS later, Labrys, Vince, and I were in my Dodge Omni, rattling toward Spiresville. The dog whined in the back seat and thrust her head between Vince and me until I surrendered the last of my Egg McMuffin. I was still hungry, but I was afraid Labrys would make me drive into the ditch if I didn't appease her. Plus I felt bad for all she'd been through.

"Your freckles are showing," Vince said, studying my forehead. "I should have used a darker foundation."

Before we'd hit the road, we'd hit the community theatre and transformed ourselves into church ladies — the better to sleuth incognito in Spiresville. Vince shaved his beloved goatee and searched for frocks that would help him inhabit Lady Bracknell. Finding none, he settled for wannabe Jackie Onassis, a plum wool jacket and skirt, a shoulder-length brunette wig, a pillbox hat, and a strand of pearls. Me, I looked like a bespectacled Hillary Clinton complete with a blond wig, body padding, and a pant suit. I couldn't help thinking that the disguise Vince had chosen for me was payback for our argument about Justine.

"This is going to be an adventure," he said.

"Yeah," I grumbled, "Thelma and Louise, the frumpy years."

"Come, come, Mar-Bar. Frumpy is as frumpy does." Vince pitched his voice higher and tugged his skirt toward his knees. "Let's get in character."

He took two deep breaths and closed his eyes, so he didn't see me rolling mine.

We crested a hill. Nestled between corn fields ready for harvest were trees the color of cinnamon, pumpkin, and red wine. A hawk sliced the blue above them. How could such beauty exist when Grace was no longer part of it? My nose tickled and burned, and I was afraid I'd start crying. The last thing I wanted was Vince fussing over me or insisting he redo my makeup. I rolled down my window and tried to focus on the chilly air.

"That gale is decimating my do," Vince said.

Labrys panted in my ear as she sought the open window.

I shut it. From the top of the next hill, I could see the construction site we were headed for, the one where Kyle had received the briefcase. The directions in Zoey's email were spot-on. A bulldozer was pushing dirt toward a huge pile, maybe the one Zoey and Reed had hidden behind. Near the front of the lot was a sign, but I was too far away to read it.

"Look out!" Vince yelled in his full baritone.

I wrenched the steering wheel. The road zigzagged more than most highways in Iowa, and I'd almost driven off it. Vince fanned himself with a white-gloved hand. "Goodness," he said, back to his church-lady voice, "my poor heart is racing faster than you were."

I rode the brakes down the rest of the hill and pulled into the site—not too far, though, lest I destroy any footprints. But I needn't have worried. When Labrys bounded out of the car, tugging at her leash, her paws left no trace. The soil was too cracked and hard. Labrys barked at the bulldozer's obnoxiously roaring engine and yanked me toward the biggest pile of dirt. I struggled to keep up, my toes smarting in too-small pumps. At the base of the pile were cigarette butts. I bent over as far as my padded belly would allow. A Camel filtered and a Virginia Slim. I announced that Zoey and her boyfriend must have been smoking there last night.

"Kids'll do that." Vince shouted over the bulldozer. He squinted into the sun, and then raised his hand to shield his eyes.

"But she's only fifteen. It's so unhealthy."

"You sound like your mother."

Vince was right. There I was again, going maternal. What was my deal?

"Lighten up," Vince said. "You've toked a few things in your life."

Labrys barked more fiercely as the bulldozer droned closer to us.

"Come on," Vince shouted, "we're not here to investigate teen smoking."

What were we there to investigate? Mostly we'd stopped because the site was on the way to Spiresville and I'd hoped that seeing the place would give me some sort of insight about Spires or Kyle, some flash of intuition that great detectives always get when visiting the scene of a crime. If that's indeed what this was.

Vince and I headed toward the sign. Happy Valley Condominiums. Soon Iowa would be all subdivisions and strip malls.

"There are oodles of deserted places between here and Iowa City," Vince said. "Why would anyone want to meet here?"

Labrys strained at her leash, eager to chase the bulldozer. My phone rang. I gave Vince the leash and answered.

It was Anne. She sounded distraught, but I couldn't make out her words. I told her to hang on and dashed to the car as fast as my old-lady footwear would allow. With the windows shut tight, my Omni was semi-soundproof.

"The Center has been robbed," Anne said. "My computer is gone."

I was torn between wanting to comfort her and wanting the details. "What about the other computers?"

Hers was the only one missing. The Center didn't have any cash, and the police hadn't yet arrived. She must have called me first thing. Or second — right after the cops. "Annabelle," I said quietly. "What do you need?" I imagined her gazing out her office window, her hair in a messy top-knot, fussing at it with her long slender fingers like she always did when she felt lost.

"Meet me later?" Anne asked.

I could sense the desperation underneath her casual tone. "Sure," I said, keeping my own voice light. So what if I was going to spend a chunk of the day in Spiresville and I wasn't the least bit ready — psychologically or sartorially — for Grace's visitation that evening.

I stepped out of the car and saw Vince and Labrys heading toward the bulldozer. Vince was attempting to snare the operator's attention by waving his gloves around in the air. The operator, a skinny man with a bright orange baseball cap, gaped at Vince and exchanged a few words with him before backing the bulldozer away.

When Vince returned to me, he was smiling smugly. "Guess who used to own this land," he sang out. "Reverend Leo Spires."

VINCE AND I were fast approaching Spiresville, but we were no closer to agreeing on Justine.

"Teeney is no robber or vandal," Vince said.

"She was up before me," I argued. "She could have broken into the Women's Center this morning."

"The thief probably struck last night when Teeney was at rehearsal."

"She could have done it afterward."

"Why are you so determined to think the worst of her?"

Labrys whimpered. Vince reached back and stroked her. "There, there. Uncle Vince is simply trying to reason with Auntie Mar-Bar."

I squeezed the steering wheel. "What about those sperm vials in her purse? You've got to admit that's weird."

"Weirdness does not a robber or killer make."

We topped a hill, and I could see Spiresville on the horizon. At the town's center was a church with a giant steeple. A logo of the steeple adorned the water tower near the east edge of the town.

"What about Justine's argument with Roger's daughter?" I asked.

"*We* argue," Vince said, looking pointedly at me. "It doesn't mean we're criminal conspirators."

He was right, but I still didn't trust Justine and I still wanted her out of the house. "She'll use you like her own personal ATM," I said.

Vince shook his head dismissively. "You just want her to leave so our guest room will be available for Anne."

I started to protest, but he cut me off.

"You've told me ten million times that she and Orchid are having problems. Don't you see where you're headed?"

"4217 James Avenue, the residence of Kyle Bremmer's grandmother."

"If you don't want to talk about it—"

"There's nothing to talk about. Where are those directions I printed?" I braked at an intersection. My engine rattled and shuddered.

"You're in denial about your car too," Vince said.

I concentrated on Spires' mini empire. To my left was his radio station and welcome sign, "Spiresville—Home of 3,356 Souls & the World's Sweetest Cookies."

Past the sign loomed the source of the aforementioned cookies and most of Spires' worldly success. Sugar Spires, a factory that looked like a sugar cube, had been turning out cookies since the Keebler elves had been in diapers. Even the reverend's many enemies had to admire his business acumen. He sold the bulk of his wares—which were basically Girl Scout cookie knock-offs shaped like crosses—to churches for fundraisers. Most of these fundraisers occurred during the Girl Scout cookie off-season. Quoth my mother when her Altar and Rosary Society decided to sell Mint Miracles, "They may be sacrilegious, but they sure are good." I stopped eating them in fourth grade after my aunts told me how Spires used his radio station and his church—and the money from his cookies, they carefully explained—to harass people like them. It was my first boycott.

Vince sniffed the air. "Shortbread?"

I shrugged.

"If I lived here, I'd gain twenty pounds just like that." He snapped his fingers.

"They'd run you out of town first." I stopped at a light, relieved that my engine kept chugging. "Not shortbread," I said, breathing in the scent. "Chocolate chip."

Vince jabbed my shoulder. "Roger Lipinski is in the car next to us."

I shifted my eyes to the right. The man at the wheel wore sunglasses, but it was Roger alright. Thin silver ponytail, thick neck. Holy coincidence, Batman.

I gave Vince the number for Grace's lab and asked him to call and see why Roger wasn't at work.

Cell phone in hand, Vince asked for Roger, using his church lady voice. "Out sick, you say. Oh, dear. Nothing serious, I hope."

The light turned green. Roger shot across the intersection.

"Then may I please speak to Justine Nissen?" Vince falsettoed to the receptionist at the lab.

"What are you doing?" I hissed.

"Hey Teeney," Vince said in his regular voice. He asked if she'd accidentally grabbed his script, and then he hung up and turned to me. "Ye of little faith, now we know that Teeney's right where she's supposed to be."

"There's something going on with those two," I said. "Mark my words — Roger and Justine are in cahoots."

Instead of heading straight for James Avenue, we followed Roger's car, and he led us downtown. I had to give the reverend credit for a thriving one. Most Iowa towns the size of Spiresville are lucky if they have a Mini-Mart. We passed a quilt shop, a salon, and several clothing stores. The streets were lined with potted pines in the shape of — you got it — spires. Roger whizzed by them.

I tried to tell myself that he was simply passing through, trying to escape his grief by skipping work, but then he slowed down. Maybe he was planning to investigate like we were. I didn't want to believe that Grace's longtime office assistant had anything to do with anyone in Spiresville. Anything to do with her death.

As I braked behind Roger, I saw Celia Spires emerge from a corner bakery. She had a laptop under her arm, and the sun glinted off her auburn hair. Without signaling, Roger pulled into the nearest parking spot. I followed suit about five cars down. Roger jumped from his car and barreled toward Celia. If this surprised her, she didn't show it. From my parking space, I could see Celia clearly as she faced Roger. Shod in her alligator stilettos, she literally looked down on him. She didn't say a word, and her face was about as easy to read as a computer manual. His face, I couldn't see at all, but I imagined he was accusing her of rifling through his office or telling her what he thought of her protests.

But much to my surprise, she smiled and spoke, and then turned and entered the bakery. As Roger followed her in, I could see his profile. He was grinning.

Chapter Twenty-one

STUNNED, I GAZED at the bakery door.

"I'll go in," Vince said. He pulled down the car visor and checked his makeup in the mirror. "I just need to powder my nose."

Rather than arguing with him, I simply waited for him to begin rummaging in his handbag, and then I exited the car. I could hear Labrys barking and Vince tapping angrily on his window. As I turned to scowl at him, I smacked right into a real church lady. Her hair was sprayed within an inch of its life, and her mouth was pursed in the style of Dana Carvey. "Sorry," I said, hoping she wouldn't make me for a lapsed Catholic.

She narrowed her eyes at me, and her pursed mouth tightened. "You need to be more careful," she said.

I smiled as if I were grateful to her for stating the obvious, and I scuttled toward the bakery. The door stuck, and I didn't want to manhandle it too much lest I blow my cover. When I finally got it open, I was rewarded with the scent of fresh donuts, but no Roger and Celia. They must have slipped into the bakery's kitchen or back office. The only person in the bakery proper was an elderly prune-faced guy at the counter. He was humming as he worked a crossword. I dallied over my pastry selection, but there was still no Roger or Celia. No voices from the back of the bakery either. The counter guy fell silent and eyed me suspiciously. Stalling for time, I asked about his puzzle.

"Gotta do something to keep the old noggin' sharp," he said, "but it's a losing game, sweetheart."

I was playing a losing game too, so I accepted my defeat, purchased some donuts, and left.

Vince accosted me as I slid back into the driver's seat. "You should have let me go in," he said.

"Nobody's stopping you." I offered Labrys a bite of donut. As the dog and I carbo-loaded, Vince entered the bakery. Fifteen minutes later, he returned with nothing but a bag of day-old croissants and some humble pie. Ten minutes after that, Roger's reappearance was equally unrevealing. He got back in his car and headed toward Iowa City. So Vince and I resumed our original plan, visiting Kyle's grandmother.

She lived on the outskirts of Spiresville in a well-kept old farmhouse. Purple asters lined the gravel drive, and potted mums brightened the front porch.

We knocked, and she greeted us with a young boy her at her side. They both wore football helmets. Hers pressed against her oversized glasses and topped an ensemble that consisted of support hose and a floral dress. My gender-bending friends had nothing on this woman.

Forcing my attention away from her wardrobe, I launched into the story Vince and I had concocted. We were on our way home from visiting my brother at the university hospital. He was so grateful for all the visits from Reverend Spires and other church members, and so were we because the hospital was miles away from our own church. So we'd done a little sleuthing to see who organized Spires' hospital ministry — that last bit was true — and it turned out that Mrs. Bremmer was the very one. Since we were passing through, we hoped it wasn't too much of an imposition if we offered our thanks in person.

"Not at all, sisters." She beamed and removed her helmet. The braid atop her head was slightly askew, but her dark eyes were even more remarkable in person than they had been in Kyle's photo. "My great-grandson and I were just getting ready to practice our passing, but it can wait, can't it, Christopher?"

The chunky lad at her side nodded. His helmet hid half his face. The football he hugged was longer than his entire torso.

She nodded toward the boy and the unwieldy ball. "They may as well get used to regulation size, don't you think?"

"Size does matter," Vince answered.

Double entendres weren't Mrs. Bremmer's strong suit. She simply ushered us in. "Surprise company is a blessing from the Lord, isn't it?"

Her living room appeared to be a shrine, not to the Lord, but to her numerous descendents and the art of photography. Kyle figured prominently.

"Have a seat," she said, "and please call me Gertie. I'll get some coffee. It's already made. I always keep a pot ready. You never know when you'll need it, do you?"

A woman after my own heart. But then I remembered her protest signs. I wondered if Christopher accompanied her to the protests. I didn't think I'd seen him.

He and Vince followed Gertie into the kitchen. As she regaled Vince with her thoughts on whether coffee hour was best scheduled before or after the main Sunday service, I wondered what Roger Lipinski and Celia Spires had been doing in that bakery. Surely *they* weren't having an affair.

Christopher exited the kitchen without his helmet. He was clearly not the skinny carrot-topped boy in the photo Zoey emailed me, the one in Kyle's front seat. Nor was that boy in Mrs. Bremmer's photo collection.

"Wanna see something?" Christopher started pulling picture books off a shelf until he found one about wild animals. "Uncle Kyle has been teaching me about hippos. They have humongous teeth, and sometimes they kill people. But they don't eat them." He sounded disappointed about that.

Gertie appeared with the coffee, and Vince was behind her with a plate of cookies. Mint Miracles! He scarfed one down in a decidedly unfeminine manner before Mrs. Bremmer finished pouring the coffee. Me, I was torn. Be polite and eat a cookie? Or stick to my principles?

My mouth watered.

Mrs. Bremmer extended the plate to me.

"Calories," I said, patting my padded stomach.

She wasn't the type to argue with her guests' dietary choices. I forced my eyes away from the plate.

Vince nodded toward the biggest photo of Kyle. "He's handsome."

"My youngest grandson. He's smart too. College educated. We don't know what we'd do without Uncle Kyle, do we Christopher? Couldn't keep the place up without him. I always tell him so every time he visits, and I make his favorite meatloaf too, don't I?"

She paused for a sip of coffee. Vince and I exchanged glances. Getting the scoop on Kyle was going to be easy. The hard part would be extricating ourselves once we had it.

"He comes at least once a week," she said. "Sometimes more if I need him. Rain or shine."

"Like a mailman," Christopher added.

"Remember that blizzard last winter?" she asked.

"I do, I do!" Christopher said. "The snow got taller than me!"

"It was a weekend I had Christopher and his two sisters." She lowered her voice. "Sweet things, but a handful. All three of them got high fevers. Baby aspirin wasn't doing any good."

"I'm a rhinoceros, Grammy." Christopher crawled on all fours and tossed his head around menacingly.

But Grammy was lost in her story. "I needed to get them to a doctor, but I couldn't get the driveway shoveled, not by myself, and everybody from church was just as snowed in as we were. I called Kyle to see what he thought I should do."

The rhino attempted to pick up a book with his teeth.

"I never intended him to come in all that snow — especially with that old car of his — but he insisted. I prayed and prayed until he got here, don't think I didn't. But he got us to the doctor and stayed until the children's fevers broke."

"He made a snowman outside my window," Christopher said. "Its nose was celery because we didn't have a carrot."

"He sounds like a real blessing," Vince said. "Where does he live?"

"Iowa City." She took another sip of coffee. "I wish he were

closer and in a less sinful place. But he knows how to resist tempta-
tion."

"So many young people drift away from the church," I said,
shaking my head slowly and trying not to gag on my own words.

Gertie added sugar to her coffee. Four teaspoons full. This was
the first conversational ball that she had dropped. Despite Kyle's
obvious devotion to his grandmother, maybe he really had rejected
her homophobic church and minister.

"Reverend Spires was like a father to Kyle," she said. "To all my
boys — sons and grandsons. My youngest son, Kyle's father, was only
eight when my husband went to see his maker. There I was with five
boys — the oldest only fifteen — and a farm to manage." She nodded
outside. "All this used to be farm. A big part of Spiresville used to be
our farm." Her voice was proud, but her eyes looked sad. "After my
Walter died, I don't know what I would have done if it wasn't for the
reverend. He took my boys under his wing — showed them right from
wrong — and organized men from the church to work our land. Corn
and beans grown right out there helped put a new steeple on our
church."

Vince and I exchanged glances. How much of the farm's profits
had gone to Leo Spires?

"But then prices went down so far I had to sell. My only comfort
was that the church bought most of it. Walter," she glanced skyward,
"is happy his land is serving the Lord."

"During the eighties?" I asked.

She nodded.

I grew up in rural Iowa, so I know about the farm crisis. My
cheeks burned with anger at the thought of Spires purchasing this
woman's land for half of what it was worth.

"What about your grandson?" Vince asked. "You were saying
that the reverend was like a father to him."

"Grammy," Christopher said, "when can we start throwing?"

"Soon as I'm done talking with these nice ladies. You go on out
and practice kicking, but stay in the yard, you hear?"

As Christopher slammed the door behind him, her smile faded,
and she dropped her gaze. She clasped her hands together in her lap
as if she were praying. "Kyle's father died when Kyle was sixteen."
She looked up, her face ravaged with sorrow. "But Kyle and the reverend were always close. When Kyle was about Christopher's age, he
wanted to be a minister when he grew up. Just like Reverend Spires,
he'd say." She smiled faintly. "He never missed a Bible study or a
youth meeting, and soon as he was old enough, he started teaching
the little ones and being a camp counselor. Kyle always wanted to go
with the reverend to visit shut-ins, and sometimes the reverend
would take him. Other times they'd just spend time together fishing
or hiking, discerning the Lord's will for Kyle."

"Did he ever participate in the reverend's demonstrations?" I asked.

"Oh sure."

Apparently all children protest the "gay lifestyle" even if they're not destined for the cloth. "Are they still close?"

Gertie raised her eyebrows.

"I don't mean to pry. It just sounds like such a lovely relationship. My daughter never even wants to go to church."

"That's a pity, isn't it? How old is she?"

"Fifteen."

"Kyle was in a Revelations phase when he was fifteen." Gertie reached for her coffee. "He kept talking about the four horsemen of the apocalypse and giving his sister nightmares."

"And now?" I prompted.

"He has his own life in Iowa City."

"Did he become a minister?" Vince asked.

"No." Kyle's grandmother once again clasped her hands in her lap. "But I'm so proud of him. He works in a blood bank."

"EITHER SHE WAS lying about his job, or she's absolutely clueless about his life." I slammed my car door and cranked the engine. "What a bust."

"The cookies were good," Vince said.

I ignored him and steered us back toward downtown Spiresville. We passed a hardware store, a pharmacy, and—wouldn't you know it?—a cookie shop. The clerks might know something about Kyle, but the church office was a better bet. Unless Spires was there and saw through our disguises. Contrary to Vince's belief, disguises don't work as well in real life as they do in Shakespeare.

"The kid was adorable," Vince said, "a budding thespian."

I halted at a four-way stop and studied the pedestrians. Mostly pairs of grannies and women with strollers. There was also a slender young woman with a baseball cap and cigarette. A very familiar young woman. I headed toward her and pulled into a nearby parking space. The cap hid most of her red hair, but not all of it.

"Zoey," I said, getting out of the car. "What are you doing here?"

Her eyes ping-ponged between Vince and me, and I realized that my disguise was good enough to fool Zoey.

I lowered my voice, revealed my true identity, introduced Vince, and explained what we were up to.

"Nice drag," she said to Vince.

He bowed his head in thanks.

"Great dog too." Zoey nodded toward Labrys in the back seat of the car.

Labrys barked and wagged her tail.

I wanted to ask Zoey why she was skipping school and ruining her lungs, but I settled for something more neutral. "What brings you to Spiresville?"

She didn't answer right away. "Those women across the street are giving us the eye."

"Probably admiring my ensemble." Vince batted his eyes.

"I hope they haven't noticed me following that minister dude. He's in there." Zoey subtly nodded toward the bookstore across the street.

"How long have you been following him?" I asked.

"He's only been on the move since 8:00, but me and Reed started staking out his house at 5:00 this morning."

I resisted the urge to ask her whether she'd gotten any sleep last night. "So where's Reed?"

"I told you," she said, "he has a calculus test. He'll pick me up later."

Spires emerged from the bookstore and paused to speak with the women who'd been watching us.

"He has a white SUV," Zoey whispered, "like the one me and Reed saw last night."

One of the women glanced our way again. I hoped Spires wouldn't.

"Me and Reed have used a lot of gas following this guy. First, we drive from Iowa City to this place. And when the guy finally leaves his house, where does he go? Iowa City. He went to the university hospital and made some visits. I wrote down every room." Zoey smiled proudly and handed me a list.

I should have told her that she and Reed had been foolhardy, that Spires could have seen her, that the cops might have caught her skulking about the hospital. Instead, I thanked her and skimmed her notations. She'd kept track of how long he stayed in each room. One visit lasted nearly two hours.

"Minister on the move," Vince sing-songed. "I'll follow him. Zoey, you fill Mar-Bar in on your sleuthing."

"Only if I can eat while I'm talking," Zoey said. "I'm starved."

I offered to treat her and surrendered my car keys to Vince. "Try to blend," I told him.

"Of course," he said, looking hurt.

As I searched for a restaurant, Vince sashayed after the minister, drawing stares from every single pedestrian.

THE GOOD NEWS was that the diner we found featured all-you-can-eat pancakes. The bad news? It also featured Leo Spires' radio station. The worst news? Spires himself was on the air railing about sperm donation.

As Zoey and I settled into a booth, Spires' voice boomed from a speaker above us. Had the reverend headed to his radio station right after we saw him, or were we being subjected to a tape? Maybe the other diners were hearing this spiel for the hundredth time. No wonder they all seemed brainwashed.

"Make no mistake," Spires' said, "a man who sells his seed is no better than a prostitute. And a business or a hospital or a doctor that profits from that seed is no better than a pimp. These people may think they mean well — they may think they're helping others — but what they're really doing is decimating the American family."

"We don't have to stay here," I said.

Zoey grabbed a menu, but didn't open it.

"How are they destroying the family?" Spires asked. "By destroying fatherhood. By destroying manhood. When a man's genetic inheritance is bought and sold, all men are diminished. When a man becomes nothing more than an inseminator, fatherhood is demeaned and devalued, degraded and debauched."

"Zoey?" I said.

She fiddled with her largest ring and scowled at her unopened menu.

"Let's go," I urged, "we'll find somewhere else to eat."

She shushed me.

Great. I was introducing a troubled young girl to ideas that would make her feel even worse about herself and her family.

"God wants us to be responsible for our genetic offspring," Spires said. "The Bible celebrates fatherhood. It celebrates traditional families."

"Yeah," I said, "Jesus and Moses had real traditional families."

Zoey smiled faintly. A perky waitress took our order, and Spires went on and on about lost seed. It was almost like a garden show.

"Brothers and sisters, consider the children born of trafficked seed."

Zoey sat up straighter.

"Those born to single women or pairs of lesbians have no fathers. Research shows that fatherless children experience greater poverty and lower self-esteem. Fatherless girls become unwed teen mothers, and fatherless boys become violent."

"He's distorting the research," I said. "But what can you expect from a man who twists the words of his own holy book?"

The waitress delivered our drinks and eyed me uneasily.

"What about donor offspring who are fortunate enough to have both a father and a mother?" Spires asked. "I tell you, these children suffer too. No matter how close they are to the men who raise them, no matter how good these men are, the children feel confused and incomplete. They know that something is missing."

Zoey picked up her straw and bent it. She swallowed hard.

"They're missing half their genetic identity, half their biological origins, half the history and stories they need to shape their self-understanding."

I gently took Zoey's knotted straw from her and waited until she met my eyes. She did so for only a second, her face contorted with pain. And anger, perhaps, that a stranger had laid bare her sorrow for both of us to see.

"Don't let him tell you who you are," I said. "You're hurting, and you want to know your bio dad, of course you do, but biology isn't everything. You're not missing half your stories. You're not half a person."

She gazed at her Coke. The waitress brought two steaming plates of pancakes and asked if everything was alright. I lied and said it was.

We sat there in silence a long moment before Zoey started speaking. "I wouldn't even know about my donor dad if I hadn't eavesdropped on the judge and my aunt. She was pissed off about his speedy marriage to Trophy Wife. She said maybe he'd care more about my feelings if I was his real daughter." Zoey cut her pancakes into tiny pieces. "My aunt knows about how I was born, but I don't? That is seriously fucked up."

"Brothers and sisters," Spires' voice thundered from the speaker. "God instructed us to be fruitful and multiply. The biological urge is strong. The desire to conceive and give birth is fierce. But should a woman satisfy this desire by any means necessary? I say no. Not if she purposefully conceives a child who will never know his father. Not if she and the medical marketplace treat this father like a commodity. Not if she cheapens the notion of fatherhood and family."

I thought of Anne, the donor she so clearly admired and respected, the child she so badly wanted.

"God is calling us to act on behalf of children and fathers. He has recently struck down Dr. Grace Everest, a scientist who did much to create their suffering and who had planned to do much more."

His characterization of Grace was so egregiously unfair it left me speechless. My fury grew as he urged his listeners to speak out against her endowment. And to protest her visitation and funeral.

Protest, my ass. Spires and his cult would be there to celebrate. But I'd be ready for them.

Chapter Twenty-two

THE RECEPTION AREA of Spires' church office reminded me of a dentist's waiting room, clinically white walls, soulless furniture, and magazines no one had the heart to read. But the receptionist herself didn't seem to fit. She was a square-shouldered sixty- or seventy-year-old with sunglasses hanging around her neck. They perched on a large sweatshirt-clad bosom and pitched up and down with her breath as she listened to someone on the phone. When I cleared my throat, she waved me to a chair and turned her back on me.

So much for a Christian welcome.

Before I sat, I scanned the hallway behind the receptionist's gargantuan desk. All the doors that I could see were closed. Celia Spires' name was on the closest one.

"I can't believe it," the receptionist said into the phone, "he promised my granddaughter that promotion and then he gives it to Holly Bremmer of all people."

My ears perked up at the mention of Kyle's last name.

"Holly's a nice girl, but she's not management material. She can't even handle her own husband."

Was this Kyle's sister? I listened closely, pretending to read a magazine.

"Gertie will brag the girl up all over town. I can't imagine why the reverend would favor her Holly over my Sara. Gertie doesn't do half the stuff for the church that I do."

Hell hath no fury like a church-lady scorned. My mom once boycotted the Altar and Rosary Society's annual bazaar because she wasn't elected to the floral committee.

"It's no wonder we're struggling financially if that's the kind of decisions he makes." The receptionist tapped her fingers on the desk and listened briefly. "He may be a prophet," she said, "but he can't stick to a budget. My Isaac says the church's endowment has been shrinking for the last decade."

Maybe because the reverend was passing out briefcases filled with cash.

I studied Spires' face in the huge family portrait hanging near the reception desk. Despite his rust-colored hair and his unshapely nose, his charisma was obvious even in a photo. Daughter Celia seemed to be the only one who inherited it. She and the reverend both stood tall and smiling. "Bring it on," their grins said. The wife and other two daughters, all sitting, looked soft and boring by comparison. None of them looked eager to befriend you, persuade you, destroy you.

The phone topic shifted to food prices, and I turned my attention to the brochures on the table in front of me. "There are millions of orphans in the world," one proclaimed. I picked it up and opened it. "Why purposefully create children who will never know half their genetic parentage?" it asked. "Why objectify men and weaken the definition of fatherhood?"

I was extra glad Zoey wasn't with me. I'd talked her into going with Vince to Kyle's high school to see if his former teachers knew anything about him. It hadn't been an easy sell. I explained that I'd shown her sketch to the reverend and that if he was at the office, he might recognize her. I explained that he could be Grace's killer. What I didn't explain was that I didn't want her swallowing any more of his poison. And poison it was. The wall nearest me was covered with photos of him smiling with the likes of Pat Robertson, James Dobson, and Fred Phelps. These so-called evangelists were his heroes. Men whose good news was bad news for people like me.

"You want my two cents," said the receptionist, "Celia Spires has no business judging. She has trouble enough with her own daughter."

I reexamined the Spires' family portrait. Several little girls huddled around Celia's sisters and their husbands, demonstrating their family values, but Celia and her man had only one daughter. I'd seen that girl before. I remembered her fighting with Celia at the hospital protest the day Grace died. The daughter had wanted to protest hunger instead of homosexuality. Poor thing was probably the black sheep of the entire Spires clan. I wondered if Celia and her husband had been unable to conceive a second child. Celia had searched the main office at Grace's lab and met with Roger at the bakery. Was it possible she was secretly using the lab's services?

"Sister? Can I help you?" The receptionist had once been a looker, cheekbones to die for and commanding violet eyes. I told her I needed to locate a member of the church. "I'll do my best," she said, "but I'm a sub. And I got called in at the last minute."

That explained the sweatshirt and sunglasses and the lack of discretion on the phone.

"I give my time generously for the Lord," she said. "I'm not like some that pick and choose. I volunteer when I'm asked whether I like it or not."

This was clearly a case of not liking it. Her eyes bored into me as I stumbled through my story. My nephew's Eagle Scout ceremony was coming up, and I was trying to arrange a surprise party for him. When he was younger, he had a camp counselor who made a large impression. Kyle somebody. I couldn't remember the last name, but the young man was devoted to his grandma and to Reverend Spires.

The receptionist scowled.

"He'd be about twenty-five," I said. "Good looking."

"Kyle Bremmer. That's who you mean."

"Do you know how I could contact him?"

Still the scowl. "I could find out," she said. "I know his grandmother, but how about I give you a good piece of advice instead? If your nephew is a Christian boy, you don't want Kyle Bremmer in his life."

I gave her a puzzled look, and she gleefully forged ahead. "He quit the church and broke his grandmother's heart. She tries to hide it, but I know for a fact that he's always telling his sister she should quit too, and I wouldn't be a bit surprised if he tried the same with Gertie—that's his grandmother. He helps her out financially—he's real good that way—but you know what?" She paused dramatically. "He won't give her cash. Only gift cards." This last bit of information she whispered. "I've been with her when she's spent them. Gift cards for everywhere—the grocery, Walmart, Casey's. He doesn't give her cash because he doesn't want her giving money to the church—that's my theory." She took a deep breath, relishing her role as sage. "You ask me, Kyle Bremmer started losing faith around the time his father died. Some say it was an accident—some say different." Again the whisper. "But we all knew he drank too much. Always had, but it got a lot worse after his wife left. Kyle and his sister went to live with Gertie long before his accident." She gave the word *accident* a good spin, letting me know what she really thought.

I recalled Gertie's pain when she told Vince and me about her youngest son's death. "When did Kyle's mother leave?"

"He was ten or eleven." She shook her head. "A bad business. First she went and left them—that was a scandal—then a few months later, she got herself killed in a car accident. A *real* accident, hers was."

"Aggie," a deep voice said. "I'm sure our visitor has had enough of your gossip."

Reverend Leo Spires stood near the front door of the reception area. I must have been so absorbed in Aggie's "theories" that I hadn't heard him come in. As he studied me, my face flushed beneath what I hoped was a heavy layer of foundation.

"What brings you to us, Sister?" he asked.

Why hadn't I used a fake voice? If I altered my voice now, Aggie would know something was up, but if I used my own, Spires might recognize it.

I had only one choice.

I clutched my throat, doubled-over, and went tubercular, coughing harder than a pack-a-day smoker. As Aggie went for a glass of water, Spires headed toward me. I sure hoped he wasn't going to try any healing business. I eased up on my coughing and held out a hand to stave him off.

Aggie arrived with the water.

"Ladies room?" I croaked.

Once inside, I kept coughing until my throat hurt for real. I took a huge drink of water and listened. There were no voices, but I was taking no chances. Besides, I was hoping Aggie would come check on me so I could ask what she was about to say when the reverend interrupted. I also wanted to get the name of the tiny bald guy from the protests.

But after ten minutes, I left the ladies room and tiptoed back to the reception area. I peeked in and saw that it was empty. I called several hellos, each one louder than the last, but no one answered.

How lucky could a girl get?

I darted past the receptionist's desk toward the hallway with closed doors. Celia's was unlocked. I slipped into her office and headed to her desk, past massive ferns and an espresso maker worth more than my car. A dark computer screen taunted me, as did a stack of financial records way beyond my scope. Two photos revealed no surprises. In one, Celia posed with the evil Phyllis Schlafly. In the other, she grinned and hugged her mother.

The top drawer contained nothing but office supplies, a couple lipsticks, and an unopened package of prunes. A side drawer revealed an Ann Coulter book inscribed for Celia, "my dear friend and beautiful champion of the family." Resisting the urge to puke, I opened another drawer. All its files were labeled with dates. Except one.

It read "Bremmer, Kyle."

My heart pounding, I shuffled through the file's contents. A résumé, an academic transcript, a record of overtime and sick days. Kyle's personnel file from the lab! Was that what Celia had been searching for in the lab's main office the day Grace was killed? Why on earth would she want it?

A fax machine rang, and my heart raced as a paper slowly emerged. I seized it as soon as I could. It was an insemination report from Grace's lab. The patient's name and signature had been blacked out, but Kyle's had not. I didn't recognize the phone number at the top of the fax, so I memorized it as the fax machine churned out two more insemination reports with Kyle's name and signature.

A door slammed. I shoved the reports back into the machine's tray and raced out of the office into Celia herself.

She brushed at her blazer as if I'd sullied it. "Who are you?" she demanded. "What were you doing in my office?"

"Aggie needed stationary. She said it was back here."

"My office is not a supply closet," Celia snarled. "Where is Aggie? Why isn't anyone at the front desk?"

I opened my mouth, but Celia shot out another question. "Where's my father?"

"He was here a little bit ago," I said.

"Where'd he go?" she asked. "The hospital again? The university hospital?"

I shrugged. "I bet Aggie knows. Want me to call her?"

"No," Celia said wearily. "Just go."

Even though I'd been hoping that my helpfulness would net me Aggie's number, I was happy to just go. I whipped out my cell as soon as I was outside and punched in the number I'd memorized.

"Office Depot," said a guy with a cheery voice.

I assumed a Southern accent. "This is Detective Dallas Henry with the Iowa City Police Department. I'm attempting to identify the individual who sent a fax from your location about fifteen minutes ago."

"Sorry, ma'am. He paid cash."

"What did he look like?"

"An old hippie. He had a beer belly and a long silver ponytail."

Chapter Twenty-three

BACK IN IOWA City, there were plenty of worthwhile things I could have done. Confront Roger about the faxes. Interview the people Leo Spires had visited at the hospital. Gird my psychological loins for meeting with Anne or for going to Grace's visitation. Instead, I found myself with Zoey on Grace's front porch, her front door key in my hand. I felt horrible about what I was doing. Grace had given me the key years ago so I could water her plants when she was out of town. When I offered to give it back to her in between trips, she said, "Keep it. I trust you." She wouldn't have if she knew I was going to use the key uninvited.

"Open the door," Zoey urged.

"Her daughter could be here," I said. "We can't just walk in."

"The driveway is empty."

I knocked. The only sound I heard was a faraway leaf blower.

Zoey heaved a sigh. "You said we needed to hurry."

"We also need to be careful." At one corner of the block, an elderly woman and her dog walked away from us. Near the other corner, a couple of boys were tossing a football. I unlocked the door.

Grace's living room was strewn with DVDs, blankets, and Uno cards. "See this?" I nodded toward the grandchild detritus. "They could be back any minute." I'd never met Grace's daughter, but I felt a kinship with her every time Grace criticized her lack of routine and discipline.

Zoey and I headed upstairs to Grace's office. Its door was closed. The room was not a part of her home that Grace liked to share with others, but there I was opening it up and giving Zoey free rein.

Her face alight with hope, she turned on the computer.

I was surprised that it came right on. Grace compulsively unplugged everything that wasn't in use. But maybe the cops had searched the computer and left it plugged in, or maybe Grace's daughter or grandchildren had been on it.

"The doctor has lots of files." Zoey clicked away at the mouse.

"Grace probably didn't keep lab stuff at home," I said. "She was big on boundaries." Unlike me, apparently. Zoey gazed at the computer monitor, and I kept talking. "The cops probably already searched here and removed anything related to the lab."

"You've said."

"I just don't want you to—"

"I need to look wherever I can," Zoey insisted.

I headed toward Grace's wooden file cabinets. "Never settle for function," she'd say, "if you can have beauty too." What would I do without her pronouncements?

"You gonna help or not?" Zoey asked.

I nodded and opened a drawer. There were several files that began with the word *auto* followed by subcategories, such as consumer reports, insurance, oil changes, other maintenance. If Zoey's donor dad was in Grace's files, he'd be easy to find. I opened the next drawer and looked in the *D*'s. My heart fluttered. Several were labeled Donor. But then I noticed women's names. I pulled out a file with a male one, and it was just as I feared. The guy donated money, not sperm. I skimmed the names on the other files, and there it was. Hargrove. Grace had contacted the judge about donating to her endowment. He had declined.

"Did you find something?" Zoey's voice was painfully eager.

I shook my head. I wasn't lying. Not really. The file had nothing to do with Zoey's donor dad, and I could imagine the torturous logic it would inspire. The judge did not value the lab where she was conceived; therefore he did not value her conception; therefore he did not value her.

As I returned the file, I bent its label over so that if Zoey had her own go at the cabinets, she wouldn't see it. But I couldn't protect her from disappointment forever. In fact, I was setting her up for it. I had been ever since agreeing to help find her donor dad. And now I was allowing her to violate Grace's privacy.

The air in the office felt close, so I cracked a window. Then every car that passed by put me on edge. Zoey's relentless tapping of the mouse did nothing to help. I announced that I was going to get a drink of water, but Zoey just kept tapping.

I EXPECTED TO feel Grace's presence in her kitchen, but the animal crackers on the counter weren't hers nor were the jelly fingerprints on the fridge. Grace would never have left her toaster oven, coffee maker, and food processor plugged in. She would never have left a cupboard door open. I studied her Tupperware. There was no way I could tell whether any of it was missing. I went through a stack of papers on the table. None of them would help Zoey—junk mail, *The Utne Reader*, a flyer from someone who wanted to rake Grace's leaves, a list of books she planned to get at the library. Two of them I'd recommended.

Most of the time, she made recommendations to me. I teared up, recalling how Grace had urged, prodded, and nagged me. Once, when I was fed up with her skyscraper expectations, I blurted, "Why don't you just tell me to get a life." She looked at me with pity. "Oh, kiddo, you don't get a life, you make one."

The phone rang, and my heart sped. It took a couple more rings before I spotted it between a loaf of Wonder Bread and a box of crayon nubs. I let the machine pick up, bracing myself for Grace's voice. But there was no declaration that the caller should enunciate, that brevity is the soul of wit. Some automated voice simply asked the caller to leave a message. The volume was painfully loud, like Grace needed it, but the cops must have taken the tape with her voice. What else had they taken? What else would I find missing?

The answering machine tone sounded, and Roger's voice filled the room. He told Grace's daughter how sorry he was, how shocked and devastated she must be. "I'm sorry to intrude on your grief," he said, "but my daughter Lizzie left a history paper in your mom's home office, and it's due tomorrow. The teacher is a real stickler, and Lizzie has her eligibility to worry about." Roger cleared his throat. With the machine's volume on high, it sounded like a tidal wave crashing the kitchen. "I'd like to stop by and get it for her."

Roger was lying. When we had coffee, he all but admitted that his daughter wanted nothing to do with Grace. So what did he want in her office?

ZOEY SAT CROSS-LEGGED on the floor pouring over one of Grace's photo albums. "She's got pictures of all the babies she helped create and letters from their parents too."

"Have you found yourself yet?"

Zoey gave me a wry smile and turned the page.

Listening for cars and footsteps, I searched through more files. There was nothing out of the ordinary, nothing that could have prompted Roger's phone call.

"I don't look like my mom or the judge." Zoey peered at me from the room's darkest corner. I thought about turning on the floor lamp. Its unplugged cord snaked near my Birkenstocks. But Zoey and I were leaving soon, and I didn't want anyone outside to notice a light inside. A thought—something about the lab—formed at the edge of my consciousness, but when Zoey spoke again, it vanished.

"My mom was beautiful—really beautiful." She closed the album and moved toward the computer. "Not like Trophy Wife."

"You must miss her."

Zoey flicked her eyes toward me, removed a flash drive, and slipped it into her hip pocket.

"What are you doing?"

"I copied the files," Zoey said. "There are too many to look at here."

"We're not taking anything from this house."

"It's not like I'm ripping her off."

"There's private information on that,"

"I'm not gonna sell her social security number. As soon as I'm

sure a file doesn't have anything to do with my donor dad, I'll delete
it."

"What if you lose it?"

Zoey started to protest.

"What if it gets stolen?" I continued. "What if whoever trashed
my office—and my friend Anne's house and office—comes knocking
on your door?"

"Chill," Zoey said. "I'll keep it at Reed's."

"How about I keep it?" asked Detective Dallas Henry in an
unfriendly drawl.

Chapter Twenty-four

"I HAD A key," I said. "I'm Grace's house-sitter. We weren't breaking in."

Detective Henry ushered me into a tiny room at the back of the police station. An interrogation room low on furniture and high on what Anne would call toxic energy.

Anne. I was supposed to meet her in five minutes. I pulled out my cell phone.

"You don't need a lawyer," Detective Henry said, "You're not under arrest."

I started to explain about coffee with Anne.

"You were just caught searching the home of a murder victim with a minor who was at the scene of her homicide, and you're worried about a coffee date?"

"I have the right to make a call."

"Keep it short." Detective Henry headed to the door.

Anne was already at Fair Grounds. When I told her about being interviewed at the police station, she started interrogating me herself. I dodged the questions and asked Anne to tell Bridget I'd meet her at the visitation. I hoped I would make it.

Detective Henry returned as soon as I hung up. She must have been spying through the "mirror" on the opposite wall.

She sat across the table, her hands folded in front of her, and fixed me in her crosshairs. Refusing to blink, I took in her grim expression, her overdone makeup. My chair squeaked as I shifted. Detective Henry reached into her jacket pocket and set a small tape recorder in the center of the table. Her recorder made me think of my own and of the vitriol I'd captured during my conversation with Spires at the police station. Let the detective listen to *that* and still dismiss the reverend as a suspect. I slipped my hand into my jacket pocket and found the recorder. I squeezed it as if it were a talisman. I'd give it to Detective Henry when the time was right.

As she stated our names and the date and time for the recorder, she spoke louder than usual and with less of an accent. Her official voice. "What is your relationship with Zoey Hargrove?" she asked.

I wondered if Zoey were in a nearby room being questioned by some other cop. If so, the judge was probably with her, making sure she exercised her right to remain silent.

"What is your relationship with Ms. Hargrove?" Detective Henry repeated.

"I'm helping her with a research project."

"What kind of research?" The detective's gaze was more intense when she wasn't writing in her notebook. I decided to focus on the pencil tip behind her ear.

"Zoey is writing a report on reproductive technology," I said.

"Why did she seek your help?"

"She heard me on the radio interviewing people about it."

"Are you aware that she's searching for her sperm donor and that she threatened the victim and her colleagues at the lab?"

My concentration shifted from the pencil tip to the detective's determined eyes. "Zoey never told me that," I said.

"But Roger Lipinski did, correct?"

I nodded.

"Please speak your answer into the recorder," Detective Henry demanded.

"Roger Lipinski told me that Zoey Hargrove sought information from the lab."

"He also told you that she has no legal right to that information. Of course, given your collaboration with the victim, you're familiar with donor anonymity."

"I'm familiar."

"Why were you at the victim's home with Ms. Hargrove this afternoon?"

"I thought Grace would have some sources that would help Zoey with her research."

Detective Henry narrowed her eyes. "Why did Ms. Hargrove copy the contents of Dr. Everest's computer onto a flash drive?"

"Ask her. She made the copy. I was out of the room. I tried to dissuade her from taking it."

"Was she combative with you?"

"We argued. You heard us as you snuck up the stairs."

"Was she angry?"

"She's fifteen. Her mother just died, and her dad has married a bimbo."

Detective Henry rested her elbows on the table and leaned forward. "Ms. Hargrove has been involved in several altercations at school. Physical altercations. Her principal has concerns about her temper and mental stability."

"She's having a hard time." But even as I defended her, I couldn't help but think that Zoey had been in the lab the morning Grace was killed and that teenagers have lousy impulse control.

"If she's told you anything related to the murder, you have a legal obligation to tell me." Detective Henry folded her arms over her chest. "Otherwise you're obstructing justice."

Part of me wanted to tell Detective Henry everything I knew. I wanted to help her catch Grace's killer, I really did, and I wanted to stay out of trouble. But part of me resisted. I couldn't picture Zoey killing Grace. Throwing a punch at some kid who made a crack about her dad's second marriage? That I could see, but not what happened to Grace. Not that.

"You could be charged as an accessory," the detective said.

If I kept quiet, I would betray Grace for a girl I'd just met. But I felt like I'd known Zoey a long time. I wanted her to find her donor dad, and I wanted him to care about her. I wanted her to find what she needed to move past the lies and losses she'd endured.

"Has she told you anything?" Detective Henry asked.

I'd made Zoey a promise. She was counting on me. She didn't need another betrayal.

"Ms. Gilgannon?"

I offered up a half-truth. "Zoey says she wasn't at the hospital the day Grace was killed. She says she was with her father."

The detective's eyes lasered me.

"But I've been doing my own investigating. Independently." I offered Detective Henry the tape of my conversation with Spires. I described the reverend's money problems and his plans to protest Grace's visitation and funeral. Without implicating Zoey, I described the briefcase exchange.

"You've been following the reverend?" she asked.

"Yes," I lied.

She closed her eyes and rubbed her forehead as if she was getting a headache.

I quickly revealed all the other scoop I could without getting Zoey or myself in further trouble—Grace's plans to fire Roger and Justine, Roger's meeting with Celia, his crush on Grace and his desire to search her home office, Justine's acting skills, her money problems and the sperm vials in her purse.

Something flickered across Detective Henry's face when I told her about Roger's meeting with Celia. "You discovered all this information—everything you just told me—on your own?"

"My housemate helped. Vince Loyacano. You met him at the radio station."

She smiled faintly. "I remember Mr. Loyacano."

"What about you?" I asked. "What have you learned?" Ballsy, yes. But I had to give it a shot.

Detective Henry's eyebrows arched.

"What were you doing at Grace's this afternoon?" I asked.

"Do you really expect me to answer?"

"Can't blame a girl for trying."

"Did you and Mr. Loyacano discover anything else?"

I wanted to give Detective Henry the list of people Leo Spires visited in the hospital, but it was in Zoey's handwriting. I wanted to reveal what I'd found in Celia Spires' fax machine, but I didn't want to be accused of breaking and entering again. And I wanted to tell the detective about Liz Lipinski's anger at Grace, about her confrontation with Justine at the theatre, but I couldn't—not without giving Bridget a heads-up about her player first.

After I pretended to tell Detective Henry everything I knew, she turned off the tape recorder. I expected her to escort me out, but she just sat there. I made a show of checking my watch. There was only half an hour until Grace's visitation.

"I've been listening to your interviews." Detective Henry's vowels lengthened and honeyed.

"Have they helped your investigation?" I asked warily.

She pulled the pencil out of her hair and tapped it on the table, keeping her eyes on me the entire time. I thought about how she had laughed at the idea of someone without kids doing the series. And I was angry at myself for remembering, for caring.

"They're fascinating," she said. "You're a wonder at getting folks to open up."

Her flattery made me even more suspicious.

"You should interview some grandparents," Detective Henry said, "the grandmothers of the babies conceived in the lab."

"Maybe I will." It wasn't a half-bad idea.

She smiled coyly. "Of course, a professional like you doesn't need someone like me telling you how to do your job."

MY VISA MAY not get me everything I want, but it got me into Roger Lipinski's apartment. My hands sweating in Vince's Jackie Kennedy gloves, I slid the card in between the door and the frame, and I worked the plastic until the latch gave. Grace's visitation had just started. I figured Roger would stay at least half an hour, so I had thirty minutes to search. Priceless.

Locking his door behind me, I flipped the light switch and gazed at Roger's pastel floral prints. If only I could unearth some clue that would explain Roger's connection with Celia Spires. Or his eagerness to search Grace's home office. I wanted to go back there, to search for more clues, but Detective Henry confiscated my key and threatened to arrest me if she caught me there again. So I opted for Roger's place instead. I told myself that Roger might have retrieved whatever he wanted from Grace's while I was at the police station.

But if he had, it wasn't on the dining room table. The kitchen counters were bare too except for a stack of bills and the remains of Chinese carryout. Most of the kitchen drawers and cupboards were empty although the two largest were stuffed with mismatched Tupperware containers. Had Roger come by this collection honestly, or had he stolen some of it from Anne and Orchid?

The coffee table in front of Roger's couch sported several magazines and McDonald's cups and a legal pad with something written on it. "Dr. Grace Everest was a magnificent woman and scientist."

Then, on the next line, "Dr. Grace Everest was a magnificent scientist and woman." My stomach flip-flopped. Roger was drafting a eulogy. His tentative jotting made Grace's death achingly real. Witty, acerbic Grace was going to be eulogized by humorless, earnest Roger. She would have nothing to say about it, nothing to say ever again.

Brushing away a tear, I went to Roger's bedroom. Except for Vince's, I'd never been in a man's bedroom before. I'm not sure what I expected, but what I found was a partially made double-bed strewn with ties and belts. Perhaps he'd been trying to decide what to wear to Grace's visitation. If so, he'd wisely left behind the belt buckles featuring horses and buffalo.

On his nightstand was a large stack of self-help books. I took a deep breath and opened the drawer beneath it. There were no condoms or porn — things I imagined every man kept near his bedside — just a huge three-ring binder. I pulled it out and opened it. Taped on the first page was a yellowed newspaper article about the opening of the Advanced Center for Reproductive Care. A forty-something Grace, with fuller cheeks and darker hair, sat in front of a microscope flanked by the university president and the governor of Iowa.

I didn't have much time, but I couldn't resist thumbing through the scrapbook for other glimpses of Grace. It didn't disappoint. Roger must have clipped every single article featuring his boss. Sure, it was strange that he kept the collection by his bed, but I was enjoying it until I came to the obituary for Grace's late husband. The pages after that were one big creep fest.

Chapter Twenty-five

THE CREEPY NOTEBOOK was a scrapbook alright. Roger had literally stolen scraps of Grace. Hunted and mounted her leavings. Anything with her handwriting—office memos, supply lists, post-it notes—each item displayed as if it were a miniature masterpiece. There were photos of her working in the lab, unaware she was being watched, and things he must have taken from her purse. Monogrammed handkerchiefs, lipsticks and powders, a comb with a strand of her silver hair lodged between its finest teeth. These personal items were preserved in see-through pencil bags attached to the binder, the final "pages" of Roger's book.

Kyle had said that Roger had it bad for Grace, but Kyle didn't know the half of it. Roger even saved the letter Grace sent warning him to behave more professionally for the sake of his family, for the sake of the lab, for his own sake if that's all he was selfish enough to care about. She didn't want to lodge a formal complaint, but she would if he didn't keep his distance. Grace didn't know the half of it either. A man who puts a letter like that in his scrapbook is not going to listen to reason. He is not going to respond to threats.

Or is he? I considered the argument that Zoey overheard between Roger and Grace. She threatened to fire him. No more income, no more scrapbook material, no more fantasies about him and Grace. No more Grace.

I thought about his call to Grace's home, his claim that his daughter left her homework there. Either he wanted to make sure that Grace's home office contained no evidence of his obsession, or he wanted to feed that obsession.

Keys jingled outside Roger's apartment door.

Crap! I needed to hide. The bed was pressed against the wall. I threw myself to the floor, ready to roll beneath the bed, but the space was filled with boxes. No doubt full of whacko scrapbooks and stolen Tupperware.

I'd have to talk my way out. I work in radio. How hard could it be?

Turns out, pretty hard.

Liz Lipinski stood staring at me. "What are you doing in my dad's bedroom?" Her gray eyes were wide, her cheeks flushed above her pink sweater. She looked so young—she *was* young, just a few years older than Zoey—I could see why Bridget wanted to protect her. I squeezed the scrapbook to my chest.

"What's that?" she asked.

"Nothing," I said. "It's mine. Your dad borrowed it from me and said I could stop by to get it." I started to move past her.

"How did you get in?" she asked. "Why are you wearing gloves?"

I kept moving. She lunged for the book. I twisted away, but I'm no match for a Division I point guard. She wrenched it from me. The book thudded to the carpet and opened to one of Grace's handkerchiefs.

Liz gaped at its monogram, statue-still. Her mouth and forehead twitched. Her emotions seemed to boomerang. Confusion. Anger and pain. Confusion. She knelt over the book and paged through it. I tried to stop her, but she swept it up and turned her back to me. Turned page after page.

I tried once more to stop her, then resigned myself to watching her lose whatever hope she had for her parents' marriage, whatever faith she had in her father.

Her page-turning steadily slowed, and her shoulders tensed. In the apartment above us, someone surfed through laugh tracks and commercials. Then Liz shut the book and turned around.

She tried for a game face, but there were tears in her eyes. "You can't tell anyone about this," she said. "If you do, I'll tell the police you were here. I'll tell them you broke into my father's apartment and attacked me."

"I was trying to keep you —"

"Get out," Liz said quietly.

"But your god-mother —"

"Leave now," she said, "or I'll call the police."

"Go ahead. I can't wait to see their reaction to your father's scrapbook." I pulled out my cell. "In fact, I'll call them myself."

Liz fixed me with an icy stare, daring me to make good on my bluff.

"Okay," I said, "so neither of us is going to call the cops. What are you going to do with that?" I nodded toward the scrapbook.

She held it tightly to her chest with one hand and opened her father's apartment door with the other.

I didn't budge. "Did you know about your father's feelings for Grace before today?"

"Get out," she said, her teeth clenched.

"What about his relationship with Celia Spires?"

Liz looked at me as if I were insane. She opened the door wider.

I needed to get to the visitation anyway, so I exited the apartment. Liz followed me out and shut the door. As she checked its lock, she kept her eyes on me, and she kept the scrapbook tucked firmly under one arm. When she left, she would take the scrapbook with her and hide it or destroy it. I felt sick, knowing that I'd discovered important new evidence only to lose it. But I forced myself to concentrate, to ask one last question. "What about the lab tech, Justine Nissen? Did your father have some sort of relationship with her?"

Liz looked like she'd just tasted rotten meat. "You're disgusting," she said. "Justine is my cousin."

Chapter Twenty-six

I DROVE TO the visitation on auto-pilot, trying to make sense of Justine's kinship with the Lipinskis and fretting about Liz and her father's scrapbook. Less than a block away from the funeral home, Spires' groupies waved their hateful signs. I couldn't spot Kyle's grandmother, but the streetlights shone on the puny bald guy's pate. He grinned obscenely at the counter-protestors across the street. The reverend and Celia conferred a few paces behind him, their heads nearly touching. The cops were keeping everyone the legally mandated 500 feet away from the funeral home. Spires was wasting police time. Time that could have been used to find Grace's killer. And Detective Dallas Henry, she was wasting her own time harassing Zoey and me. I pushed the cop out of my head as my car sputtered and wheezed into the parking lot. I pushed repair-bill worries away too. This evening was for Grace.

My phone rang, and I was greeted by a stern baritone. "Mara Gilgannon?"

"Yes?" I answered in a tiny voice. Disgusted with myself, I assumed my radio persona. "This is she."

"This is Judge Paul Hargrove. I'll thank you to stay away from my daughter, or you'll be facing a restraining order."

"But she —"

"No contact. No phone calls, no emails, nothing."

"I never —"

"Zoey is in a vulnerable place, and she doesn't need some newsperson fueling her fantasies. Are we clear?"

I started to tell him we were not, but he hung up.

A SMALL CROWD huddled on the front steps of the funeral home. Diego Sanchez-Smith was sandwiched between his mothers, sobbing. His head was buried in Becky's lap, and his body was locked in a fetal position.

"This is Leo Spires' fault." Kyle suddenly appeared next to me, his voice hushed, his jaw muscle working overtime. "They were walking to the visitation." He jerked his head toward Diego and his moms. "One of the protestors got right in the little guy's face and told him his mothers were going to hell."

Kyle's words made me spin. I felt dizzy and sick, trapped on an out-of-control carnival ride with nothing solid or sane to save me. Spiresville, Roger's scrapbook, the judge's threat, Grace's death. Grace. I went rigid with fury. This was supposed to be a time to honor her, but instead, an innocent child had been terrorized. A child she'd help bring into the world.

Diego hiccupped wildly. He would probably have nightmares.

I strode toward the protestors, unsure of what I'd do, but I had to do something.

Kyle tugged at my shoulder, but I shook him off.

I was going to rip their signs to shreds and wipe the smirk right off the bald guy's face.

Kyle grabbed my arm and whirled me around. "Don't give them the satisfaction." He tightened his grip, his fingers digging deep into my bicep.

"You're hurting me," I said.

He let go and apologized. Leaves swirled around our feet, and I wondered what Spires had taught Kyle about hell. I wondered lots of things about Spires and Kyle. But before I got the chance to voice any of them aloud, Kyle stepped away from me and toward Diego. He squatted down, nestled his own jacket around the boy, and went through the funeral home door. Most of the crowd followed Kyle inside. Becky stroked her son's head, and he quieted.

Next to the guest book was a sign, "Memorials may be directed to the Grace Everest Endowment for Reproductive Technology, providing fertility treatment to low-income Iowans." Even in death, Grace pursued her life's work. But her name on the endowment— that must have been her daughter's decision. I wondered if she knew about Zoey and me searching her mother's home.

My hand shook slightly as I signed my name. The person above me had written "Dr. Everest will be missed!!!" I wanted to add a message too. But how could I capture what Grace meant to me with a few words, a single sentence, a row of exclamation points?

"You can just sign your name."

I turned around, and there was Zoey. "Are you okay?" I asked.

"The cops took my flash drive, and they're not gonna give it back."

"How long did they keep you?"

She shrugged.

An older couple stood behind her in line, so I pulled her into the nearest hallway. "What are you doing here?" I asked.

Another shrug.

"Does your dad know you're here?"

"The judge thinks I'm in my room."

I told her about his threat.

Her eyes widened, then narrowed. "He doesn't want me to find my donor dad."

"Did you tell him I was helping you?"

"No. Why would I?"

"What about the cops?"

She shook her head, exasperated.

A man passed us on his way to the restroom. I lowered my voice. "This isn't a good place to talk."

"We could meet tomorrow."

I shook my head. "Grace's funeral."

"The day after," Zoey offered.

I hesitated.

"You're not gonna bail on me?"

"Mar-Bar!" Vince and Justine converged on us, and Vince gave me a huge hug. "You've escaped the long arm of the law."

Justine gave me a cool nod and shifted her hefty purse from one shoulder to the other. I wanted to ask her what she and Cousin Liz had argued about at the theatre. But, if I tried to get Justine to talk now, I'd only add to the tension between Vince and me. So as he introduced Justine and Zoey to each other, I excused myself. I wasn't two steps away when I heard Zoey ask Justine if she had access to the lab's records.

Bridget stood in the main room, cornered by Roger Lipinski. I tried to catch her eye, but she was intent on his agitated monologue. Nobody focuses like Bridget. I wanted to get her alone, tell her that her star freshman needed her, that Liz's father was a complete and total head case. And sure, I'll admit it, I wanted to tell her about my encounter with Liz before Liz could. The girl wasn't among the mourners, but I worried that she had phoned Roger about my B&E and that he was telling Bridget.

"Is there cake?" asked a little boy.

It was the kind of thing Diego would say, and I felt another jolt of anger about what Spires' follower had done to him. This boy's parents smiled apologetically as they herded him toward the line of people waiting to offer condolences. Anne and Orchid weren't in it, but there were lots of other folks from the baby-naming ceremony. Felicity Cheng was near the front cooing at Michael and Penny's daughter. The baby lifted her flaxen head and went back to dozing on her dad's shoulder. A few people behind them, Kyle listened to Lindsey Hoover. Little did he know that she coveted his sperm. Or that I'd spent part of the day investigating him. He nodded politely at Lindsey, but his eyes were on Grace's grandkids. The boy's tie was askew, and the youngest girl had taken off her shoes. The oldest girl stood motionless near her mom. They both had Grace's curls.

Once again, I wished I knew whether the cops had told Grace's daughter about the "break-in." I didn't think she'd press charges — not after I explained — but as I headed to the back of the line, I wondered how she'd welcome my sympathy. I passed Sophie, Esther, little Stormy Grace, and a diaper bag that looked like it could hold a complete set of Harry Potters and a month's worth of Gerber. After a group hug, including the diaper bag, I found the end of the line. A

husband and wife were trying to decide if they should buy milk on
the way home. I thought of Auden's poem, "Musée des Beaux Arts."
A winged boy, Icarus, falls out of the sky; an expensive delicate ship
sails calmly on. "Of course it kept sailing," Grace once said. "That's
what ships are for."

I snapped to and studied the room again. There was still no sign
that Roger Lipinski was ready to release Bridget. Still no Anne. And
as far as I could tell, no cops. Certainly, no Detective Dallas Henry.
You'd think she'd want to observe the mourners, scrutinize her suspects. If she had any besides me.

Zoey talked with Justine, whose black dress was way too skimpy
for a visitation. Note to self—talk to Zoey and enumerate the ways in
which Justine is a bad influence, emphasize that Zoey should never
loan Justine a single dime, try to avoid sounding maternal.

Vince visited with Kyle, who was now near the front of the line.
Grace's daughter smiled sadly at Michael and Penny's little girl and
patted her head. Had the couple quietly revealed that Grace helped
create their family? Would such knowledge fill Grace's daughter
with pride or add to her sorrow? After my Aunt Glad's murder, I'd
been pained by each new thing I learned about her, overwhelmed by
my failure to know her.

A baby cried, and other members of the pack picked up the call.
The sound of Grace's life work. I started laughing. The woman closest to me stepped away, pulling her toddler with her.

"Mommy!" Grace's youngest granddaughter stood tall as she
could, sock-footed, hands on her hips. "Mommy, it is too loud in
here." The stance and tone were pure Grace.

I fled.

MY CAR WOULDN'T start. Well, it would start, but it wouldn't
keep going. Vince was right—I'd been ignoring its cries for help. Yet
as I stood alone in the dark parking lot, I couldn't help wondering
whether someone had sabotaged my engine.

"Car trouble?"

I started at the sound of Kyle's voice. He apologized for scaring
me, and when I affirmed my car trouble, he asked if I wanted a ride.
I was exhausted, and my feet hurt from the so-called sensible shoes
I'd worn in Spiresville. Could I trust Kyle? I now knew that he
wans't in cahoots with Leo Spires, but something was going on. Otherwise, why had Celia Spires been collecting his paperwork?

"Maybe you'd rather ride with a friend," he said, backing up a
step and loosening his tie.

If I asked Vince, I'd be subject to Justine's antics, and if I asked
Bridget, I'd risk a run-in with Roger. If I asked anyone else who was
still in the funeral home, I'd have to go back in there.

I told Kyle a ride would be great.

We walked past a couple of white SUVs, and I wondered if Spires had the gall to park in the funeral home lot. A little boy sprinted across the lot, leaving his shouting mother behind. Diego was probably already home. I imagined his mothers tucking him in, still trying to soothe him with a beloved book or teddy bear.

"Lots of kids in there." Kyle's voice was strained. He had suffered a lot of loss in his young life. His mother and father. His faith in Reverend Spires. And now Grace.

"How are you doing?" I asked.

"Hanging in. You?"

"How was reopening the lab?"

"Okay." He picked up his pace.

"Justine is staying with me."

"Yeah, she said."

"I found some empty sperm vials in her purse."

He stopped and narrowed his eyes at me.

"It fell. They just spilled out."

We walked a few steps in silence. The wind whistled through the trees. I felt a raindrop on my face, then another on the top of my head. We dashed to Kyle's car. It was a small beater like mine, but much tidier. Not a single pop can or candy wrapper. No telltale briefcase either, and no photo on the front seat.

"Justine is a sweet girl," Kyle said, "but she has this bizarre habit of swiping containers. Her big thing is Tupperware."

My pulse quickened.

"You bring it to work," he said, "and it's history."

Justine had to be behind the break-ins. "Did Grace know about it?"

"Roger didn't want to bother her."

So, I thought, Roger knew that his niece was swiping stuff, but he didn't say anything. "Why do you think she takes it?" I asked.

"No idea." Kyle wheeled out of his parking spot. "How's your investigation going?"

"Slowly," I said. Like crap, I thought to myself. I was the cops' public enemy number one, and I had nothing but wild theories and a thespian kleptomaniac invading my home and seizing people's Tupperware.

"What about that girl in the sketch," Kyle said, "you ever talk to her?"

"She claimed she wasn't there." Mara Gilgannon, Queen of the Half-Truth.

Kyle idled at the lot's exit, his windshield wipers beating a slow rhythm. He checked his rearview mirror and frowned. Behind us was a souped-up truck. The driver was short and bald like Spires' scariest protestor. I couldn't see his face, but I could imagine his furious eyes and frightening grin.

As Kyle pulled onto Muscatine Avenue, Spires' group was straight ahead, still spewing their hate. Sure enough, the tiny bald guy was not among them. Kyle turned onto a side street, and by the time we returned to Muscatine, the protestors were well behind us. But the truck was not.

"I think one of Spires' men is following you." I tried to keep my voice calm.

Kyle glanced at his rearview mirror and turned onto Burlington Street.

"Maybe he knows you work at the lab," I said.

We crossed Summit Street, and the rain came down harder. The guy behind us high-beamed his lights. Kyle cursed and sped up. The truck edged closer. The driver honked, then flicked his lights off and on.

"I don't want him to know where I live," I said. "Take me to the police station."

Kyle agreed and switched to the right lane. The truck switched with us, lights still manically strobing. Closer and closer.

We zipped through a yellow light, the truck on our bumper.

Other drivers honked in protest. I twisted around to get the truck's license plate. Then I was thrust into a screeching tornado of pain.

Chapter Twenty-seven

A HAND COVERED my face. An oxygen mask smothered me. "Please," I begged, "take it off."

"Sorry ma'am."

I heard one Sorry-ma'am after another. Sorry ma'am, we need to start an IV, stabilize your neck, lift you, move you. Each touch hurt. Each breath ached. The ambulance howl seemed like it was inside me.

At the hospital, I endured x-rays, CT scans, test after test until I was thoroughly diagnosed. Lateral whiplash, blunt chest trauma, possible pulmonary contusion. Bridget held my hand and pummeled the staff with questions. Vince shrilly proclaimed that Leo Spires was responsible for my injuries, that the police must arrest him this very moment. Me, I just wanted to go home.

"SSH," BRIDGET SAID. "Kyle is fine. He accidentally ran a red light because of a pickup behind him. You're the only one with serious injuries, but you'll be okay. Go back to sleep."

I was lying in a hospital bed. Something was on my finger. I tried to look at the contraption, and pain shot through my neck.

"Your hand is fine," Bridget said. "They're monitoring your oxygen levels."

"That truck..." I said.

"Try to rest, babe."

My meds were not strong enough to stop all the pain, but they were strong enough to make me feel thick and sleepy. The blinds in my room were closed. "What time is it?"

"Time to sleep."

"Grace's funeral," I said.

"Ssh." Bridget gently rested her hand on my shoulder.

"Your player, Liz, her father—"

"Sorry ma'am," said a nurse, "but I need to take her vitals."

Bridget brushed her lips against my forehead. "I'll be back," she whispered.

"But your player—"

"I'll call her," Bridget said. "You sleep."

WHEN I WOKE again, my neck felt worse, and my mood deteriorated with each tick of the clock. It was 9:30 in the morning, half an hour until Grace's funeral, and there was still no doctor to discharge me. "He'll be here soon," Bridget said. "I brought some clothes for you." She herself was wearing a gray wool suit and a silk shirt that brought out the blue in her eyes. I told her she looked beautiful.

"That's the pain meds talking," she said.

I chuckled and winced. "Who knew bruises could hurt so much?"

"Rib contusions," Bridget amended.

"Bruises. All those tests, all this for bruises." I glanced at the outfit she'd placed at the foot of my bed. The thought of changing my clothes made me want to whimper.

Bridget sank into the chair nearest me. "Bad news," she said. "The pickup driver who caused your accident fled the scene, and the cops still haven't found him." She took my hand. Hers was warm and strong.

Mine was clammy and trembling. I did not want to think about some crazy man lurking around every corner, but I refused to be intimidated. "Did you talk to Liz?" I asked.

"I'm telling you, babe, you need to be careful."

"I don't want to talk about it."

Bridget withdrew her hand. "Liz isn't answering her phone or her door. None of the other players know what's going on with her."

The last thing I wanted to do was add to Bridget's worries, but she needed to know about Liz and the scrapbook. As I spoke, Bridget's expression darkened. Outside the room, the PA sounded, but Bridget remained silent.

"I'm sorry," I said.

WHEN BRIDGET AND I arrived at the funeral, Roger was delivering the eulogy. Bridget sat with her fists clenched during the entire speech, her eyes scanning the crowd. I saw Kyle, Justine, Anne and Orchid, but I didn't spot Liz, thank God. She didn't need any more evidence of her father's skewed vision of Grace. Roger painted her in broad idealistic strokes—her dedication to work and family, her meticulous attention to detail, her passion for justice and helping others. There was no mention of her impatience, her snobbery, her bulldozing will. Nothing about her love of sonnets and canapés, her penchant for Talbots' sale rack. By the time Roger finished, I felt like I'd lost Grace all over again.

Bridget proclaimed me unfit to attend the burial and luncheon. I suspected that she herself was unfit—too worried about Liz, or too angry with me—but I didn't argue. Vince gave me some more pain meds and tucked me into my own sweet bed.

I STOOD ALONE on the deck of an old ship, madly spinning the helm, but I couldn't steer the ship away from a gaping whirlpool. A winged boy fell from the sky and spiraled down the watery vortex. On board the ship, a baby cried. Snow filled the sky. All I could see was white. I ran toward the baby's cries, but they came from every-where. The whirlpool roared. A teenage Jodie Foster appeared and told me to check for misused equipment. Then she vanished into the snow. The baby wailed, and the whirlpool bellowed. The ship tossed, whipped my neck from side to side, banged my head, my ribs. I hurt everywhere, but the noise stopped. Then I heard a bell. A rescue ship. The bell again. Heavy footsteps.

Vince. My housemate was answering the doorbell. I was in my bed. Safe and sound. No, not sound. Pain shot through my right side as I tried to turn on my lamp. I gave up and gazed through the dark until my eyes adjusted. A golden pothos from one of Aunt Glad's vines spilled over the top of my bookshelf and grazed the edge of my curtains. They were open. It was dark outside. I braced myself for more agony and reached for my glasses. My clock said 9:12.

"I just want to see her," a voice demanded. "I'm not gonna wake her, dude."

Zoey.

Vince murmured something.

"If she's okay, why can't I see her?"

"I'm awake," I shouted. "Give me a second." Yelling hurt, and so did getting up and maneuvering into my robe.

I was halfway down the stairs when the doorbell rang again. Vince went to answer it, and Zoey gaped at me. Then she and I both froze as Detective Dallas Henry drawled her way into the living room. "Good evening, Mr. Loyacano. I see that your housemate is receiving visitors."

"She most certainly is not. This young person showed up unan-nounced."

Zoey gave Vince a poisonous look.

I was tempted to climb back up the stairs and under my covers, but that would just delay the inevitable.

"Ms. Hargrove," Detective Henry said, "are you aware that your presence in this household could cause legal trouble for Ms. Gilgan-non?"

Zoey looked up at me expectantly. But what could I say?

Norma Desmond leapt onto the desk near Zoey, mewing plain-tively.

"A cat has more rights than I do." Zoey stomped past the detec-tive and out the front door.

I tightened my robe and resumed my descent.

Vince turned toward the cop. "Have you found the truck driver?"

"Not yet." Detective Henry opened her notebook and helped herself to Vince's chair.

He and I took the futon. As the detective inquired about my injuries, I tried to imagine what she really wanted. Surely my contusions gave me a decent alibi for anything that had transpired in the last twenty-four hours. She asked for my version of the accident, and I gave it to her.

"Were you planning to ride home with Kyle Bremmer?" she asked. "Did anyone know you were going to be in the car with him?"

Hadn't she talked to Kyle himself? Did she have to verify every nitpicky detail about a car wreck while Grace's murderer still roamed free? "I didn't know my car was dead until I left the visitation."

"Did you notice anything unusual near your vehicle or the funeral home?"

I shook my head. Ouch.

"Are you sure?" Vince asked.

Detective Henry ignored him. "What about on your way there?"

"The protestors," I said. "I think the guy in the truck might have been with them."

"Edward Faust," Detective Henry said. "We've verified that he accosted a young boy earlier in the evening."

Diego. I blinked back tears.

"Did Faust ever protest at your radio station?" Detective Henry asked.

I thought about the crowd that dogged me from my car to the station entrance. I couldn't remember faces. I had tried to ignore them. But I told her what I did remember. "He was protesting at the hospital the day Grace was killed." I shivered. If he had killed Grace, then maybe Vince was partly right. Maybe he had been trying to kill Kyle and me.

"We're aware of that," the detective said, "and we're interviewing the other protestors."

"Was he there the whole time?" I asked.

She tapped her pen against her notebook — one, two, three — like she was ready to conduct a symphony. I knew she wasn't going to answer my question. "Edward Faust is unstable and dangerous," she said. "Reverend Spires tried to convince him to seek counseling, but he refused."

Spires telling someone else he needs help — that was rich.

"I'll bet Leo Spires counseled him himself," Vince said. "Counseled him to murder."

Detective Henry closed her notebook. "Edward Faust has been in and out of psych hospitals and prisons. He has a record of assault and battery." She locked eyes with me. "You've been clever enough to uncover some important information, but you need to stop. The more time I have to spend worrying about your safety — and the safety of young Ms. Hargrove — the less time I have to build a case."

"Then quit worrying," I said, "and quit patronizing me." But I was worried, plenty worried. And I would stay that way until Edward Faust was apprehended.

Chapter Twenty-eight

AFTER VINCE CLOSED our front door behind Detective Henry, I eased myself to my feet and asked him to take me to the hospital.

His eyes filled with panic. "Are you having trouble breathing?"

"I want to talk to the people Spires visited."

"Are you serious? You just got out of the hospital. There's a crazy truck driver out there. He tried to kill you."

"Kyle," I corrected. "He tried to kill Kyle."

"*And* you," Vince insisted. "Besides, it's after 10:00. Those people are sleeping just like you should be. They're sick. That's why they're in a hospital."

"I've got to do something."

Vince sat on the futon and patted it. "You've done enough," he said. "The detective is starting to take Spires seriously as a suspect."

"Maybe."

Vince patted the futon again. "Rest tonight, Mar-Bar, and tomorrow I'll drop you at the hospital before I go to work."

I thought about calling a cab, but Vince was right. You shouldn't disturb the slumbers of the sick. The nurses probably wouldn't even let me try. And truth be told, I was far from eager to step into another car or revisit the hospital.

TEN MINUTES OF Nick at Nite, and Vince was snoring on the futon. I sat at the computer and surfed the Donor Sibling Registry, a site created in 2000 to help connect people like Zoey with their donor dads and half-siblings. I knew it wouldn't help me find Zoey's donor, not directly. Zoey would have already scoured the site. But I could learn what we were up against and trace part of her search. I typed in her birth year and the University of Iowa Hospital. "There are a total of 3 offspring," the screen said. "0 sibling matches, and 0 donor-to-offspring matches from this clinic." The list of offspring read like belated birth announcements.

I'm a boy born 1982.

I'm a boy born 1983.

I'm a girl born 1995.

To the left of the list was a column where they could post their donors' ID numbers.

Unknown

Unknown

Unknown

Each offspring also had a code name, a message you could click on, and a post date. The oldest post was from six years ago. Zoey had posted nearly half a year ago, probably right after discovering that she had a donor dad, probably telling herself that she wouldn't have to wait six years. But the truth was she might have to wait forever. Zoey had been conceived after the AIDS crisis, after Grace's lab quit collecting and selling sperm. The university lab processed the sperm that helped create Zoey Hargrove, but the sperm itself—them-selves?—could have come from anywhere, or at least from any sperm bank that the university contracted with. Zoey's donor, assuming he wanted to find her, would have a hard time doing so via the registry unless she could post his donor ID number. No wonder Zoey was desperate for Grace's records.

I clicked on Zoey's message title and learned that if I wanted to read the message itself or any other messages I'd have to fork over forty bucks and become a member of the registry. I didn't want to drag my aching bones upstairs just to get my Visa, so I kept surfing the free pages.

The blog section started with an entry about identity rights. "The medical establishment and individuals desiring to be parents cannot create a binding contract that precludes the offspring's rights to knowledge of his genetic heritage." Despite the legalese, I felt a twinge of guilt. *Trying Times* examined the struggles of fertility spe-cialists and potential parents. I hadn't even thought about the chil-dren and their struggles. Before I met Zoey, the oldest donor-conceived kid I knew was Diego. Until Edward Faust had terrified him, Diego's biggest issue seemed to be his mothers' ban on refined sugar. I always thought he was lucky to be born to women who wanted him so badly, who were raising him to be open-minded and joyously himself. But that was only half the story. I saw that now. I'd been a lackadaisical journalist, a lazy thinker. I'd gotten too caught up in Grace's zeal.

What would she say to that?

Tears blurred the computer screen. I squeezed my eyes shut. This very day, while I was sleeping, Grace had been buried. I would never know what she had to say about anything ever again. No, that wasn't true. I did know one thing. "Quit dithering." For once, her command made me smile.

There were posts aplenty on the success stories page. A few sounded like tabloid headlines—"Twin sons from different moth-ers!", "God used Oprah to answer my prayer." But most must have made Zoey wild with hope— "My daughter found me." "I found five siblings in less than a week." "It took only four hours to receive a response." Zoey must have felt cheated when her four hours passed, when months slipped away, and she heard nothing.

I read the blog entries from around the time she registered. Most were written by the site's founder. She announced the number of countries where matches had been achieved, she urged members to update their email addresses, she criticized the American Society of Reproductive Medicine (an organization Grace had belonged to) and she chided its spokesman. He had said, "A lot of traditionally-conceived children don't know their parentage, so why should gamete-donor children?" My eyes grew heavy. I was about to call it a night when an entry from a member snapped me awake.

Warning!

Be careful who you tell about your conception and attempts to find your donor dad. I made the stupid mistake of talking to Leo Spires. I knew he was a whack job, but he said he knew lots of sperm donors who wanted to find their kids and he said he would help me. But all he did was twist my words on his web site so he could attack donor conception. I will never forgive him for using me to make my mother look selfish. She was the best and bravest person ever.

This had to be Zoey. I thought about our pancake session and her careful attention to Spires on the radio. She hadn't simply been moved and curious; she'd been listening for him to use her words. For all I knew, he had. Why hadn't she told me? Was it pride—not wanting to admit she'd been tricked—or was there a more sinister reason? Maybe she was trying to get revenge on Spires and frame him for Grace's murder. Rolling my chair away from the computer, I took a deep breath. Pain blossomed on my right side. I'd spent a lot of time pondering the briefcase exchange between Spires and Kyle, but I had no real evidence of it. Only Zoey's word.

I shuffled upstairs to get my Visa and my Vicodin. When I came back down to the living room, Justine was trying to steal Vince's wallet while he slept. She was so intent on maneuvering it out of his back pocket that she didn't hear me approach. That or she was just too out of it. "I told him he was a fool to trust you," I said.

Justine extracted her hand from Vince's pocket and faced me, red-eyed and unsteady. "My friends took my car keys. I got a cab to pay."

It honked in my driveway.

"He won't leave til he gets paid," Justine said.

Vince shifted on the futon and flung an arm over his face. The man could sleep through Armageddon.

"Tell you what," I said, "I'll pay if you answer some questions about Uncle Roger and Cousin Liz."

She didn't answer, and that surprised me. I thought she'd sign away her first-born for a fiver.

"I'll also forget about the whole pickpocket thing," I said.

The cabbie pounded on my front door.

Justine stumbled toward the kitchen and raided it as I paid her debt. When I joined her at the table, she kept her eyes on the barricade of junk food between us. A can of Coke, a bag of Cheetos, half a donut, and a slice of leftover pizza. The scent of pepperoni made me queasy. I slid the pizza closer to her and found a clean spot on the table to rest my elbows.

"You look like crap," she said, cracking open her Coke.

"Thanks. That means a lot coming from you."

She ignored my barb and picked the sprinkles off the donut.

"Did your uncle Roger get you the job at the lab?"

She nodded, but didn't meet my gaze.

"Why?"

"To help me out." She opened the bag of Cheetos, popped one in her mouth, and eyed me nervously. "Aunt Deb asked him to. She always looks out for me."

"Roger's wife?"

"They're separated." Justine's voice was colder than usual.

I decided to take a chance. "I've seen the scrapbook."

Justine froze, her hand in the bag of Cheetos. "What scrapbook?" But she was a beat too late, too drunk or high to use her brilliant acting skills.

"Keep lying to me," I said, "and I'll tell Vince you were trying to lift his wallet."

She crunched another Cheeto and licked the orange residue from a taloned finger.

"I'll tell the cops that Grace was planning to fire you and your uncle," I continued, "And I'll tell them about the scrapbook."

"You searched his apartment," she said. "That's illegal."

Had the cousins been chatting or had Justine made a lucky guess? "Whatever I've done," I said, "is small stuff compared with your uncle's motives for murder."

"He'd never kill anybody." She slumped in her chair. "What a freaking idiot," she mumbled, "what a slimeball."

"If he's such a slimeball, why keep his secrets?"

"Aunt Deb," Justine said. "For some reason, she still loves him. When my 'rents split, she took me in, and she was nice about it. She made it seem like it was a big treat that I'd come to live with her and her family."

I felt sorry for Justine. It hurt a lot when I'd chosen to exchange my parents' homophobia for a spare room at my aunts'. I couldn't imagine what it would have felt like if I hadn't done the choosing.

"I thought Aunt Deb and Uncle Roger were a great couple. In love." Justine yanked the pull-tab off her pop. "What a joke." She fingered the plate the pizza was on and spun it slowly, a dishwasher-safe wheel of fortune.

After three revolutions, I prompted her. "What happened with them?"

Justine held onto the plate. "A few months after Dr. Everest's husband died, Uncle Roger started going ape-shit over her."

Grace's husband had passed away about four years ago, yet according to the scrapbook, Roger had been carrying the torch for Grace long before then. If Justine was telling the truth, maybe Roger had tried to conceal his obsession with Grace until after she was widowed.

"He was all Grace-this, Grace-that," Justine said. "I wanted to puke. Aunt Deb was clueless for like eons."

"How long, really?"

Justine nibbled her lower lip. "A couple years. Then she begged him to get a new job."

"Did he try?"

Justine scoffed as if I'd just asked the world's dumbest question. "Aunt Deb finally kicked him out. She said she'd take him back only if he got Grace out of his life. But she was stupid. She listened when he said he loved his job, and she let him convince her that he should be able to stay at the lab if he got me a job there. He told her I could keep an eye on things, make sure there was no funny business." Justine made air quotes. "Funny business," she repeated, mocking her uncle's euphemism for cheating. "The plan was for a three-month trial. If I reported no funny business," she used her mocking air quotes again, "then Aunt Deb would let him move back in."

"Did Grace agree to this?"

"No. She was clueless. Uncle Roger told her that if he could get me a job, it would help him score some points with Aunt Deb." Justine paused. "True, I guess, but not the whole story."

Not the whole story indeed. I thought about the argument Zoey overheard, Roger's claim that Grace would destroy his family if she fired Justine. "Does Roger want to get back with your aunt?"

"He wants to live in the same house as his kids," Justine said. "His son, anyway, since Lizzie is in college. My mom says he wants to have his cake and eat it too."

"What happened at the lab? Why did Grace want to fire him?"

"I didn't want to work there and play spy, but I couldn't say no to Aunt Deb. And I needed the money."

"What happened?"

"He found ten million excuses to talk to Dr. Everest every day. It was disgusting. She clearly had no interest in him, but he was clueless."

"So why did she want to fire him?"

Justine studied her fingernails. "It was my fault. I was at his apartment, and I found the scrapbook."

I didn't ask how she found it. No doubt she was raiding his

Tupperware collection or trying to use her Uncle Roger as an ATM.

"It was crazy," she said.

For once, I had to agree.

"When I saw it, I knew he'd never get over her. So I talked to Dr. Everest. I told her that Roger had feelings for her and that it would be better for him and his family if she helped him get a transfer to some other part of the hospital."

"When was this?"

Justine waved her hand through the air. "A few days ago—I don't know—I don't keep a diary."

"You showed her the scrapbook?"

Justine reddened. "No. I couldn't. It's so...well, you've seen it." She took a long drink of Coke.

I gave her a few moments to gather herself. It had been bad enough when I'd found the scrapbook, and I wasn't related to the man who'd made it. "So what happened?" I asked.

"Dr. Everest didn't take me seriously. So I knew I'd have to go back to her with some kind of evidence." Justine shifted her attention to the Cheetos and rolled the top of the package into a tight scroll. "I should have bailed on the whole thing. But I was stupid. I went back to Uncle Roger's apartment, and I took this bracelet that had Dr. Everest's name engraved on it. I knew he'd stolen it. I showed it to her, and I told her where I found it."

"She didn't accuse you of taking it?" I asked gently.

Justine released her hold on the Cheetos and gave me a dirty look. "Uncle Roger swiped it before I started at the lab. My first week, there was a note about the missing bracelet above the microwave." Justine dropped her gaze and spoke her next words softly. "The bracelet was from her husband."

"How did Grace react?"

"She didn't say anything, but she looked furious. I was afraid she'd decided to fire him. Maybe even press charges. I didn't want him in trouble. I just wanted him to get a transfer."

Again, I recalled the argument Zoey overheard. "One more incident," Grace had said. "Pathetic. Get some help." If her rejection—her revulsion—had gotten through to Roger...

"I begged her to help him get a transfer," Justine said. "I told her that if she didn't, he and Aunt Deb would never get back together. Grace said my aunt had a right to know what was going on." Justine's face puckered. "I told her Aunt Deb would be completely hurt and humiliated, but she didn't give a shit. I told her to think about their kids, her own freaking goddaughter. I told her they didn't need to know that their father is a complete twat. She told me to watch my language, and she waved me out of her office like she was queen of the freaking universe."

Justine's anger unnerved me, as did my realization that she

cared about her cousins. "I saw you arguing with Liz at the theatre."

Justine looked surprised. "Were you stalking me?"

I ignored the question. "What were you fighting about?"

"She wanted to know what was up with her dad and Dr. Everest. I told her I didn't know, and she called me a liar."

"I heard she was really angry with Grace," I said, "that she blamed Grace for her parents' separation."

"Yeah," Justine admitted, "but Lizzie had nothing to do with Dr. Everest's death."

"How do you know?"

"You mean because I like did it myself?" Justine smiled faintly and shook her head. "You're crazy."

"You're fond of Liz, aren't you?"

"Whatever."

"You'd lie for her."

"I don't need to. Lizzie is a good person," Justine said. "Sweet and boring. End of story."

"Why didn't you destroy your uncle's scrapbook?"

"I was going to after the murder, but I never had the chance."

"I saw Roger meet with Celia Spires."

"The minister's daughter?" Justine sounded surprised. She clutched her Coke and pushed herself to her feet. "Uncle Roger is probably just trying to be a hero. Find Dr. Everest's killer or confront her enemies or some bullshit like that." She shook her head. "I thought that once the doctor was dead, he'd finally quit being such a fool."

Chapter Twenty-nine

LATE THE NEXT morning at the hospital, I found the boy from the photo Zoey had emailed me, the one she'd seen in Kyle's car. He was sleeping in Room 245 of the Colloton Pavilion, where, according to Zoey's notes, Reverend Leo Spires had spent two hours on the day she'd followed him. That had been Wednesday, the day before Grace's visitation and my own emergency trek to the hospital. It was Friday now. How long had the boy been sick? The nameplate next to his door revealed that his first name was Seth. His last name rang no bells. As I peeked into Seth's room, he shifted slightly but didn't wake. His rust-colored hair made him look extra pale, and he had an IV and a bruise on his hand where he was hooked up to it. Maybe Seth was too sick to answer any of my questions.

"Can I help you?" The voice belonged to a stocky woman with a well-lined face and frizzy gray hair. Her t-shirt read "Honor the Dead, Heal the Wounded, End the War." She'd been wearing tie-dye the day Grace was killed. She'd argued with Celia Spires and spoken to me as we watched the protest in front of the hospital.

"My great-grandson needs his sleep." She motioned me into the hall and looked me up and down.

I hoped she wouldn't remember me as I lied through my teeth. "I'm Deacon Emily Webbing, chaplain." I extended my hand, and she took it reluctantly, introducing herself simply as Seth's great-grandmother.

"We're not religious," she said.

Then why had Spires spent so much time with them? "My mission isn't to convert," I reassured her, "just to offer assistance and support. A listening ear."

Great-grandma narrowed her eyes.

"How long has Seth been here?" I asked.

"Almost a week. His appendix ruptured. He had a terrible infection, but he's on the mend now." She looked past me into his room.

"I understand you want to get back to him, but if you could do me a quick favor first..."

Again, the narrowed eyes.

"The chaplaincy is doing a survey to see how many visits pediatric patients typically receive and to determine how many of those visitors need our ministry."

"We're not from here," Great-grandma said.

I feigned a look of concern. "So your great-grandson hasn't had any visitors?"

"His parents have been with him," she said defensively.

"Anyone else?"

She gazed past me, suddenly alarmed.

I turned and saw two lanky red-headed women barreling toward us. The older one, about my age, lead the way. The younger one, twenty-something, tugged at her, distraught. "You're not supposed to be here," she whined. The older one pulled away. "I have a right to see my grandson." She had a toothy overbite and a nose that only a plastic surgeon could love. And her hair was rust-orange just like Seth's. That made sense, she was his grandmother. Was she the daughter of the woman I'd been talking to, or was she from the other side of the family? The real question, though, was why Great-grandma looked so terrified as the other women descended and brushed past us into the boy's room. Great-grandma just stood there, gaping, rooted to the spot—a big change from the way she'd reacted when she'd seen me near the room. When she finally closed her mouth—closed it hard and tight, grinding her teeth—I stepped into Seth's doorway.

He was just waking up. His grandmother and—who? his mother?—loomed over his bed. As Seth sat up, he leaned forward slightly, and both women leaned toward him. That leaning reminded me of something I'd noticed recently. I recalled that when I'd seen the photo of Seth, he, too, had reminded me of someone, but I couldn't put my finger on who. Now, as the boy pushed his covers away, I could see that he was thin and long-armed. His grin revealed Bugs Bunny teeth. Seth was a younger version of Reverend Leo Spires.

But the boy hadn't been in the proud Spires family portrait I'd seen at the church office and neither had the two women standing over him.

I stepped back into the hallway and faced Great-grandma. Just as I was about to speak to her, a leggy nurse dashed past us and then stopped. She was movie-star gorgeous even in scrubs that featured Micky and Minnie Mouse. "Mara?" she asked.

There was no use denying it. She quickly reminded me that we met at Kyle Bremmer's. She was his girlfriend. We talked about poor Dr. Everest and the Lipinskis. Didn't I remember?

Great-grandma studied us, looking puzzled, then worried.

But I didn't care that my cover was blown. The series of events that led Leo Spires to pay off Kyle Bremmer lay before me, a clear untrammeled path. Leggy Nurse Toni endures her boyfriend's constant complaints about Reverend Leo Spires. She sees the minister make an unusually long visit and mentions it to said boyfriend. The boyfriend, Kyle, checks it out. He sees the toothy red-headed boy with his toothy red-headed grandmother and reaches the same conclusion I did. Mr. Fixated-on-the-Family has an illegitimate daughter—nay, an entire extended family—that he has not publicly acknowledged. Lo and behold, Kyle has a new source of income.

Nurse Toni went to help a patient.

"I saw you arguing with Celia Spires," I said to Great-grandma, "and I think I know why."

"You don't know anything."

Two nurses zipped around us, one on each side, their shoes squeaking on the floor.

"Why don't you enlighten me?"

Her glare intensified. "Leave my family alone."

"Leo Spires's family, you mean," I said loudly.

"*My* family." She stepped toward me.

Another nurse hurried past. "Ladies!" she said. "Keep your voices down."

I waited until the nurse was out of earshot. "It's hard for me to speak softly because I work in radio." I held Great-grandma's eyes. "You can either tell me about your relationship with Leo Spires, or I'll broadcast my own theory over the airwaves."

"You wouldn't dare."

"Try me," I said. "The man made a career out of harassing one of my dearest friends, and now she's dead."

The woman paled. "Leo hates violence. He'd never hurt anybody."

I resisted the urge to argue. "If you're so sure he's innocent, talk to me."

"You want to ruin him. Drag his name through the mud."

"That's exactly what I'll do if you don't give me the truth."

She looked as if she wanted to toss me out with the week's garbage, but then she slumped in defeat and headed down the hall. I followed her into the unit's playroom and shut the door. Despite the adult-size couch at the far end, she stopped amid knee-high chairs. A magnetic board rested against one of them. Bright plastic letters kaleidoscoped across its white surface.

"You could start with your name," I said.

Outside the room, a cart rattled past. As the woman glanced toward the sound, I surreptitiously turned on the mini tape recorder in my pocket.

Great-grandma studied me and gnawed the inside of her lip. The PA summoned one doctor and then another before the woman admitted that she was Helen Drake. "It's not what you think," she said. Even though we were alone, she kept her voice hushed. "Leo and I, we were kids together. Summer days, I'd spend sunup to sundown with him and his brother Larry. Fishing, biking, making forts."

I shifted my weight. What I needed was a hefty dose of Vicodin or something incriminating about Spires, not a cheesy reminiscence about his rural boyhood.

"See this?" Helen held out her left thumb. There was a tiny scar, like a crack on a bird's egg. "A blood pact. Leo and I were eight. Larry was five. We vowed eternal friendship." She shook her head sadly. "Back then, that meant sharing your ice cream money, the rocks and feathers you found." She paused, plucked up a stray Fisher-Price person, and slowly rolled it back and forth in her hands. "You despise him. With good reason, I suppose. But he wasn't always like he is now. He used to have an open heart. Wide open. And he was sweet too unless someone messed with Larry or me. Then watch out."

"So what happened?" I wasn't sure what I was asking. What made Spires such a jerk? Or what prompted her to sleep with him?

"Leo and I drifted apart in high school. I was wilder than he was." Helen smiled faintly. "And we lost touch in college. We went to different schools. He was studying to be a minister, and I was protesting the war. After graduation, I stayed in California, and I didn't see him again until after Larry was killed in Viet Nam." She pressed her lips together a long moment. "It was almost a year after he died. I was home visiting my folks, and I ran into Leo at the super market. He said he wanted me to have something of Larry's, so I went back with him to his parents' place. They were gone, and we were sitting in Larry's old bedroom, looking at the medals his mom had placed on his dresser. Leo started weeping. I'd never seen him cry before." Helen's face crinkled with pain. "He said nobody knew how much he missed Larry, not even his wife. She just wanted him to move on, to focus on their daughter and their future together. At first, I was just comforting him, holding him while he cried..."

The last thing I expected to feel was pity for Leo Spires. The man had used Zoey. He had fueled hate against me and my community. He had protested Grace's lab and her funeral. I gazed at Helen. "He's kept you and your family secret all this time."

She looked at me defiantly. "My choice. My secret. I never told him I was pregnant. I knew he'd try to do the right thing. But it would have been wrong. For both of us. He had a family, a church and a town he was building. I had my freedom and independence, a life in California."

"But he found out," I said.

She squeezed the toy in her hand. "Not until Lee was grown, a mother herself. Her daughter Niki—you saw them both in the hall— when she was twelve, she was diagnosed with cancer. She needed a bone marrow transplant. Lee and I weren't matches, and Niki's father was out of the picture. None of our blood relatives were matches."

"So you asked Spires."

Helen's eyes drilled into mine. "He saved her life. And he tried to do it on my terms. He pretended to be a random donor, but you've seen for yourself how much he looks like Lee."

I tried to imagine how father and daughter must have felt. Lee—her own child's life at risk—discovering that her father is a radio evangelist who rails against single mothers such as herself. And Spires, with a surprise daughter and granddaughter.

"My darling Lee. She'll never forgive me for not telling her about Leo. And she'll never forgive Leo for not somehow magically knowing about her." Helen shook her head sadly. "He'll never forgive himself. But there's no guilt or anger between Niki and Leo. They adore each other. And Seth, of course. Leo worships Seth."

I thought about Spires' family, the one he used to bolster his image as super-dad. Three daughters. No grandsons. "Does his wife know?" I asked.

"He wanted to tell her, but I said no."

I bet Helen didn't have to argue too hard.

"What good would it have done?" Helen asked. "I told him that if there was anything he needed to atone for, he'd already done it by saving Niki. But he also helped her and her husband start their salon, and he contributes to Seth's college fund. He's even helped Lee out a few times."

No wonder the endowment at Spires' church was shrinking. "What about his daughter Celia?" I asked.

Helen curled her bottom lip as if she'd just smelled something rank. "That woman hired a private investigator to spy on my family. He scared Niki to death. She thought some pervert was stalking her."

I asked how she knew the private eye was working for Celia.

Helen grinned. "I hired one of my own. Soon as I knew the truth, I told Celia to call off her detective or I'd go public with my family story." Helen sighed. "But she knew it was an empty threat. He's still spying on us."

"Is that why you were arguing with her last Sunday?"

"She kept calling," Helen said, "asking what it would take for me and my family to disappear from her father's life—to vanish. Vanish! Can you believe it?" Helen's face flushed with anger. "No one buys me. And Niki and Seth, it would break their hearts to lose Leo. But that woman wouldn't give up. People like her, they think they can have anything they want. Such arrogance."

To me, Celia Spires seemed desperate, so desperate to protect her family's reputation that she was using its dwindling resources to bribe Helen and pay a private investigator.

"I kept telling her that we were just passing through when Seth got sick, that we're going back to California, but she wouldn't believe me," Helen said. "She thought we were trying to insinuate ourselves into her father's life." Helen stared past me, lost in her own indignation. "When I ran into her in the hospital lobby—"

"You weren't planning to meet?"

"With that woman?" Helen said. "No way. But I saw her get off the elevator and decided it was time—"

"The elevator," I said. "You're sure?"

Helen nodded, and my pulse quickened. The day Grace was killed, Celia had been on the elevator that went up to the lab. And Zoey had seen alligator stilettos there. "How did she seem? Emotionally, I mean?"

Helen ignored my question. "I told her that if she and her PI didn't leave me and my family alone, I'd tell her father what she'd been up to."

I wondered how Helen could be so sure that the reverend didn't already know.

She must have read the doubt on my face. "Leo is a decent, loving man. A good man."

I resisted the urge to roll my eyes.

"He's spent every morning in the hospital with Seth—with Niki and me—even though—"

"Every morning?" I asked. "Last Sunday?"

"He came around 11:30—right after his last morning service—and stayed until mid-afternoon. Ask Niki. She'll tell you. Ask the PI for that matter."

So much for the newspaper photo of Leo Spires entering the hospital while his flock protested. The minister was guilty of many things, but killing Grace wasn't one of them.

Chapter Thirty

BACK HOME, I slammed my medicine cabinet shut. I thought I'd stashed my Vicodin in my backpack, but it wasn't there. It wasn't anywhere. My neck and my right side keened. I grabbed some Advil off the counter and swallowed half a dozen without water. Coughing and choking, I stumbled downstairs and rifled through the cupboards until I found Vince's peach schnapps. It would do. A couple sickly sweet chugs, and warmth engulfed me. The pain receded. I wanted to drain the bottle, but I screwed the lid on tight. Clear thinking, that's what I really needed. Part of me felt gleefully vengeful. I wanted to send my scoop on Spires to every tabloid that ever graced a checkout lane. Another part of me was disappointed and defeated. I'd wanted the bad guy to be the bad guy, but Spires hadn't killed Grace. I needed to accept my mistake and tell Detective Henry about the minister's alibi.

The light on my answering machine flashed. Its red pulse reminded me of heart monitors and ambulance lights. When I hit the play button, I heard Bridget's luscious voice accompanied by the rumbling of basketballs. She had called from practice—the first time ever—to see how I was doing and to say that she would stop by later. Anne was next. "Mara, I hope you're feeling better and that you're resting. I'm so sorry about your accident. I still want to talk if you're up to it."

I wondered what she wanted to talk about. There was certainly no shortage of topics to process—the thefts, the funeral, my injuries. I hoped there wasn't anything new.

"I'll bring Labrys," Anne continued, "and some soup. I'm sending you good energy."

Soup. She'd never brought me soup before.

There were also check-in calls from Aunt Zee, Sophie and Esther, my parents, Felicity Cheng, Kyle, Zoey, and Orchid. Then Vince, "Mar-Bar! Either you're still at the hospital sleuthing your little heart out or resting like a good girl. I'm betting on the former." Dogs yelped in the background, and he asked me to call him at the shelter with a full report. I was about to oblige when another voice thundered from the machine.

"Miss Gilgannon," Leo Spires said. "We need to speak about a mutual acquaintance." I flew to my front door and checked the lock. Ditto the back door and the latches on my first-floor windows. My heart pounded wildly. Sure, Spires hadn't killed Grace, but he might have sent a crazy truck driver after Kyle. Now Spires might send Edward Faust after me.

I looked out my front window. There were no monster trucks or white SUVs, only a man and a little girl shuffling through leaves on the sidewalk.

Father and daughter. Celia Spires also knew Edward Faust. And she was the one with Kyle's résumé on her desk. She was the one receiving faxes of lab reports he'd signed. She was the one with the private investigator. What if her PI spotted Kyle haunting Seth's hospital room? Best case scenario, Celia would have worried about Kyle discovering her father's secret. Worst case, she would have discovered that Kyle was blackmailing her father.

Still, that didn't explain why she'd want Kyle's résumé and lab reports. Or why Roger would send them to her.

I sat down and massaged my forehead. I needed to do something besides think. Searching Justine's room would be just the thing.

DESPITE THE CHILLY breeze from the open window, the room smelled of menthols. To my surprise, the bed was neatly made. Bottles of lotion, perfume, and nail polish lined the dresser top. I resisted the urge to check myself in the mirror. Bruises and anxiety do not a beauty treatment make. The top drawer squeaked as I opened it, revealing a riot of thongs. The next two drawers were jampacked with purses. Since my own collection contains only a single backpack, I marveled at Justine's. Inside a sequined clutch was a note written on animal shelter letterhead. Vince's handwriting. Vince's purse.

I zipped open two other purses, but they were empty. A large white leather one—too conservative for Vince—contained his Betty Boop cookie jar. The red bag next to it revealed empty pencil boxes. The next purse? A canning jar. When Kyle said Justine had a habit of swiping containers, he didn't know the half of it.

The last purse was filled with pill bottles, including my Vicodin. I shoved it into my pocket, too freaked out for anger. What would I find in the bottom drawer? Thermoses? Petri dishes?

Sweaters and jeans, it turned out. A carton of cigarettes. But the normalcy stopped there. The drawer of one nightstand contained empty vials and test tubes. The other, a ceramic vase my sister had given me. The closet housed a fleet of Tupperware.

But I didn't find Anne's computer, my computer, or our work on *Trying Times*. Of course, this contraband could be in the trunk of Justine's car or some other hidey-hole.

Under the bed, I discovered more vials and test tubes, some housing tiny paper scrolls. I grabbed tweezers from the dresser and plucked some of the papers out. There were a few newspaper articles about Liz's athletic triumphs, but most were horoscopes or fortune cookie messages. "Prosperity and wealth will find you." "Happiness is a day away." Maybe these vials were inexpensive gifts, Justine's attempt to trim her budget. Or maybe they were part of some ritual or spell. Justine Nissen, creative craftswoman? Witch? Or complete and total nut case?

A car door slammed. It was just a guy across the street. Still, there was no reason to dally. I returned the vials and smoothed the bedspread where I'd disturbed it. Maybe something was hidden in the bed itself, and that's why Justine made it so neatly.

Bingo! In between the mattress and box springs was a manila file folder crammed with papers from Grace's lab—donor insemination reports from the eighties and nineties. I remembered Grace's visitation and Zoey asking Justine about the lab's records. I impatiently shuffled through the reports in my hands. And there it was. A 1994 report for Monique Hargrove inseminated by donor number 12785 of the California Cryobank.

Zoey's donor dad. 12785. I committed the number to memory. I was about to slip the reports back under the mattress when I saw Justine.

She blocked the doorway, hands on her hips. "What are you doing?" she asked.

"Retrieving my Vicodin."

Justine lunged for the papers in my hand. I dodged her. Pain blazed through my right side.

"Those are mine," she said.

I resisted the urge to back away. "Did Grace catch you stealing them? Is that why you killed her?"

Justine gaped at me.

Outside a car roared past, leaving a faint trail of rap, then nothing.

"Those are just copies." Justine went for them again.

I swept them behind my back.

"I didn't steal anything," Justine said. "And I didn't hurt anyone. I made those copies. They're mine."

I didn't bother to argue. The nuances of ownership, privacy, and hurt were way beyond Justine's scope.

"This is crazy," Justine said. "Give them back."

"Does anyone else know about them?"

Justine ignored my question and edged closer.

I considered bolting for the hallway, but I wouldn't be fast enough, not in my bruised condition. I could surrender the papers. But then what? Justine wouldn't let me phone the police. "I know why you made the copies," I said. "You saw Zoey Hargrove confront Dr. Everest about her donor. Why not give the kid a chance to find her father, you thought. If the price is right."

Justine folded her arms over her chest.

Behind my back, I rolled the lab reports into a tight tube, careful to keep my motions hidden from Justine. My right shoulder throbbed with the effort. "Why stop with Zoey," I said, "when there are so many other people searching for their donors. When there's so much money to be made."

Justine launched herself at me. I threw the paper tube across the room. It thwacked against the window and dropped to the bed. Justine stopped. The tube came undone, and the breeze blew the top page out of sight. Justine glanced at me. Then at her precious papers. Another one floated off the bed.

She went for the papers, and I dashed to my room, locking the door behind me. I was too sore to move the dresser in front of it, but I did manage a chair. I was about to call 911 when the phone rang.

"Hey. Is like Justine Nissen there?"

I told Stoner Boy this wasn't a good time, but he kept talking. The thing was Justine might not totally remember his name because she was like having a pretty wild time and all. But they'd spent Saturday night and most of Sunday together. He didn't know her cell number, so he tracked down this friend of hers and found out that Justine was hanging at my place.

"This past Sunday?" I asked. Was Stoner Boy Justine's alibi?

Yeah, absolutely. And could I do him a solid? Could I like ask Justine if she accidentally took his housemate's purse? It was missing.

I was about to inquire about his Tupperware when Justine peeled out of my driveway.

Chapter Thirty-one

"CALL ME THE next time your driveway is filled with black and whites," Bridget said. "They scared the crap out of me."

She'd shown up right when Detective Henry finished taking my statement. The detective had told Bridget what happened, begged her to keep me out of trouble, and explained that fellow officers would remain upstairs, processing my guest room. Now they thumped and thudded as Bridget and I sat in silence. Not the comfortable, companionable kind, but the where-do-we-start kind.

I reached my hand across the futon and laced my fingers in hers.

She pulled me toward her, gently because of my injuries. "I really was scared," she said. "I thought something had happened to you. Besides your contusions."

"Bruises," I said. "Mere bruises." I wanted to nestle into her with my good side. I wanted to forget about everything except how her heart beat faster when we were close. But, alas, my neck hurt.

"You okay?" she asked.

I knew she wanted to talk about Liz, and I loved her for holding back. "I'm glad you're here," I said. "How was practice?"

"I talked to Liz after. The kid is worried sick about her father and her cousin."

She should be, I thought. Instead, I asked if Liz had talked about the scrapbook.

Bridget pulled her hand away. "Did you tell the cop about it?"

I didn't answer.

"Babe?" Bridget's voice was far from tender.

"I had to. It gives Roger a huge motive." I shared the dysfunctional family saga I extracted from Justine the night before. Then there was more silence. Upstairs, the cops bantered and laughed.

Bridget sighed. "Liz used to adore Grace."

I didn't know what to say. It was hard to imagine a happy ending for Liz.

"She's such a great kid," Bridget said. "She deserves better."

"She has you."

Bridget smiled sadly. "And I guess Grace has you, trying to bring her killer to justice."

I couldn't tell if that was a compliment or a criticism.

Bridget studied me a long moment, her face expressionless. "When you and I first got together," she said, "I thought it was an opposites-attract thing. But we're a lot alike."

I still couldn't read her tone.

"You think all I care about is the team." She paused briefly, and when I didn't deny it, she went on. "You can be just as dedicated — or obsessed, whatever you want to call it — when you think you're doing the right thing."

I wanted to say that I *was* doing the right thing, but that would have proven her point. "I admire how you are with the team," I said, "I just wish there was more time for us."

"Do you really?" Bridget asked.

Her question surprised me. I shifted slightly, and my injuries protested.

"Babe," she said. "You need some more pain meds?"

"Why did you ask that?"

"Because you winced."

"No," I said, "why did you ask if I really want more time with you?"

Bridget studied me again, her eyes troubled. "Because sometimes I wonder."

"Why?"

She dropped her gaze to my hands and took them in hers. "We're both stressed out of our minds, and you're in pain. Let's talk about this later." Then she leaned in and kissed me softly and slowly.

I let her deflect my question, but I couldn't stop thinking about it.

VINCE AND ANNE half-heartedly played tug-of-war with Labrys while Bridget paced behind the futon and the cops continued processing the contraband upstairs in my guest room. It had been nearly two hours since Detective Henry had taken my statement and put out an all-points bulletin on Justine. The cops still hadn't found her. Nor could anyone locate her Uncle Roger, who, according to Kyle, left the hospital shortly after Justine left my place. Edward Faust, he of the scary truck, was also still at large.

The phone rang, and Labrys barked. We all looked at one another. Maybe Justine was returning one of Vince's calls. I picked up and managed a hello.

"Ah," Leo Spires said, "I finally got you."

I hung up and summoned my thespian training. "Wrong number." I tried to look disappointed.

Vince raised an eyebrow at me and hefted himself off the floor. I moved in between him and the phone so he couldn't check the caller ID. Part of me wanted to spill everything I'd learned about Spires. I wanted advice about what to do with his secret, but if I confided in my friends, it wouldn't be my secret any more. It wouldn't be my decision. And I knew what they'd say anyway. Spires deserves to be exposed. He's devoted his life to attacking Grace's lab, to bashing us—all in the name of family values. What an outrageous hypocrite! He's using his church's money to support his secret family. What's to decide?

But they hadn't seen Helen and her family. Her great-grandson in that hospital bed. Yes, Spires had cheated on his wife. Yes, he was a liar and a hypocrite. But once he learned that he'd fathered a daughter, he'd done everything he could for her, for her daughter and her grandson. Helen's story made me hate Spires less, not more. It made me think about his motivations. Maybe his campaign against sperm donation was fueled by more than misogyny, homophobia, and misguided Christianity. More than the lesbian baby boom or the triumph of gay marriage in Iowa. Maybe Spires had also been motivated by the fact that for nearly thirty years he had been denied his own fatherhood.

The phone rang again, and Vince grabbed it. He listened and frowned, flicked his eyes toward me. "She's not available right now. May I ask what this is about?" Vince's frown deepened. "Please don't call again tonight. We have houseguests. Oodles of them." Vince hung up and turned to me. "What does Spires want with you?"

Anne and Bridget shot each other puzzled looks.

"What did you learn at the hospital?" he asked.

Outside, headlights cut through the darkness. "He didn't kill Grace," I said.

"So why is he calling?" Vince asked.

I contemplated my housemate, my lover, and Anne. Their strained faces. If I told them about Spires, they'd fret about my safety. If I kept quiet, they'd stew about what I wasn't telling them. Either way I would add to their worry.

"Well?" Vince said.

I shrugged.

"Fine. Withhold from your dearest friends."

I tried to dismiss his words as the antics of a drama queen, but I knew I'd hurt his feelings. Probably Anne's and Bridget's too. Upstairs the cops slid furniture around. Labrys barked, and Anne stroked the dog's head. The scent of the vegetarian chili she'd brought wafted from the kitchen. She announced that she was going to give it a stir and left with Labrys at her heels. Bridget said she was going to call Liz again, but she made no move for her phone. Her face was a mixture of worry and resolve, as if she were coaching a losing game. In a way, she was. If Roger had murdered Grace, Bridget's star freshman would have to grapple with the fact that her father was a killer. The rest of the team—eleven young women—would have to shoulder the burden that a man they'd known, and possibly liked, had done the unthinkable.

"You can use my room," I said, "if you want privacy."

As Bridget headed upstairs, Vince turned away.

"You want to run lines?" I asked. "Try out your Lady Bracknell on me?"

He sighed and shook his head. "Justine was going to be a great Gwendolen Fairfax."

Was. I wished I could reassure Vince and tell him that Justine would soon be treading the boards again, but I knew she probably wouldn't be. The cops would find her eventually, and her legal problems would keep her far from the stage.

"She was obviously no poster child for mental health," Vince admitted.

"You couldn't have known." I fought to keep my voice even. Maybe Justine couldn't help it, but she had betrayed Vince and made him doubt himself. She'd violated Grace's trust. And she'd brought the police into my home.

Anne and Labrys returned with a bowl of chips. Bridget trudged back down the stairs and shook her head glumly. Liz still hadn't heard from her father or cousin. If the silence got any heavier, it would crush us.

"I saw some of the lab reports Justine took," I said. "I know the ID number of Zoey's sperm donor."

More silence.

"I'm thinking about giving it to her so she can post it on the Donor Sibling Registry."

Anne set the chips on the coffee table, and I explained how the web site worked.

"So," Bridget said, "she'll post his number there and wait for him to respond?"

I nodded.

"And if he doesn't?" she asked.

"It could increase her feelings of rejection and abandonment," Anne said.

"But now she's in limbo," I argued. "She's lonely and lost."

"You could get in major trouble," Vince said, reaching for a chip.

"What about Grace?" Anne asked. "And honoring her memory?"

Bridget and Vince nodded in agreement.

They were right. Grace wouldn't want me sharing that number with anyone. But I'd promised to help Zoey. "What if it were you?" I said. "Wouldn't you want a shot at knowing your biological father?"

Before anyone could answer, the cops—a hefty thirty-something and a lanky man near retirement—came down the stairs and announced they were finished. The older one apologized for the mess. Once they were gone, Vince used a stage whisper to pronounce my plan illegal.

"You should at least look into the psychological impact of posting and not getting results," Anne said.

"How about crappy results?" Bridget asked. "What if the guy is a jerk?"

I headed to the computer. Ever since Justine disappeared, I'd been itching to do something. Now I had a tiny action plan. As my friends went to the kitchen, the better to criticize me, I went to the Donor Sibling Registry and clicked on "Articles and Issues." A California sperm bank — not Zoey's — was barely beginning to research its identity release program. "What happens when adults with donor origins learn their donor's identity? What happens when an adult offspring and donor meet?"

Great questions. But what about younger offspring? What about Zoey? I clicked on another article and learned that donor offspring often feel angry and betrayed if their parents lie to them about their genetic origins. You think? This research was as helpful as me sitting on my ass while Roger roamed free. I really wanted to search his apartment and office. But the cops were no doubt ensconced at both locations, and my friends were intent on keeping me out of trouble. In other words, keeping me a prisoner in my own home.

I decided to spring for a membership in the registry so I could read Zoey's message to her donor dad. My friends' voices ebbed and flowed as I got my Visa and registered on the site. Then I browsed by clinic and scrolled down to the University of Iowa. Once on the hospital's page, I saw that Zoey's post was still there — "I'm a girl born 1995" — but to the left of her information in the Donor ID column, where it used to say unknown, was the number 12785. I felt a split-second of relief — there was no longer any need for me to make a decision on Zoey's behalf. But then I realized that the only way Zoey could have posted her donor's ID number was if Justine had sold it to her. What if Zoey were with Justine? What if they were both missing?

Chapter Thirty-two

THE NEXT MORNING was a Saturday. It hadn't yet been a week since Grace had died. As I entered her lab, I heard Kyle chatting up a patient about sperm motility. Since he often worked weekends, I figured he might be there. I hoped he'd be cool with me poking around Roger's things, but I tiptoed just in case. Fortunately, I didn't have to walk past the prep room where Kyle was working to get to Roger's desk in the main office.

Roger's computer was gone, presumably taken by the cops. The notations on his desk calendar shed zero light on his connection with Celia Spires. Near his phone was a take-out menu for El Ranchero, but I doubted that Roger was hiding from the law among the chips and salsa. I star-69ed his phone and discovered that he'd last called some other office in the hospital.

The phone gods had not been kind to me since Justine went missing. I'd spent half the night waiting for Zoey and Detective Henry to return my calls. When Bridget finally dragged me to bed, I still had no idea where Zoey was or who she was with. Justine? Or the math-geek boyfriend Reed, whose last name I'd been too stupid to ask? The morning brought more bad news. A livid Judge Hargrove reported that his daughter hadn't been home all night. Detective Henry revealed that the cops had found Justine's car—but no Justine—in the Iowa City Walmart parking lot and that Judge Hargrove thought I knew his daughter's whereabouts. A note on my pillow stated that Bridget couldn't sleep and had gone to the gym. Vince, of course, was still snoozing, providing me with the perfect opportunity to borrow his car.

So there I was, gazing fruitlessly at Roger's desk. Family photos, neatly stacked Post-it pads, and a paperweight from Branson, Missouri. I tried a drawer, but it was locked. They all were. Ditto the file cabinets and metal closets.

I entered the hall. There had to be a clue somewhere that would lead me to Roger. My shoes squeaked on the over-waxed floor as I headed across the hall to Kyle's prep station. I wanted to see if Kyle would be willing and able to open some of Roger's locks for me, but he and the patient were gone. Kyle must have been so focused on the patient that he hadn't noticed me in Roger's office, and I must have been so intent on Roger's office that I hadn't noticed Kyle and the patient leave the lab. If indeed Kyle had.

I went back into the hall and studied the lab's main entrance, its metal double doors the same institutional beige as the walls. Near this entrance was another door that led to the cryo room. Kyle could be in there, but I had no desire to enter that place ever again. I looked down the hall in the other direction, toward the window. A smidgeon of sunlight was trying to work its way into the lab. I called Kyle's name and got nothing in response. The silence was unnerving. I told myself that I was fine. I had watched carefully for Edward Faust on my way to the hospital, and I'd seen no sign of him. Of course, I hadn't seen Kyle leave the lab either.

Wondering if he would return, I went back to his work station. Posted on the wall above his microscope were photos of his nieces and nephew and a crayon drawing of a snowman with a celery nose. "For Uncle Kyle," it said in huge lop-sided letters. I almost smiled at the thought of Kyle making the unconventional snowman for his nephew. Then I turned my attention to Justine's station. Everything had its own plastic container, including an ancient stapler, but there was nothing that suggested where she'd gone.

My phone wasn't working — I was too deeply entombed in the hospital — so I used Roger's to check for messages on my cell and on my home and work phones. Nada on all three counts. I paced the hall, glancing at the sperm cartoons and hoping that Kyle would return soon. Then, in the prep room next to the main office, across the hall from where Kyle had been working, something caught my eye.

A tiny orange light on a hot plate. Grace had said that it should only be on for diagnostics, only when the lab is open. Never on weekends. Never unattended. But I remembered that it had been on the Sunday she was killed. It was on now.

I peered inside the container on top of the hot plate and sniffed. The contents looked like water, and there was no smell. The container itself was warm to my touch. I thought of what Grace always said about sperm. "Nothing is harder to store or easier to kill." What could be easier than boiling it? In my mind, I saw the insemination reports on Grace's desk the day she died. I thought about Sophie and Esther and their Stormy Grace. About Felicity and Anne. I knew who killed Grace, and it wasn't Roger.

I TURNED TO flee, but Kyle's lab-coated shoulders filled the doorway. His eyes darted between me and the hot plate. "Just like Dr. Everest," he said. "That's how she figured it out." He unplugged the hot plate and removed the electrical cord from its base. "You wouldn't give up. I knew you wouldn't." He wrapped each end of the cord around a hand and pulled it tight.

Fear anesthetized me, numbed me, dumbed me. I needed to say something — talking would be my only salvation — but I couldn't manage a single word.

"You're like me," he said. "We take matters into our own

hands." He edged closer.

I stepped back, but eventually, he'd have me cornered. "You said you hated Spires. You quit his church."

"I do hate him." Kyle's face and words were hard. I could feel his hate—a sheer, jagged crag of rage.

"Why did you sabotage Anne and—"

"Kyle?" A woman's voice came from the hall.

He relaxed the cord slightly and looked over his shoulder.

It was his grandmother—no football helmet this time and no smile either. Behind her glasses, Gertie's eyes widened in horror. "What are you doing?"

Kyle's jaw muscle pulsed. He glanced at me. Then back at her.

When he wasn't looking, I turned on the tape recorder in my jacket pocket.

"Go back to your protest, Grandma. Don't say anything to anybody. We'll talk later."

"I saw you in the lobby," she said. "I decided to prove Aggie and her rumors wrong. Tell me you don't work here."

"He does," I said. "He killed—"

"Shut up." He tightened the cord and stepped toward me.

"Kyle," Gertie said, "You're not going to hurt her."

"Grandma, I need you to leave. This is my business."

But she moved closer and peered around him. When our eyes met, I could tell she recognized me, even without my church-lady costume.

"Your grandson is in a lot of trouble," I said. "He murdered Dr. Everest."

"I told you to shut up." He raised the cord toward my neck.

"You didn't," Gertie sputtered. "Tell me you didn't."

Kyle refused to look at her. He stared past the cord. Right through me.

"Kyle?" Her voice trembled.

"I had to. I was doing God's work. Dr. Everest was going to stop me."

"God's work?" she said. "Here?"

"Nothing gets done in church. Just talk and wishful thinking. While Spires was preaching and protesting, I was actually doing something. I was taking direct action."

I felt gut-punched by my enormous mistake. Kyle hadn't turned his back on Spires' beliefs—just on the man himself and his methods.

"I've prevented suffering," Kyle said. "I've stopped ten lesbians from having babies."

Anne, I thought, Anne was one of those ten. She'd squandered her money and her hope. She'd wondered what was wrong with her own body. "Those women trusted you," I said. "They thought you were on their side."

Kyle twisted slightly toward his grandmother. "Saving ten children from unhappiness—that's more than Spires has ever done."

His boast sickened me. How could he think anyone would be happier if Stormy Grace hadn't been born? And she wouldn't have been if there hadn't been a blizzard the day Sophie was inseminated, if Kyle's grandma hadn't needed his help in all that snow. Less precipitation, and Sophie and Esther would still be trying just like Anne.

"I killed the sperm," he explained, "before the women were inseminated."

"You killed a person," Gertie whispered.

"To protect our family. I would have gone to prison. Then where would we be—Holly and the kids?"

"I raised you to be a good man. I taught you right. So did the reverend."

"He's never done anything except take your money."

"He taught you right from wrong. He cares about you."

Kyle shook his head.

"He uses that money for good," Gertie insisted. "He helps people. He built that camp you loved so much."

"It's gone, Grandma, you know that. He sold it to a developer. It's going to be condos."

I recalled the bulldozed lot where Kyle had taken Spires' cash, a lot that Spires used to own. The camp site, I'd bet my life on it. Although that wouldn't be an option if I didn't think fast.

"He still prays for you," Gertie said.

Kyle's face reddened. "Did his prayers stop Dad from drinking? Or from beating the crap out of Holly and me?"

Gertie flinched.

"Did he try to stop Holly from marrying someone just like Dad? Does he do anything for her kids? For any kids?"

As Kyle raged about Spires' inability to help children, I thought about Kyle's devotion to his nieces and nephew, his empathy for Diego and Zoey, the time he spent talking with Roger's young son. I thought about the only object left undisturbed in my ransacked office, the photo of my nieces on a carousel.

"Does that quack teach kids how to help themselves?" Kyle asked. "Has he ever saved one single kid from going through what Holly and I did because of our mother? I have. I've saved ten kids."

When Kyle mentioned his mother, Gertie paled.

If she fainted, there would be nothing to keep him from killing me. I needed to remember what Spires' substitute secretary told me about Kyle's mother. She'd been killed in a car accident. How was anyone supposed to prevent that? Then it hit me. Before dying, she had left Kyle and his family. There was a scandal, a scandal that Spires had not wanted the secretary to share.

I asked Kyle if his mother was a lesbian.

He whirled toward me.

"Kyle," Gertie said. "Listen to me. There's something you need to know about your mother."

"She left without saying goodbye," Kyle said. "She abandoned us."

"She was planning to come back for you, for you and Holly. She loved you."

Kyle squeezed his eyes shut.

I shoved him into Gertie. I pushed away the pain that flared on my right side. And I ran.

My shoes screeched across the floor. Kyle's shrieked right behind me. I wouldn't be able to make it out of the lab, not before he tackled me. I grabbed the closest door, wrenched it open, and locked myself inside.

The cryo room.

Kyle would have keys, but I would have a few moments, a chance to think. I couldn't count on Gertie's help, and I couldn't overpower Kyle by myself. I flipped on the lights, and my eyes went to the floor. To the spot where Grace had lain. How much of Kyle's betrayal had she absorbed before he struck her down?

And how had he done it? I scanned the room, the many metal canisters. Kyle might have hit Grace with one of them before he'd strangled her. But he was way taller than Grace—taller than me. I couldn't go for his head. I'd have to aim for something else. The smallest canister was the size of a milk crate and as heavy as a box of books. When I lifted it, pain careened through me. There was no way I could throw it or swing it hard enough. I set it down and tried to think.

"Kyle," Gertie pleaded on the other side of the door, "listen."

The door handle twisted, but the lock held. There was a thud against the door, a curse, footsteps. Kyle going for the keys.

"Mrs. Bremmer?" I asked.

No answer.

"Gertie?" I hoped that she'd followed her grandson or that she was trying to determine her next move. I hoped that Kyle hadn't hurt her. "Your grandson needs help," I said.

Nothing.

And nothing in the cryo room but canisters of liquid nitrogen and the cauldron-like freezer filled with sperm. Atop it were giant tongs, goggles, and padded gloves that looked like industrial-strength kitchen mitts. I thought of Grace donning them, opening the freezer. Liquid nitrogen fogging the air. Liquid nitrogen, so cold it burns.

I put on the goggles and the gloves.

"Grandma, come on, move." Kyle's voice was surprisingly gentle.

I released my breath, nearly overwhelmed with relief. Gertie was okay. Kyle hadn't completely lost it.

"Come on, Grandma, get out of my way."

Please, Gertie, I thought, hold your ground. Use those football skills. Block your grandson. Just a few more seconds.

"You need to hear the truth," she said. "After your father died, I found a letter for you and Holly in his things. From your mother. She was coming back."

The goggles dug my glasses into the bridge of my nose, and they blurred my vision slightly. I squatted next to the smallest canister and studied its gauges and valves. If I released the wrong one, would the whole thing explode?

"Did you hear me?" Gertie asked.

I twisted a valve. It hissed. I picked up the canister, managed to carry it a few steps, and set it down. My side throbbed, but I was ready. When Kyle opened the door, my canister and I would be hidden behind it. In the same spot where he'd waited to kill Grace. He must have left the door open, the light on, or a canister out of place, knowing Grace would need to restore order.

Fighting a wave of nausea, I listened for Kyle's key in the lock.

"You lied to me," he said.

"I didn't want you to think any worse of your father than you already did, and when I asked—" Gertie stopped herself. "Please understand. She hurt your father. My son! She destroyed him, and she disgraced our family."

"Spires told you to lie." Kyle's voice was flat.

I imagined the minister's advice. "Children need to believe in their fathers. What was this mother, after all, but an abomination?" I imagined Spires trying to comfort and counsel young Kyle after his mother left. "It's not your fault. Homosexuals are not meant to be parents." And after her death? "The hand of God." Those twisted lies had led Kyle to this place.

"I've still got the letter," Gertie said. "At home. I'll show you."

Kyle didn't answer. His mother had not betrayed him, but all the other adults he'd loved and trusted had. His deepest hurt—the hurt that birthed his desire to stunt other families—had been based on a lie.

"Come on," Gertie urged. "We'll show Holly too."

Kyle remained silent a moment more. When he spoke, his voice simmered with fury. "Get out of my way, Grandma, or I'll move you myself."

"This is wrong."

"If I let her go, I'll go to prison."

"We'll get you a lawyer. A good one. The reverend will—"

Gertie gasped and scuffled with her grandson. Keys rattled. There were no more words. There was no more time. I prayed that she was unhurt. I squatted next to my canister and opened it all the way. I stood up, holding it with both hands.

A key slipped into the lock.

I prayed for good aim. Me, the one lesbian in the world who doesn't play softball.

Kyle crept into the room, the cord taut in front of him. The moment he passed the door, I tossed the canister's contents. Liquid nitrogen arced through the air and splashed him. He shrieked, crumpled against the freezer, curled up like a baby on the floor. Gertie rushed to him, and I escaped.

Chapter Thirty-three

GRACE'S VOICE SOUNDED from the radio in my living room. "I don't have time for people who question my family values. I'm too busy creating families."

Then my own voice, "For NPR, I'm Mara Gilgannon."

As Melissa Block announced the next story on *All Things Considered*, my friends cheered wildly and raised their glasses to me. Diego Sanchez-Smith nearly spilled his chocolate milk on my computer keyboard, and Anne steered him away from it. I thought about Kyle swiping computers, desperately trying to discover whether their hard drives revealed any hint of his sperm tampering. I thought about him trashing my office, hoping to cast suspicion on Leo Spires, then stealing Tupperware, trying to focus attention on Justine. The attention was on him now. It had been ever since he was arrested six months ago. While he awaited trial, he granted one media interview after another.

Vince pulled me into a bear hug and handed me a fresh Corona. I sipped it and gingerly tilted my head from side to side. My neck still hurt sometimes. A reminder of my run-in with Edward Faust. Detective Henry had found him living in a partially constructed apartment building owned by Celia Spires. Celia claimed ignorance, but there was no denying her other transgressions. After she discovered that Kyle knew about her father's secret family, she stole Kyle's personnel file from the lab and convinced Roger to provide her with further evidence of Kyle's employment. With these, she tried to get some leverage with Kyle, threatening to show them to his grandmother. Kyle didn't bite, but Roger, poor sap, had actually believed Celia when she promised she'd stop protesting the lab if he faxed Kyle's insemination reports.

Detective Dallas Henry exited my kitchen, and I headed toward her to see what she thought about my segment with the grandmothers. But the phone rang, and Vince handed it to me.

"You rocked the air waves, babe. Congratulations." I was happy to hear from Bridget. Relieved too. We hadn't broken up—we still had fun together—but we had been drifting apart.

She was calling from Georgia. In a few hours, she and her girls had a second-round NCAA tournament game. In their first-round game, Liz Lipinski led all scorers with 34. Roger Lipinski had given Justine cash the day she disappeared. Then he headed to Milwaukee, where he failed to persuade his in-laws that they should persuade their daughter to take him back. Justine herself had been chauffeured out of Iowa City courtesy of Zoey and Reed, but their assistance only delayed the inevitable. Like Celia, Justine was arrested for stealing hospital records, and she was out on bond. Unlike Celia, she was living with her father in suburban Chicago and receiving much-needed help with her Tupperware issues. Vince claims that Justine steals containers and fills them with messages in order to fill her own emptiness; I claim that he watches too much Oprah.

"Grace would be so proud of you," Bridget said.

I battled tears. When someone you love dies, you miss them the most when you're the happiest. It doesn't make sense, but it's true.

"Your series was a real tribute to her and her work," Bridget said. "I bet lots of listeners will contribute to her endowment."

Ironically, *Trying Times* would probably never attract as many donors as Kyle had, first with his arrest and then with all the dirt he revealed about Reverend Leo Spires. The minister no longer had time to attack Grace's lab. He was too busy defending his reputation and his bank account. Members of the man's own flock, including Gertie Bremmer, were suing him silly. Not just for financial malfeasance, but emotional damages. Talk about poetic justice. Grace would have loved it.

And there I was again, missing Grace.

"Babe," Bridget said. "I gotta run. We'll celebrate you when I get back."

I wanted to say that we'd celebrate her too, but Bridget gets weird about jinxes. "I'll see you on ESPN2," I said. "Break a leg."

Like always, she chuckled at my way of wishing her luck.

After I hung up, Vince raised his champagne to propose another toast. He cleared his throat dramatically, and the doorbell rang. "Ah," he said, lowering his drink, "the high price of fame."

Zoey stood on my front porch, her coat unbuttoned despite the chill March air. "I've got a surprise for you," she said. Her presence itself was shocker enough. Although we texted a lot, I hadn't seen the girl since interviewing her for *Trying Times*. When I invited her in, she gave me a coy look. "I've got someone with me." She stepped aside and gestured toward the mysterious someone. A young woman with Zoey's red hair, round face, and blue eyes.

"My sister!" Zoey said triumphantly.

The girl—shorter, older, and better-mannered than Zoey— extended her hand. She introduced herself as Mellette Meyers and explained that they met via the Donor Sibling Registry.

"Let me tell it," Zoey said. "Mellette's parents are way cool. She got her donor's ID number as soon as she asked."

"When I turned sixteen," Mellette added.

"Come inside," I urged. "It's freezing."

"Can't," Zoey said, "the judge is waiting for us in the car."

"So your father is okay with—"

"He loves her," Zoey explained. "My big sister, the law student." Zoey gave Mellette a teasing smile. "He wants me to grow up and be just like her. Only I already am. We both play bass guitar, and we both love thrift-shopping and pineapple pizza. And I get to visit her at Harvard on my spring break. On the judge's dime."

I didn't ask about their donor dad. If he'd contacted them, Zoey would have announced it to the world. For now, he wasn't registered. He didn't want to be found. But for now, Zoey didn't seem to care. She had Mellette.

When the sisters left a few minutes later, I returned to the party, my mind reeling with Zoey's happy discovery and my own triumph. Vince once again raised his champagne. Michael and Penny's little girl, secure in her dad's arms, hoisted a Tipee cup and grinned. The room was filled with people I loved — friends from the station and the theatre and people who shared their lives and struggles with me so I could make *Trying Times*. There was Felicity, not yet showing, in a bright cashmere sweater, and Lindsey, rumored to be expecting, sharing some cheese and crackers with her partner. Esther eased Stormy Grace into Sophie's arms and raised a glass. Diego Sanchez-Smith was, for better or worse, back to his old self. He petted Labrys a tad too vigorously as Dallas Henry's granddaughter grabbed the dog's tail. Dallas herself caught my eye and gave me a thumbs-up.

Then there was Anne, standing next to Vince. She'd been living with us — in the guest room — ever since Orchid told her she wasn't up to co-parenting after all. Despite Vince's warnings about tossing my emotions in a blender, my sole reason for inviting Anne back into our home was so that she could save money for a new dream donor. Even Vince knows that she can't count on her lawsuit against the hospital — it could go on and on like a Dickens novel. Vince, of course, keeps beating his chest and insisting that her dream donor is right in front of her. All four grandparents, he boasts, are alive and kicking, and he has a great aunt who, at ninety-three, still swims a mile every morning. "How about these looks?" he says to Anne. "This sense of humor? How can you resist?" How indeed? Especially since his swimmers are free and he's willing to have any kind of test and sign any kind of legal agreement Anne wants. "Why?" she asks. "Pure hubris," he says, "a chance at immortality, a chance to help a friend." She shakes her head, exasperated. "You're too serious," he says. "Trust me, your kid is gonna need my genes."

Okay, so I know they're joking. Or half-joking. And I know that even if Anne did allow Vince to help her conceive, she wouldn't stay here — in this home where she and I used to live together. But I imagine it sometimes — her, me, Vince, a quiet and well-behaved baby. All of us together. A family. Then I tell myself to get a grip and let Anne go. And I try. I really do try.

Other Mary Vermillion titles
you might also like:

Death By Discount

Nothing short of homicide is going to drag headstrong Mara Gilgannon back to her dinky hometown. So homicide it is, as Mara finds herself back in Aldoburg, Iowa, unraveling clues surrounding the death of her aunt Glad. Mara soon begins to suspect that Glad's vocal opposition to the opening of a local Walmart may have led to her murder. But nothing is ever as simple as small-town life would have you believe. First, Mara butts heads with police chief Chuck Conover, who stole her girlfriend when they were both in high school. Then she becomes rattled by the attention of a beautiful rookie police officer, Neale Warner, who's conducting her own investigation on the sly. On top of all that, Mara loses her prime suspect, a key supporter of Walmart, when he's run over by a car—twice! Someone has taken the issue of the corporatization of rural America to a deadly new level.

This title will be released in eBook format only.

ISBN: 978-1-61929-047-1

Murder By Mascot

Dave DeVoster, star of the University of Iowa men's basketball team, is found dead beneath a statue of Iowa's mascot, his blood dripping from Herky-the-Hawkeye's curved beak. Arrested for the murder is Anne Golding, director of the UI Women's Center, who led a protest against the university when it allowed DeVoster to remain on the team while under investigation for the rape of a member of the women's basketball team. To the rescue comes radio talk-show host Mara Gilgannon. She is not only Anne's ex, but also carries a bit of a torch for Bridget Stokes, the cute assistant coach of the women's team. Mara soon butts heads with overprotective parents, tight-lipped players, university administrators, and Bridget herself, whose interest in protecting her team's heterosexual image may mask motives much darker.

This title will be released in eBook format only.

ISBN: 978-1-61929-048-8

ANOTHER QUEST TITLE YOU MIGHT ENJOY

Hearts, Dead and Alive
by Kate McLachlan

When fifth grade teacher Kimberly Wayland finds a human heart in the middle school dumpster, she has some explaining to do. Like why she was in the dumpster in the first place, and why she didn't tell the police about her gruesome find. But after giving the police a fake alibi, explaining is the last thing Kim wants to do. Instead, with the help of her friends—hot "best friend" Becca, co-worker "lesbian wanna-be" Annie, and lawyer "stickler-for-rules" Lucy—Kim sets out to solve the mystery of the missing heart. Along the way, she unexpectedly solves another mystery, the mystery of her own heart.

ISBN 978-1-61929-017-4

Buyer's Remorse
by Lori L. Lake

Leona "Leo" Reese is a 33-year-old police patrol sergeant with over ten years of law enforcement experience. After she fails her bi-yearly shooting qualification due to a vision problem, Leo is temporarily assigned to the investigations division of the state's Department of Human Services. She's shell-shocked by her vision impairment and frustrated to be reassigned to another department, even temporarily. On her first day on the new job, she's saddled with a case where a woman at an independent living facility for elders has been murdered by an apparent burglar. But all is not as it seems, and it will take all her smarts to outwit a dangerous criminal. Will she uncover the murderer before other people are robbed and killed

First book in the Public Eye series

ISBN 968-1-61929-001-3

OTHER QUEST PUBLICATIONS

Brenda Adcock	Pipeline	978-1-932300-64-2
Brenda Adcock	Redress of Grievances	978-1-932300-86-4
Brenda Adcock	Tunnel Vision	978-1-935053-19-4
Victor J. Banis	Angel Land	978-1-935053-05-7
Sharon G. Clark	Into the Mist	978-1-935053-34-7
Michele Coffman	Veiled Conspiracy	978-1-935053-38-5
Blayne Cooper	Cobb Island	978-1-932300-67-3
Blayne Cooper	Echoes From The Mist	978-1-932300-68-0
Cleo Dare	Cognate	978-1-935053-25-5
Cleo Dare	Hanging Offense	978-1-935053-11-8
Lori L. Lake	Buyer's Remorse	978-1-61929-001-3
Lori L. Lake	Gun Shy	978-1-932300-56-7
Lori L. Lake	Have Gun We'll Travel	1-932300-33-3
Lori L. Lake	Under the Gun	978-1-932300-57-4
Helen M. Macpherson	Colder Than Ice	1-932300-29-5
Linda Morganstein	Harpies' Feast	978-1-935053-43-9
Linda Morganstein	On A Silver Platter	978-1-935053-51-4
Linda Morganstein	Ordinary Furies	978-1-935053-47-7
Andi Marquette	Land of Entrapment	978-1-935053-02-6
Andi Marquette	State of Denial	978-1-935053-09-5
Andi Marquette	The Ties That Bind	978-1-935053-23-1
Kate McLachlan	Hearts, Dead and Alive	978-1-61929-017-4
Kate McLachlan	Rescue At Inspiration Point	978-1-61929-005-1
Kate McLachlan	Rip Van Dyke	978-1-935053-29-3
C. Paradee	Deep Cover	1-932300-23-6
Keith Pyeatt	Struck	978-1-935053-17-0
Rick R. Reed	Deadly Vision	978-1-932300-96-3
Rick R. Reed	IM	978-1-932300-79-6
Rick R. Reed	In the Blood	978-1-932300-90-1
Damian Serbu	Secrets In the Attic	978-1-935053-33-0
Damian Serbu	The Vampire's Angel	978-1-935053-22-4
Damian Serbu	The Vampire's Quest	978-1-61929-013-6
Mary Vermillion	Death By Discount	978-1-61929-047-1
Mary Vermillion	Murder By Mascot	978-1-61929-048-8
Mary Vermillion	Seminal Murder	978-1-61929-049-5

About the Author:

Mary Vermillion is the author of the Mara Gilgannon mystery series. Her first novel, *Death by Discount*, a finalist for two Lambda awards, portrays Walmart's impact on small-town America. Her second novel, *Murder by Mascot*, provides a darkly comic look at homophobia and sexual violence in the world of Division I basketball. Mary is a professor of English at Mount Mercy University in Cedar Rapids, Iowa, and she lives in Iowa City with her partner and three cats. She loves to hear from her readers, so please visit her web site, www.maryvermillion.com or email her at maryvermillion@hotmail.com.

VISIT US ONLINE AT
www.regalcrest.biz

At the Regal Crest Website You'll Find

- The latest news about forthcoming titles and new releases

- Our complete backlist of romance, mystery, thriller and adventure titles

- Information about your favorite authors

- Current bestsellers

- Media tearsheets to print and take with you when you shop

- Which books are also available as eBooks.

Regal Crest print titles are available from all progressive booksellers including numerous sources online. Our distributors are Bella Distribution and Ingram.

CPSIA information can be obtained at www.ICGtesting.com
Printed in the USA
LVOW101044030812

292717LV00003B/4/P